D0050035

THE
SPEED
OF
LIGHT

Hillsboro Public Library
Hillsboro, OR
A member of Washington County
COOPERATIVE LIBRARY SERVICES

THE SPEED OF LIGHT

A NOVEL

ELISSA GROSSELL DICKEY

LAKE UNION
PUBLISHING

This is a work of fiction. Names, characters, organizations, places, events, and incidents are either products of the author's imagination or are used fictitiously. Any resemblance to actual persons, living or dead, or actual events is purely coincidental.

Text copyright © 2021 by Elissa Grossell Dickey
All rights reserved.

No part of this book may be reproduced, or stored in a retrieval system, or transmitted in any form or by any means, electronic, mechanical, photocopying, recording, or otherwise, without express written permission of the publisher.

Published by Lake Union Publishing, Seattle

www.apub.com

Amazon, the Amazon logo, and Lake Union Publishing are trademarks of Amazon.com, Inc., or its affiliates.

ISBN-13: 9781542022675
ISBN-10: 1542022673

33614082201467

Cover design by Faceout Studio, Tim Green

Printed in the United States of America

To Ted, who will always be the hero of my story

PART ONE

TRAGEDY

Monday, December 6, 8:08 a.m.

In the darkness the snowfall is hypnotic, each flake sparkling as it winds down in slow motion, like the inside of a snow globe, safe and serene. I, too, am shiny and new in this imaginary place—I am me again, normal and healthy and *his*, a spellbound princess who gets her happily ever after. Who deserves it.

"How's it going in there, Simone?"

My eyelids fly open. How easily spells are broken.

I blink against the brightness as I'm wedged within a cylindrical prison.

"Can you keep your head still, please?"

Screw you. Probably not the best response, but the radiology technician's voice in my ear is extra whiny today. Plus, imagining the delight of telling Nikki about my outburst later almost makes me say it out loud. My best friend would be so proud.

"Doing my best," I say instead, with all the fake cheeriness of a passive-aggressive text ending with a smiley-face emoji.

The music starts again: familiar pop tunes. Even though it's the holiday season, I didn't request Christmas music during my MRI—I don't want beloved holiday tunes ruined by being forever linked to this experience.

I close my eyes again, trying to return to my inner sanctuary—the dark, cozy snow globe—and yet now I can't drown out the throbbing, pounding buzzes and screams of this goddamned mechanical tomb in which I am entrapped. Jesus, now I know how poor Han Solo felt when he was encased in carbonite.

Okay, that's a little dramatic—and what is it about the MRI machine that makes me want to swear so damn much?

It has to be the drilling sounds—relentless and constantly changing, so you can never quite get used to it. At first, a series of slow, pulsing buzzes; then they start shooting out at rapid fire, like a machine gun, only to go back to the intermittent, grating bursts.

Today they're like accusatory jabs: *He's gone. It's your fault. It's better this way.*

Deep breath, in and out. *Don't think about it, Simone.* Any of it. Not him. Not what the MRI results might show—new lesions, a sign the multiple sclerosis has progressed. Not my uncertain future with this disease.

And definitely do *not* fixate on the small throb of pain in the back of my head, a nagging ache that worsens the longer I'm stuck in the same position.

Great, now my head is hurting more. Who designed these uncomfortable death traps?

I would never do well in a torture situation, that's for sure. I'd sing like a canary. What book was that where they ripped out the lady's fingernails, and she finally gave up the location of her family?

Would I do that? Could I endure that kind of torture if I had to protect someone—my parents, Nikki, my little brother? Oh God, what if I couldn't do it?

I open my eyes, focusing on the top of the white tube. It is time to shut down my spiraling thoughts—I would shake my head at myself, but that would earn another shrill warning from the technician. If I move now, we'd have to do the whole thing over. What would Nikki say about my irrational fears? She'd shake *her* head (because in the real world, nobody cares if you move your damn head) and say, *Simone, nobody's going to be tortured.*

And she'd remind me that the reward for MRI day is all the wine and chocolate I want after work tonight while watching *Bridget Jones* in my pajamas.

I just have to get through today.

With sheer power of will—and the promise of pinot noir, Hershey's Kisses, and Bridget's Mark Darcy—I'm finally able to let my thoughts drift to mundane, cheerful things like what to buy my mom for Christmas, or which cheesy sweater to wear to the office holiday party.

At last, the voice of the tech rings in my ears: "Okay, Simone, we're all done. You're free now."

Free.

The word stings, lingering within me as the machine slowly releases me from its grip, the tech waiting to help me to my feet.

In the changing room I hurry to switch back into my clothes before the chill penetrates my skin through the thin hospital gown. I work hard to avoid the reflection of the weary woman in the mirror. From my purse, a low buzzing—I reach for my phone, and Nikki's slyly smiling face glows on the screen. I answer the call, but she speaks before I can.

"Morning, sunshine. How was the tanning bed of doom?"

I snort, pressing the speaker button so I can set my phone down and hike up my jeans. "Lovely as always."

"When will you get results?"

I sigh. "Could be tomorrow; could be next week."

"Well, happy fucking holidays to you."

I laugh bitterly and Nikki clears her throat.

"So, no need to hurry into the office because—spoiler alert—Stan is MIA."

"What happened to the staff meeting?" I'd planned to take the whole day off for some post-MRI self-care—it's the first week after winter commencement, so the campus is dead anyway—but our boss had *insisted* we needed to meet this morning.

"Oh, we're still having it, unfortunately. His email said he's running late. Apparently, he's in some big meeting upstairs in Administration right now, but we are still meeting at *nine thirty sharp*—he even said some cryptic shit just to make sure we don't skip the meeting."

I freeze. "What cryptic shit?"

Nikki pauses, her hesitation flowing through the phone. "Simone, you know he's just being dramatic. He likes to feel important."

"What did he *say*, Nik?"

She sighs. "He said it's time for us to finally discuss budget cuts, because every department needs to. But he did *not* say layoffs, so don't even worry about that, okay?"

Nikki and I have been best friends for a dozen years—it's the reason we took jobs in the same department at the same university—so she knows damn well that telling me not to worry is like telling me not to breathe, but I pretend for her sake, or for mine. "Yeah, sure, sounds good. I'll be in soon."

We end the call, and I sag against the wall. I've lost so much already this year; now I could lose my job—and along with it, my health insurance. I rake my hands through my hair and consider screaming, or crumpling into the corner of this tiny radiology changing room.

The woman in the mirror beckons me to meet her gaze, but I fight to resist.

I'm saved when my phone buzzes again. Nikki, a text: Just a reminder that we got this. Get your ass in here.

The tiniest smile tugs at my lips, at my heart. Silently, I pick up my purse, pick up myself, shuffle out the door, back on my unsteady path.

As I sit at my office desk in Herald Hall, snowflakes float down through the air outside my window, almost exactly like I visualized during my MRI this morning: a falling sea of white, pure and serene. The snow-covered campus is exquisite, the towering elms of the quad veiled in white as the stately brick academic buildings stand watch. The scene should fill me with peace, even hope. But it's sad somehow, like a reminder of holidays past, something you're not sure you can ever get back.

This has been my view for almost eight years now, ever since Nikki and I took jobs right out of college in the Office of Marketing and Communications of this small university in Sioux Falls, South Dakota. We even got adjoining cubicles—in the "mega office," as we affectionately call it, a shared space with an open floor plan—so we can look up from our desks across the room at each other for a covert eye roll when our boss says something cringeworthy. I look around at this place where we sit day after day, me cranking out press releases while Nikki designs brochures.

So much of the fabric of my identity is woven into what I do for a living, and maybe that's wrong, but dammit, I'm clinging to any part of myself I can—any part my disease can't take away.

My eyes flick down to my desk, and I tap my phone, sitting on top of a pile of file folders. *Shit.* It's 9:24 already.

I take a greedy slug of coffee, trying to calm my nerves before our staff meeting, but my bladder twinges.

Ugh, my body's timing is terrible. *As always.*

I stand, craning my neck to spot Nikki across the room, hunched behind her computer monitor. "Bathroom break—I'll be quick."

7

"You're not jumping ship, are you?"

"Are you kidding? I am *so excited* for this meeting," I scoff.

She meets my gaze, eyes intense. "Listen, we don't know what Stan's going to propose until we get there, okay?"

I squeeze my eyes shut. Ripples of anxiety have been spreading like wildfire across campus this fall. Tough enrollment year, freezing positions . . . I've been ignoring the rumors for a long time because of everything going on in my personal life, but now Stan's email, and this morning's meeting, both confirm that we need to slash our budget. "I just keep thinking how Hayley heard Chet say some people would lose their jobs."

Nikki narrows her eyes. "Chet's a dick—he shouldn't be saying that. And even if it's true for a big department like Admissions, there are only three of us over here in Marketing, okay?"

My lip quivers, but she holds my gaze. "Okay. Yeah, I'm sure you're right."

"Damn right I am. Other departments are having meetings, too— I'm sure Stan just wants to be able to show he's making an effort with his own team. You know, like ordering cheaper phones instead of the mega-expensive ones when we replace the system."

I shake my head. "Yeah, I don't know why those haven't arrived yet."

"Like he cares—once his new phone comes in, he'll have no more excuses for ignoring his wife's phone calls." She rolls her eyes as I grimace, then turns back to her computer screen. "Now go pee already."

I turn away from her desk to step out into the hallway, but my left knee buckles and I shoot my hand against the wall for support, a familiar thump of worry in my chest. I proceed slowly, one foot in front of the other on the faded brown industrial carpeting. No numbness, no muscles locking up.

False alarm. Must've turned too quickly. Damn knee.

I sigh. I've come so far this past year, but I'll probably always jump to that conclusion. Probably always be waiting for the next relapse. The curse of chronic illness.

The floor creaks beneath me as I walk down the otherwise-silent hallway. This corridor is a strange beast in itself—it connects the Administration building, where our office is, to the Student Union through a door at one end and, on the other end, a doorway to an academic building teeming with classrooms. When you're waiting to pass someone walking through, the corridor seems to stretch on forever as you deliberate on when to make eye contact and extend an awkward greeting. Too soon means you have several seconds of agonizing silence before you pass each other; too late and you might miss your chance, risking rudeness, which in the Midwest is practically a crime.

But there's little chance of meeting someone in the hall today, with campus slow to wake up, now that the semester is over and the students and professors have left for winter break. It's so barren that I'm afraid when I look down the dimly lit corridor I might see something creepy, like the twins from *The Shining*.

As I near the end of the hallway, though, a soft, peppy holiday tune wafts toward me out of the break room: "Feliz Navidad." A quick wave of sadness pulses through me, a memory pricked, though it's fuzzy, and I push it aside as my bladder twinges again—sheesh, thirty years on this earth, and how many of those have been spent in the bathroom? I shake my head as I flick on the break-room light, ignoring the ancient compact radio that sits on the countertop and the scent of burned popcorn wafting from the microwave. The women's restroom is on the far side of the room—vacant, thank God—and I hurry toward it.

The heavy wooden door clicks shut behind me, and I lock it, shuffle across the black-and-white tiles to the toilet, sigh in relief when I'm done, then walk to the sink. The cruel glare of the fluorescent light is like a spotlight onstage back in our college theater days, exposing me to the judgment of a roomful of strangers. Now it's just me, and as I wash my hands, I fight again to avoid the haggard woman in the mirror.

From outside the bathroom, the muted clamp of the microwave door swinging shut jolts me—Charlene is heating up her cinnamon roll, her daily breakfast. It's her morning ritual; her afternoon ritual is stopping by our office to see if Nikki or I have any gossip to share. I smile. She's usually the one who has juicy info for us. She's the president's secretary, super friendly, and has worked here so long that she knows everybody's business.

My smile fades when I realize she's probably down here using our break room because the upstairs Administration conference room is occupied. My stomach flips as I picture the group of bigwigs gathered around the table, determining our fates. But I force myself to take a deep breath, determined not to be late for *our* meeting.

I shuffle over to the door and reach for the handle, but I pause, turning back at last to face the woman in the mirror. I owe her that much, at least. Long dark hair twisted up carelessly, tired green eyes hiding the pain, the fear. I wish I could tell her she's made the right choices about her health, about her relationship. That no matter what happens, no matter what any test results say or what any staff meeting reveals, everything will be okay.

That she could still get her happily ever after, somehow.

"You'll be fine," I whisper, but I arch my own eyebrows skeptically in reply.

Worth a try.

I flick the light off with one hand as the other presses down on the door handle. There's a soft click as the door unlocks.

But before I push it open, a jarring crack pierces the silence outside the bathroom, freezing me in place as my mind tries to identify the sound—surely it was somebody dropping a heavy object. Or maybe it was Charlene's breakfast splattering all over the inside of the food-crusted microwave.

Still, I stay immobile on the inside of the bathroom, with my hand on the handle.

A few seconds of intense quiet before a man shouts in the distance. A woman screams. Then, that popping sound again, farther away, an eerie echo of something foreign but familiar. My mind races, desperate to normalize the sound—but a sick feeling slams my gut when I realize I don't recognize it from real life, only action movies and TV dramas.

Gunshots.

I can't move—my mind is reeling, but I'm locked in indecision as I stare at the door, my hand trembling as it slowly releases the handle.

Then footsteps return, hard and fast, into the break room. Maybe somebody got away—maybe they came to help Charlene, to save us all. Maybe I should open the door. But something stops me. I wait in the heavy silence, lean forward, press my ear to the door to listen.

Another blast rings out close and loud, and my hands fly to my mouth in time to clamp back my scream.

Terror courses through me, but the feet on the other side of the door are moving again, stepping closer to the bathroom—closer to *me*—and it's like I'm in slow motion and fast-forward all at once. Beneath the surface, right under my skin, a scream is brewing, a version of me who wants to crumple to the floor in the corner, helpless. But deeper within is something harder, the version of me strong enough to walk out of the neurologist's office last year without sobbing, strong enough to walk away from *him* last summer without breaking down. This version gets me to the wooden bathroom cabinet, tall and wide, where the custodian stores the extra toilet paper and disinfectant spray.

There's only one shelf, toward the top. I'm short. I can fit. I *will* fit.

Within seconds I'm wedged inside, hunched underneath the shelf, huffing in shallow breaths of the potpourri-scented cleaner. It's too stuffy, too cramped; it's so hot in here, and I can't do this. I can't. But I suck in a longer breath, squeeze my eyes shut—and I pretend I'm back in the goddamned MRI machine. Pretend in a few minutes I'll hear the irritatingly cheerful voice of the technician reminding me to hold still.

Pretend that this will all be over soon.

The bathroom door handle jiggles, and my heart stops. A sliver of light appears through the edge of the cabinet as the door opens. I bite down on my lip to hold in any sound threatening to escape.

Please God please God please God please. It's the only prayer I can think of right now, the words playing on a loop in my mind.

The shooter must be less than a foot away from the cabinet, because I can hear breathing—so chillingly normal, almost familiar. There is just another human being standing in the bathroom right now.

Another human being with a gun.

Seconds tick by. My body shakes, but somehow I remain silent. Images swirl through my mind—not the sequential life-flashing-before-your-eyes you read about, but my mom and dad playing cards at the kitchen table, my brother, Emmett, riding next to me on the merry-go-round when he was little.

A footstep scrapes—the shooter takes a step closer to the cabinet.

My arms wrap around myself, the only protection I have.

All is lost; I'm sure of it. My mind races, swirling like the snow-flakes in the wind outside, the snow globe tipped and jostled violently. From the depths of my chaotic mind, one thought forces its way out—perhaps my last.

Connor, I'm sorry. I love you.

CHAPTER ONE

Christmas Eve, one year before

The snow swirls in the air, down through the jet-black sky, onto my windshield. As a kid I always thought driving through the mesmerizing white flakes made it seem like we were traveling at light speed, blasting through space like the *Millennium Falcon*.

Tonight, though, the snow doesn't fool me. Mostly because I'm not moving at all.

"Come on, baby," I purr to my old Honda. "Please?"

I turn the key again, but I'm met with the relentless half roar of an engine that refuses to revive. She growls at me over and over, like it's causing her pain.

I give up, slam my hand on the steering wheel. "Merry freaking Christmas to you, too."

I sigh—it's not my car's fault this happened. None of this is her fault. Not the tingle in my legs. Not my uncertain future.

I give the steering wheel a loving pat, then take out my phone. After three rings, I hear laughter and holiday music burst from the other side—the warmth and security of being surrounded by loved ones, not stranded on the side of the road.

"Hello?" There's a smile in my mom's voice, and it makes my frown deepen.

"Hey, Mom, it's me." I pause, close my eyes so I don't have to look at the swirling snowstorm against the black sky outside my window. "I'm, uh . . . my car broke down."

"Simone, honey, where are you?" The smile is gone.

"I'm still about thirty miles out."

"On the highway?"

"Yeah." My chuckle is bitter. "Well, on the side of it, technically."

"Did you have an accident? I didn't think the snow was supposed to be this bad!"

"No. I mean, yeah, the roads aren't great." I'd been white-knuckling it for about forty miles now, but she doesn't need to know that. "But that's not the problem. I don't really know what's going on with my car." The truth is, my check-engine light has been turning on and off for the past few weeks, but I've been too busy to find out why—she doesn't need to know that, either.

Mom tsks. "Simone, you need to get yourself a more reliable vehicle, especially if you insist on driving from Sioux Falls after dark."

I don't bother responding—I don't need her paranoia right now. Mom's already moved on anyway, her voice muffled as she covers the phone to speak to Dad. "Bob, her car broke down. Get your boots on and start up the truck."

"No, Mom, don't worry about it." I clench my shaking fist, clutch the phone tighter in my other hand. "You made me get AAA, remember? I should probably use it."

"Oh, honey, I hate the idea of you sitting out in the cold by yourself." There's a pause, and I know what's coming, as if I can feel the concern forming in her mind. Mom has her own form of anxiety about my recent medical issues, worrying when I do anything on my own. But it's only because she doesn't understand what's happening to me. And I can't blame her, because neither do I, really.

I sigh. "I'm fine—sitting here in the warm car." Laughter bursts out behind her. "Everybody's already there. I don't want anyone to come out in this weather. Go get dinner ready. I'll be there soon."

Mom pauses; then I hear her whisper to my dad before turning her attention back to me on the phone. "Okay, well, if you're sure. But keep us updated about how long you'll have to wait. Dad has his boots on. Just text and he'll be there, okay?"

A typical parental offering, but it makes me extra thankful in this moment. "Okay."

I end the call and dial AAA like the competent adult I am. "I'm about to ruin somebody else's Christmas Eve," I whisper into my ringing phone.

There's a click and a woman picks up. "How may I help you?"

"Um, hi, I'm wondering if there's any chance I can get a tow? I mean, I know it's Christmas Eve and everything, but, um, my car broke down and—"

The woman cuts me off—a little no-nonsense tactic to combat my flustered babbling. "What's your location, ma'am?"

"Uh, Highway 12, about thirty miles east of Aberdeen, South Dakota."

"Mile marker?"

I blink out my window, squint, but there's only darkness beyond the swirling snow. "I don't see one. I'm sorry."

"No problem, ma'am." She takes my license plate number instead. "I'm looking at your area, and there are not a lot of services available tonight."

I swallow. "Um, okay. So what should I do?"

There's a pause, and I can hear her fingers tap quickly on a keyboard. "You just might need to wait a little longer than usual, ma'am. We'll get someone there as soon as possible."

"Thank you." I add a hasty "Merry Christmas," but she's already hung up.

I sit back and close my eyes, try to think about good things. Mom's peppermint hot chocolate waiting for me at the house, Nikki opening the present I got her. She'll be so excited about the tickets to our favorite musical, *Rent*, in Sioux Falls this spring. Maybe she'll even think it's better than our own "epic" production was, the one that solidified our friendship freshman year of college—or at least close, since she designed most of the set and costumes as well as playing one of the leads.

But even as the thought makes me smile, it's there. The little flip in my chest, the knot of anxiety that never lets me forget: *There's something wrong with you. You could wake up tomorrow and not be able to walk or see, and you'll never get to see another show or travel the world or do anything, really, because your future is over.* And then the panic surges, roiling the acid in my stomach, threatening to send it up and out of me, along with tears and screams, and suddenly the fear has morphed into anger because it's not fair.

It's not fair.

Some people live long, healthy lives, and others face the possibility of an unpredictable, incurable illness.

Multiple sclerosis.

I didn't even know what it was when my doctor first mentioned it. I still don't, not entirely. Googling too much about this progressive neurological disease leaves me cursing WebMD for sleepless nights of spiraling anxiety.

God, my gut still clenches as I remember the fear and uncertainty when I'd feel it coming on—when the constant pins and needles in my legs would intensify to the point where my leg would lock up and I could barely walk. If it happened as I was leaving work, I'd stop and lean against a building—or a tree, bench, whatever was available—fighting back tears, wondering if this was the time it would never go away, if I would never walk again, but too embarrassed to call anyone for help.

Because if they asked me what was wrong, what would I tell them? I had no idea.

It's taken months for the puzzle to come together—a gauntlet of tests and appointments aimed at ruling things out, an MRI that revealed a lesion on my spine. The final piece is an appointment with a neurologist two days from now in Minneapolis, since my parents insisted I not "mess around with small-town doctors" for something like this.

Happy holidays to me. Potentially life-altering diagnosis the day after Christmas. The day before Christmas, stranded on the side of the road with nothing but existential dread to keep me company.

My eyes drop to my phone. I'm tempted to call Dad, but instead I turn on the radio. A tow truck is already on its way, so I don't worry about draining the battery.

I've just cranked up the Christmas tunes—and I'm steaming up the windows singing along to "Jingle Bell Rock"—when a pair of headlights shines in the rearview mirror. A truck pulls to a stop behind me. A man gets out, a shadowy figure illuminated by the headlights. *Wow, that was fast! But I'm also pretty sure there's an urban legend about a serial killer posing as a tow truck driver.*

He walks toward my door.

Wouldn't that be a fitting end to this year—November, devastating medical issue, December, hacked to death on a dark highway. Just my freaking luck.

I shake my head, tap my fingers against the plush seat, think. Okay, maybe a serial killer is unlikely—but he'll probably, definitely, still be creepy.

The man reaches my door, now looming on the other side of my fogged-up window. He raises his hand and raps on the glass. I take a deep breath—this is *fine*, stop freaking out, Simone—and press the button. A burst of snowflakes flutters into the car on a gust of wind as the window rolls down.

He leans his head in, smiles widely. "Hi there. Did your car break down?"

Oh God. My heart pounds even harder. He's not scary at all. He's young and surprisingly attractive.

Somehow, this is way worse than creepy.

"Uh, yeah . . . sure did," I stammer, forcing a laugh. I squeeze my eyes shut. *Come on, he's not that good looking.* But when I open them, his smile is even wider, disarming, and snowflakes are accumulating on his light-brown hair.

Oh crap, yes, he is.

"Do you need some help?"

My eyes widen. "Aren't you the tow truck driver?"

He furrows his eyebrows, and his eyes flick back to his vehicle. I crane my neck—it's definitely a truck, but beyond that I can't make out more in the darkness. "No," he says. "I just saw you here and thought you might need help."

My heart can't decide what to do—flutter at this sweet gesture or race as the serial killer possibility resurfaces.

"Um, thanks," I squeak-say, even as I'm internally memorizing his appearance for any potential police questioning. *White male, about six feet tall, obscenely handsome.* I clear my throat. "I'm fine, just waiting for my tow truck."

His eyes flick back again before settling on me, concerned. "You might be waiting a long time on Christmas Eve. I could give you a ride somewhere, if you want."

Hell no. As much as I don't want to sit here waiting all night, there is no way I am getting in this strange man's vehicle, no matter how handsome he is. I force a smile, wishing I didn't feel the compulsion to always be polite. If Nikki were here, she'd have no problem telling this guy to get lost. "Um, no, thanks. I'm fine."

"Are you sure?" He glances back again. "We've got room."

We? Before I can say it out loud, another voice pipes up.

"Can we go? I wanna open a present tonight!"

I blink, searching for the source of this high-pitched demand. Finally a small head also covered in snowflakes appears next to him in the darkness.

"Hey, I told you to stay in the truck." He's more worried than angry, which pushes him a notch toward endearing instead of threatening. "And where's your hat?"

He scoops up the youngster, and suddenly I'm face-to-face with a smiling little girl. "Hi. I'm Ella."

I smile back. "Hi, Ella. I'm Simone."

"I like your green dress. You look like a Christmas tree."

My face flushes, but I laugh. "Well, that's good because I was on my way to a Christmas party."

Ella nudges the man with a stage whisper. "Mom says we should always introduce ourselves."

He flashes an apologetic smile. "I'm Connor, and I'm sorry, but I really need to get this little one home. She lives in Aberdeen, but my offer for a ride still stands, wherever you need to go."

Aberdeen *is* where I need to go, and who knows how much longer the tow truck will be? I could call my dad, but it's clear now this man is harmless.

Unless he somehow has an elaborate scheme where he uses his child to lure women into his vehicle.

Where do I even come up with these things?

I smile as I grab my purse and shrug into my coat. "I'd love one."

CHAPTER TWO

"'Rudolph the Red-Nosed Reindeer'!" Ella hollers from the back seat of the truck.

"What do you say, Ella?" But her response of "please" is muffled by the music because Connor has already turned on the song. I chuckle as her little-girl voice turns "Rudolph" into "Woodolf" as she sings along.

"How old is she?" My purse is clutched on my lap like a protective barrier, giving me the courage to initiate small talk.

"Five."

Ella interrupts her singing to correct him: "Five and a half!"

"Sorry, El." Connor winks at me and my neck warms. "She's five *and a half.*"

"She's adorable," I say. "She looks just like you."

He gives me a strange look. *Oh God.* Does he think I'm hitting on him or something? *Am* I hitting on him? "Um, I mean, she has your eyes." I stare at the floor, wishing I could melt into it.

"Well, thanks, I guess. Ella's my niece, so no one's ever said that before."

I look up in surprise and he's smiling. I smile back, but it's shyer now. Up close there is no doubt how handsome he is.

We stare ahead and an awkward silence sets in. Or maybe it's only awkward to me. When I first got in, there was such a flurry of activity and the talking point was so obvious—*Where do you live and how do we get there?*—that I didn't have to feel nervous. Then I called AAA again to let them know I'd gotten a ride and to give them the address to deliver my car.

Then I texted my mom and told her a family had stopped and offered to give me a ride—"family" was both true and safer than saying "strange man." Because my fretful apple didn't fall far from my mom's anxious tree.

When I first got in, I thought I was sitting next to a married father, not a handsome, potentially single man who is super sweet to his niece. As the vehicle crawls along the snow-covered road, social anxiety rears its ugly head. I rack my brain for something to say.

"So you're going to a party, huh?" Connor's voice is pleasant; his eyes don't leave the road.

I tuck my hair behind my ear. "Yes. Well, I mean, it's at my parents' house. So it's the three of us and my brother, but they always invite the neighbors over for Christmas Eve. And it's our year to have my grandma, too." His eyes dart to mine, a question in them, and I look down. "My grandma's . . . health has declined. She doesn't really remember us anymore. She mainly lives with my mom and dad, but sometimes she goes to my aunt's or uncle's house for holidays. They kind of rotate."

I pause to catch my breath, and there's a beat of silence. Dammit, why do I always do that? I'm either awkwardly quiet or I spill out way too much information.

Connor clears his throat. "Well, that sounds like a great party to me."

"I want to go to a party!" Ella yells from the back, and it gives me a fresh topic.

"Where are you guys headed?"

"I'm bringing her home. We got to spend three fun-filled days together, just us and Grandma and Grandpa, didn't we, El?"

"Yup. But I have to go home because Mommy misses me, and I get to open a present from her tonight. And I have to be at home so Santa can bring me his presents, of course."

"Of course." I glance over, and Connor is staring ahead. I'm confused by the family dynamics they've described, but even my purse barrier isn't giving me enough courage to ask. "Well, that sounds fun."

Connor turns up the radio, and Ella starts singing again. His eyes dart to mine. "She's my brother's daughter. He died. Six months ago."

Perspective hits me like a brick. "I'm so sorry," I whisper.

"Thanks. Just trying to make her Christmas as normal as possible."

We stare ahead again, but a wave of melancholy has fallen over the truck, a dull ache settling in my gut. We reach Aberdeen and pass through streets I grew up around—my old elementary school, the local ice cream shop I worked in every summer—all coated with a fresh layer of white. I find myself mesmerized by the falling flakes again. A snowfall is like a fresh start, or a cover for past problems. Sometimes both.

"Payton told me Santa isn't real," Ella blurts from the back.

Connor frowns. "Who's Payton?"

"From *school*." Ella says it like it's the most obvious thing in the world. "Is that true, Uncle Connor?"

I glance over and see his panicked grimace. "Uh . . ."

Maybe it's the snow trance, but I suddenly know just how to distract her. "Hey, Ella, have you ever stared out at the snow and pretended you're flying at light speed?"

She leans forward. "Huh?"

"You know, like if you stare out the front of the vehicle, the snow hitting the windshield makes it look like you're riding in the *Millennium Falcon*." I look over, and Connor is staring at me. My voice trails off. "I mean, if you like *Star Wars*?"

"My dad loves *Star Wars*," Ella says quietly.

My hand flies to my mouth. I keep making things worse.

"And who were you for Halloween this year, El?" Connor's voice is bright, forced, but it works.

She grins. "Rey!"

"Hey, I was, too!" It's the truth and my enthusiasm is real, but I'm playing it up out of guilt over my misstep.

Ella starts naming off ideas for next year's Halloween costume, and Connor and I lapse into silence.

"There it is," I say at last. My parents' house is aglow with light from inside as well as twinkling Christmas lights strung across the entire front—a festive sea of red and green popping through the storm of white.

Connor pulls into the driveway. The snow isn't as deep here because Dad has already been out with the snowblower once—he's meticulous about his driveway and his yard all year-round.

I turn to Ella first. "It was nice to meet you, Ella. I hope Santa leaves you a lot of presents."

She beams. "Me too!"

I face Connor, and any trace of sadness from my *Star Wars* comment is gone. "Enjoy your party," he says with a smile.

"Thanks. And thank you so much for the ride."

"No problem. Ella's house is only a few blocks over, actually."

I glance outside at the snowfall, which is dangerously close to blizzard status now. "So are you staying there tonight?"

"Nah, I'm headed back up to my parents' house in Fargo." I frown and he winks. "This old truck has been through worse."

I step out, knees aching in the cold, eyes downward as I walk cautiously on the slippery ground—though I'm able to walk confidently again, my balance still isn't what it used be.

Behind me, a throat clears. I look up, blinking as fat snowflakes tickle my eyelashes, and Connor is walking toward me, my overnight bag slung over one shoulder. "Everything okay? Do you need any help with this?"

I force a smile to hide my embarrassment. "No, that's okay. But thanks again."

He hands me the bag and graces me with his wide smile one last time. "Merry Christmas, Simone."

"Merry Christmas, Connor." I shiver at the chill in the air and the thrill of saying his name out loud.

I wave as he drives away, this handsome stranger I'll never see again. Just as well. I stand out for a long time in the snowfall, no more distractions, only the thickening snow falling on this wintry night and the sadness settling back in.

Then I turn to face the house, absorbing all its warmth and holiday cheer, hoping they can give me the courage to face the questions, the comments, the prying about an illness I'm not even sure I have and don't even know how to describe.

Hoping they can give me the courage to face my future.

CHAPTER THREE

Stepping into my parents' house is like traveling back in time. The rush of warm, heated air reminds me of those exquisite moments when I'd come in after playing in the cold—red cheeked, hair matted with sweat, peeling off the outer layer of snow-caked clothing, waiting to slide a toasty coating of cocoa down my throat.

"You're here!" Mom carries a mug toward me now as she rushes across the entryway. "Bob, she's here!"

Her hug is one armed but comforting, and I inhale a spicy-sweet scent. "Mint hot chocolate?"

Mom beams. "Your favorite."

I shrug out of my jacket and drop it with my purse onto the pile of coats on the sturdy wooden bench next to the front door. My hands wrap around the warm red mug, and I smile as I survey the room. Mom has gone all out this year. White Christmas lights line the tops of the walls and continue their festive path down the hallways and around the rest of the first floor.

Mom and I follow those lights into the kitchen, where a small Christmas tree sits atop the marble countertop, alongside a group of snowmen from her porcelain collection (cute or creepy—it's hard to say). A low hum of holiday carols flows from the radio, and more tantalizing aromas waft toward me. Mom's making her famous swedish meatballs, and I'm guessing some sort of cheesy potatoes, and—wait. "Did you bake cookies without me?" I can't keep the pout out of my voice.

Her smile turns apologetic. "Sorry, hon. But we can frost them together after supper."

My dad walks into the kitchen, and I grab an olive from the tray he's holding. "Ah, Monie, you made it." He gives me a quick hug with his free arm and glances over my shoulder. "Can we thank the family who gave you the ride?"

"He had to get going."

Mom raises her eyebrows. "He?"

"A man. And his niece," I add quickly. "They had to get to their own Christmas celebration."

"Well, we are certainly grateful," Mom says.

Dad harrumphs. "Coulda walked you in."

I shudder at that picture of awkwardness—Dad would eye Connor with suspicion, and Mom would insist on giving him a tour of the house. "So, where's everybody else?"

Mom sighs, leaning back against the countertop. "Your brother is downstairs playing that video game of his."

Dad jerks his head toward her. "I told him absolutely no *Fortnite*. Not on Christmas Eve, for crying out loud."

She holds up her hands. "He helped with the cookies, Bob. I told him he could play until it's time to eat."

"He's always playing that goddamn thing," Dad mutters.

I chuckle. "Well, I'm sure he'll come upstairs when Kaley gets here."

They exchange a look. "They . . . aren't seeing each other anymore." Mom glances toward the basement door, lowers her voice. "She broke up with him."

"Oh no." Emmett is seventeen, and it's been years since we've had anything in common—when he withdrew into his teenage shell and

I into my bubble of adulthood. But he's still my baby brother. "Poor Emmett. What happened?"

Dad scoffs, shifting the tray to his other hand. "We have no idea. Doesn't wanna talk about it."

A burst of laughter floats in from the living room, and Dad sighs. "Better get back in there—if Dave tries to talk politics with Kathleen, we're gonna have to take away their steak knives."

I snort, then smile in a blaze of satisfaction. Last month I passive-aggressively unfollowed Dave on Facebook after one too many ranting political posts. "Tell Kathleen to give him hell."

Dad shakes his head and walks out, and Mom busies herself with silverware. Then she clears her throat. "The Johnsons brought Walter."

I freeze. "No."

She doesn't look up as she begins gathering silverware to set the dining table. "What? I'm just saying. He's visiting from California." She says the word like it's a fanciful, mythical island.

Mom also has fanciful, mythical ideas about Walter and me ending up together—so she can tell her friends how we grew up next-door neighbors, how we used to play together, and how we even shared our first kiss. We were eight, for goodness' sake, and it was a dare. A sloppy, gross dare.

So what if we went on one date while I was home from college one summer, and only after Mom bugged me about it for weeks? So what if we shared way more than a kiss on that date because I was tipsy and needy after a string of bad first dates and short-term relationships? That was ages ago, and Walter and I are thousands of miles apart, in every sense imaginable.

"Mom," I warn.

"He's very kind, Simone. Understanding." She clears her throat. "He works in pharmaceuticals, you know."

Heat creeps into my neck and I clench my fists. "Mom, I don't even know where to begin with that . . . and I will remind you that I haven't *actually* been diagnosed yet." A swelling in my throat, the reminder of our post-Christmas plans to trek to Minneapolis.

"I *know* that." Mom holds up her hands in defense again, now filled with spoons and forks. "I just worry about you. I'm your mother. It's my job."

We share a look, and there's so much sorrow in her eyes that for a moment I catch a glimpse of a parent's fear, a mother's love.

But then she sighs. "He really is a good boy, Monie."

An absurd chuckle erupts before I can stop it. "It sounds like you're describing a dog, Mom."

She shoots me a look, then walks toward me and stuffs a pile of silverware into my hand. "It's Christmas, dear. Let's at least be nice."

Soon the only sounds are the murmur of voices in the other room and the gentle croon of Bing Crosby's "Silent Night." I let myself relax as I focus on my task, but only after I say a quick prayer that tonight will be as smooth and uneventful as possible, that maybe I'll even have a good time.

I scrutinize a spoon in my hand. *Maybe I'll get a Christmas miracle.*

But my reflection, upside down and distorted, seems to mock me for thinking something so unlikely. I drop the spoon into the drawer and slam it shut.

CHAPTER FOUR

The table is crowded with food and people—with the heavy red table-cloth, we look like a group of dignitaries ready for a meeting, the chairs so close together you can barely squeeze in.

I scan my options. Grandma is seated at the end, with Mom and Dad on either side. Damn—the Johnsons have already lined up next to Mom and our other neighbors, the Colts, next to Dad, so I can't sit by either of my parents. That means small talk is inevitable, but I need to decide who is less annoying to sit by.

I push my hair back from my face—there's a snowstorm outside, but it's blazing hot in here. Around me, the group continues friendly chatter at the table, and I make my decision: Walter will surely sit next to his parents, so I have to sit by the Colts to avoid any awkwardness and not send my mother any unintended signals of hope. I'm confident in this choice, but as I round the table, Walter emerges from the kitchen with a drink in his hand, and it's like a warning bell goes off in my mind.

He's on the wrong side. Why is he walking toward the Colts? As he sits next to Mr. Colt, I'm a deer in the headlights, a statue frozen at the edge of the table. But I've committed. Now I *have* to sit next to him, or I'll look like a complete jerk.

The basement door opens then and Emmett walks out, his shoulders hunched over his lanky frame. We make eye contact, but if he registers my discomfort, it doesn't show—there's no sympathetic glance, not even a smirk as he slides into the seat next to Mrs. Johnson.

I face forward again, plastering what I hope is a convincing smile on my face, and Walter smiles back, pulls out the chair next to him.

Across the table, Emmett clears his throat. "Hey, sit by me, sis."

I turn in surprise, blink, then offer a shrug and a quick apologetic smile toward Walter before scurrying around the table. I don't have time to thank my brother as I sit down—Dad is standing up and leading grace, and soon we're passing plates and filling our bellies amid contented chatter. And now seated next to my brother, who has absolutely no desire to hold a conversation, I'm completely at ease.

The minutes tick by, and I fill up my plate a number of times because it's the holidays—no judgment. I'm deliberating whether I can lick my plate after my third helping of meatballs when Mrs. Johnson leans around my brother. "So, Simone." Something about the way she says my name, the slow drawing out of the syllables, makes my shoulders tense. "How are you *feeling*?"

It's dripping with sympathy, and yet there's something fake in her voice that makes my skin prickle. I take a long sip of the champagne Mom passed around the table—so long it can't technically be considered a sip, really. "I'm fine, thank you."

She beams at me, her smile garish amid fuchsia lipstick and face pinked from the heat of the room or the bubbly in her own glass. "Oh, that's *so* good to hear, dear. You know, I had an older brother with MS."

I stiffen. "Uh, well, I'm not even sure that's what I have."

Curse this long, twisting road of medical uncertainty. With all my appointments, every test to rule something out, someone else has inevitably found out what is going on—that the big, bad thing we've feared I have is multiple sclerosis. Sometimes it's been my own fault—like my awkward conversation with my boss, Stan, because I needed so much time off work for medical appointments. Other times, it was totally my mom oversharing with nosy neighbors—like Mrs. Johnson.

Her smile is too patronizing now, and as she opens her mouth to speak again, I cut her off, blurting, "So, uh, how's he doing?"

Mrs. Johnson's brows furrow. "My brother? Oh, he died years ago."

I wince, then reach for my glass, raising it to my lips as Emmett leans forward with a snort. "Gee, that's comforting."

"Emmett," Mom warns, glaring from her seat down the table as I nearly choke on the final drops of my champagne.

He shrugs and goes back to eating. I lean in, whisper, "Thanks."

"I just feel sorry for you." His eyes cut to mine, a twinkle in them. "You know, since Mom and Dad love me best and all."

I elbow him with an affectionate "Jerk." There's truth to it—he's their miracle, born years after they thought they couldn't have any more kids—but I was old enough then that he was like my baby, too. We're opposites in many ways—he's all logic and I'm all emotion; he's drawn to sports; me, the arts. We don't even look that much alike, since I'm short like Mom, my pale skin prone to sunburn, and Emmett is tall like Dad, always tan in the summer. But my brother and I are still close enough to have each other's backs like true siblings.

Despite my gratitude and sisterly pride, my appetite has vanished. I glance over at Mrs. Johnson, who's dabbing her red face with her napkin and sneaking indignant daggers at Emmett. The entire table is silent now except for the clinking of silverware and the clearing of throats, the tension so thick we could be cutting *that* with our knives instead of Mom's holiday meal.

I wipe my sweaty brow, press a hand to my cheek, but it does nothing to quell the flush on my face. I can feel everyone at the table's eyes glancing up at me every few seconds from their plates. The ungracious sick girl. Finally, I can't take it any longer. My chair scrapes against the laminate flooring as I push myself back, stand up.

"Simone?" Mom's eyes dart around the table—everyone else is now looking directly at me—before her nervous gaze lands on me. "Everything okay?"

I shove a hand through my hair, scrambling for an excuse to get the hell out of here, then narrow my eyes at the center of the table. "I forgot the buns."

My brother snorts again, and my face blazes even hotter somehow. Mom sighs, "Ah yes, the dinner rolls. Thanks, dear."

But before I can make my escape, Dad clears his throat. "The kitchen garbage needs to be taken out. I mean, since you're up and all."

I wrinkle my nose, but I'm grateful for the excuse to prolong my absence. "No problem."

Outside, I'm blasted with the cold as I clutch my jacket closed with one hand, the other firmly grasping the white plastic bag stuffed to the brim with Christmas party refuse. The snow is thick and heavy as it falls on my head, weighing down my hair, and my feet push through the ankle-deep snow already on the ground. I make my way around the side of the garage, brush off the top of the large trash bin, and pull it open to hike the bag inside.

Then I make a beeline back to the side door. Inside, it's cool but comfortable—and blissfully quiet. I sag down onto the back bumper of my mom's sedan and let my head drop into my hands.

But I don't cry. Instead, I fish inside my pocket, pull out my phone—cold but dry—then tap out a text: SOS.

It vibrates within seconds—Nikki is probably watching Christmas movies with her girlfriend, Claudia, and her family. Family drama?

More like neighbor drama.

Ooh, is Walter there? Are you going to give him a Christmas present?

A chuckle rips out of me before I can stop it—I clamp my mouth shut even though nobody can hear me out here. Very funny. He's here, and so is his nosy mother. This is pretty much the most awkward situation imaginable.

A holiday season already ruined by medical anxiety made even worse thanks to people and their insensitive comments.

Across the garage, the interior door whooshes open, laughter and light pouring in, along with a slow shuffle of feet. There's a pause—I'm hidden here behind Mom's car, I'm sure of it—then the feet scuff across the concrete floor again. The door of the old garage fridge creaks open, bottles clink, then the door pads shut again.

The door to the house opens again, and I let out a breath, home free—then my dad clears his throat. "If anybody happens to be in here, she's probably got about five more minutes before her mother notices and comes looking for her."

Then he whistles a merry tune as he retreats inside, shutting the door behind him.

I shake my head at my dad's nonwarning, then sigh and push myself to standing. *You can do this, Simone.* But even my internal pep talk is weak, and I stand there staring out the window of the garage door into the blizzard, stalling as I watch swirls of frenzied white snow against the black sky.

Then I blink, narrow my eyes, lean forward until my nose is almost against the glass. It couldn't be . . . no one would be out in that. But there it is again—a figure, tall and dark, hunched into the wind, trudging along the sidewalk across the street. As he passes by the house, he turns my way just enough, and I gasp, bolting out the side door before I can stop myself. In an almost run down the driveway, I yell, "Connor?"

I squint against the pelting snowfall, arms wrapped around myself as protection against the biting wind, and call his name again, louder. "Connor!"

His head jerks over, and for a moment he stands still, looking disoriented, but when I wave him over, he trudges across the street toward me. Up close his cheeks are pink. "I didn't even realize I was back here," he says.

"What happened?" My eyes widen. "Where's Ella?"

Connor shakes his head. "I dropped her off. Made it about two blocks before my truck got stuck."

I nod, relieved that Ella is safely home. "Where are you going?"

He glances out at the thick falling snow. "I . . . guess I don't really know."

My eyes flit to my parents' house, light and warmth pouring out through the windows. "Do you want to come inside?"

"No." He's already shaking his head. "It's not too bad out here. I'm sure I can find a gas station, or somewhere warm to wait out the storm."

The wind picks up as if in protest, and I shudder. "No way, it's terrible out here." Before he can say another word, I reach a mittened hand for his arm and pull him toward the doorway.

Inside, we're instantly enveloped by warmth, and I hear Connor exhale in relief behind me in the entryway. I smile as I turn to face him, but it quickly fades. The twinkling Christmas lights now reveal just how cold he is—he's trembling, though some macho part of him is trying to hide it, pink ears sticking out from under his hat, hands curled up into tight white fists. I gasp. "Where are your gloves?"

He shakes his head. "I guess I forgot to put them on when I got out of my truck."

Without thinking, I reach forward to clasp his cold hands in mine to share some warmth, but then I freeze—*I just met this man; what am I doing?* I pull my hands back and quickly cross my arms. "Uh . . . you . . .

you should take off your wet coat," I stammer. He nods and plucks off his hat, and I bite back a smile—even his disheveled hair is cute.

As he shrugs out of his jacket, I hurry over to the closet, soon returning with a fleece blanket. I step up on my toes to loop the thick checkered monstrosity around his shoulders. "There," I whisper. We're standing so close to each other now, and when my eyes float up to his, I can't make myself look away.

"Thank you." His voice is soft, his smile tentative, and my entire body warms. There's a beat of silence, a shiver of something silvery and light.

Behind us, a throat clears again. I turn around quickly, put some distance between us.

"What's going on?" Dad's arms are crossed.

"Dad, this is Connor. He gave me a ride. And, well, now he's stuck."

Mom—whose motherly radar must have finally kicked on—calls out from the dining room. "Bob, what's taking Monie so long?"

Dad steps back and gestures us toward the dining room with a look that's part annoyance, part amusement. I hold my head high and march into the dining room, but when Connor comes in behind me, all conversation stops. I take a deep breath. "Everybody, this is Connor. His truck got stuck, and I noticed him walking by outside when I took the garbage out, so I invited him in."

As all eyes turn to Connor, he flashes his wide smile. "I'm sorry to disturb you all. I was hoping to find a gas station or something, but I wasn't making it too far out there in this weather. I called for a tow, but we know how long that takes." He flashes me a conspiratorial wink.

Mom's face suddenly lights up. "Oh, you're the young man who rescued Simone."

Connor fixes his disarming smile on Mom, and I'm pretty sure she's already naming her grandchildren. "Yes, ma'am. And now I guess she rescued me."

Emmett smirks, and I shoot him a dirty look. Dad, too, looks unconvinced. "Why didn't you go back to your niece's house?"

Connor's eyes darken—a flash of the sadness I witnessed in the truck crosses his face but is quickly gone. "They've got a full house. My sister-in-law has her entire family visiting, so I didn't want to impose." He squeezes his eyes shut briefly. "But now I'm imposing here."

"No." I say it too quickly—I see the way Walter raises his eyebrows, the way my brother's smirk deepens.

Luckily Mom drowns me out. "Oh, for heaven's sake, *stay*. The way it looks out there, I don't think a tow truck will make it out tonight. We've got plenty of room."

She gives Dad a look, and he sighs in resignation as Mom ushers Connor toward the table. I take my seat again as Connor sits down next to Walter. As Mom fills his wineglass, Connor flashes his wide smile across the table at me. "You were right, Simone—this looks like a great party."

Heat creeps into my face and neck, but attention shifts from me immediately as Mr. Colt starts firing questions at Connor—favorite sports teams, political leanings. In my pocket I feel my phone buzz and reach in to retrieve it. Nikki: **WTF? Did you get abducted by aliens or what?**

I tap out a reply: **The party took an unexpected turn.**

Her reply comes within moments, and a rush of gratitude warms my chest. My best friend knew this Christmas would be hard and was ready at her phone. **Good unexpected or bad unexpected?**

I bite my lip, glancing at Connor before typing my response.

Good. Definitely good.

My appetite has returned, so I sneak another hefty piece of Mom's Christmas fudge. It helps to rationalize glass number four, which is going down as smoothly as the holiday tunes my parents have cranked up. We all gravitated to the living room after the meal, with murmurs of conversations now taking place around the room. Eventually it gets late enough—and the weather gets bad enough—that our neighbors decide to walk home before trekking across the street becomes too treacherous.

But the Midwestern goodbye lasts forever in the entryway, with lingering thank-yous and merry Christmases. Finally it's the cookies—Mom's dogged determination to frost them, to be precise—that gets them out the door. She steps to the door, places a hand on the doorknob with a smile. "Thank you so much for coming, everyone, but we've got to finish these cookies before Santa comes."

Dad laughs a little too loudly—he passed glass number four a few hours ago—as he ushers people toward the door. "Mone, get the coats, will you?"

"Better you than me," Emmett mutters next to me.

I punch him on the shoulder as he slips back into the living room unnoticed by my parents, then pop the last square of fudge into my mouth with a flourish. I'm in that warm, fuzzy stage of tipsiness where life is beautiful, and uncertain futures are easy to ignore.

Plus I've noticed Connor sneaking glances at me all night—oops, he's doing it right now from the back of the room and caught me looking back.

I busy myself handing out coats, saying a polite "Merry Christmas" without really paying attention to who I'm talking to, but one recipient pauses before me, jacket in hand. I look up at last, right into Walter's eyes.

He clears his throat. "Thanks for inviting me."

I didn't. I'm not tipsy enough to be that rude. "Sure. It's good to see you." *Such a good boy.* Not tipsy enough to let a giggle slip out, either, thank God.

He glances over his shoulder to where our mothers are chatting, his mom wrestling herself into her coat. When he turns back, his smile is apologetic, his voice low. "Look, about before . . . I think my mom only meant my uncle was diagnosed a long time ago. He did well for a long time. It wasn't always easy for him, but he lived a good life."

I blink, let out a breath. "Thank you."

He nods. "It was good to see you, too. Merry Christmas." Then he turns away to help his mom finish putting on her coat. A pang of guilt hits me—Walter *is* a good guy. It's too bad I don't have feelings for him. It would make sense for us to end up together. He's been a part of my life forever.

But life doesn't always make sense.

My buzz fades as I watch him go.

CHAPTER FIVE

The guests are gone; Dad shuts the porch light off, signifying the end of the night, and I follow him into the kitchen.

"We started without you," Mom says as we walk in.

I smile, expecting to see Emmett sitting next to her, but it's Connor at the kitchen bar, carefully slathering pale-green frosting onto a star-shaped sugar cookie.

He looks up at me and grins. "I haven't done this in years."

My neck warms, and I smile back but turn to Mom. "Where's Emmett?"

"Probably playing video games," Dad mutters.

"He was tired." Mom shoots Dad a warning glance as she shakes red sprinkles onto a cookie.

"Well, I might head to bed myself," Dad says. "You guys look like you can handle this, huh?"

Mom rolls her eyes, but she lets him kiss her good night, giving him permission to retreat to the bedroom.

I chuckle as I rummage through the silverware drawer for another butter knife, then sit down on a stool on the opposite side of Mom and Connor. The three of us settle in to frost, Mom breaking the contented silence to sprinkle Connor with her typical flurry of nosy questions—pointed but polite, more interview than interrogation. As impressive as it is annoying.

Mom looks out the window. "It's getting even worse out there." She turns to Connor. "You are *definitely* staying here tonight—no arguments."

He raises his hands as if in surrender, one of them holding a butter knife globbed with green frosting. "Okay."

I smile, then continue gliding the knife across each cookie methodically, slathering on frosting the way I like it—thick and plentiful, because no calories exist at Christmastime. I hum along to the holiday tunes that have been playing steadily in the background all evening, leaning back periodically to stretch and try to avoid the stares of Mom's decidedly creepy army of porcelain snowman figurines lined along the windowsill above the sink.

Finally, Mom sets her knife down with a sigh. "I think we're done." I smile at her but notice the slump of exhaustion in her shoulders. She has put together this entire party, taken care of Grandma, kept the peace between Dad and Emmett, and welcomed a stranger into her home. *And* she has frosted the damn cookies.

An impressive feat; and yet, something is different this year.

She hasn't been humming along to the holiday tunes, her laughter carrying above the music from a joke Dad told. The spark I'm used to seeing in her eyes when all of us are gathered under one roof, warm and safe together at Christmas, isn't there this year.

My mind pulls out a long-ago memory of the last time I saw this. Emmett was a baby and had gotten sick right before Christmas—*just a virus*, and yet he was feverish, miserable, crying constantly. Mom had insisted we'd still have our normal festivities, but even at thirteen I couldn't miss the forced cheeriness in her voice, the haggard look in her eyes.

Back then, my brother's fever had thankfully broken by Christmas morning.

But this year is different. Mom's worried about a sick child whose illness won't go away.

The wine, apparently, has given me clarity—and emotion. I thrust forward and hug her tightly, basking in the comfort of the flowery perfume she has worn all my life. After a moment of surprise, she hugs me back. "Thank you," I whisper. We pull back, and she wipes her eyes. "I've got this, Mom. You go to bed."

She surveys the rows of red, green, and white cookies that fill the counter, then blinks at me. "Are you sure?" She leans in, lowers her voice. "You shouldn't stay up too late, Monie. Your doctor said rest is important."

Even her comment—and the fact that Connor surely heard it—can't burst my wine bubble. "I'll go to bed right after I'm done cleaning up, Mom. I promise."

She nods, then squeezes my arm. "Merry Christmas, hon. I'm so happy you're home." Then she turns to Connor. "I'm glad you're here, too, and so grateful you helped our Simone this evening."

Connor looks down—I'm pretty sure he's blushing, but then again, so am I.

After Mom leaves, there's a beat of silence, save for the Christmas music. I take a deep breath. "My mom set out some blankets by the couch—I'll try to keep it down in here as I get this all put away."

"No way," Connor says. "I'll help."

"You don't have to."

He shrugs. "It'll go a lot faster with two people."

We're locked in an epic battle of Midwestern politeness, and the match goes to him because I can't argue with his logic. We place the cookies into faded blue Tupperware containers and stack them in the refrigerator, and within minutes the kitchen is clear of all evidence of a frosting operation.

I settle back into one of the stools at the counter and pour more wine into my almost-empty glass. "You know, we really shouldn't let this go to waste."

Connor stands on the other side of the island resting his hands on the marble top, watching me. I hold the bottle up toward him, offering to top off the glass in front of him, but it's already full.

Suddenly he stands up straight. "Wait." He turns around, opens the fridge, and pulls out two cookies. "Do you have a plate?"

I furrow my brow but stand up and pull a plate out of a cabinet. He places the cookies on it and sets it on the counter, then turns to me with a grin. "We have to leave some out for Santa, right?"

My mouth twitches, and I melt. "Right."

Our smiles linger for a moment; then we both look down, awkward for the first time that night. My eyes scrutinize the floor as if searching for my wine-induced confidence, but I look up when Connor clears his throat. "So, uh, that guy who was here . . . Walter, is it?"

I blush even brighter, holly-berry red, I'm sure. I reach for my wineglass. "Yes."

"Nice guy." He licks his lips. "So is he . . . ? I mean, are you two . . . ?"

Did his voice get a little higher? "Oh no," I say quickly. "We're totally just friends." I cringe—my voice *definitely* got a little higher.

Connor nods, smiles, and it's about to get awkward again, but suddenly he cocks his head, then walks over to the radio and turns the dial. The melody of "Feliz Navidad" gets louder.

"I like this one." Connor holds out his hand. "Dance with me?"

"What?" I scoff, but I'm already setting my glass down. He takes my hand, and soon we're spinning around the room in some sort of swing dance.

When the song ends, he dips me back with a flourish, and suddenly our faces are inches apart and I'm staring into his eyes. A thrill shoots through me, but he pulls me up and steps back, shoving his hands in his pockets, his smile cautious. "Uh, thanks. Haven't danced like that in a long time."

"I'm not sure I've *ever* danced like that." We laugh and the electric moment passes. I'm as relieved as I am disappointed.

He follows me into the living room, and we sit on the couch, wine-glasses in hand. The room is dark except for the glow of the Christmas tree, its winking lights a colorful reminder of holidays past. I let my shoulder lean in to Connor's, but somehow that's okay. The wine is kicking in now, and I'm sleepy. The silence is comfortable, but the air crackles with expectancy.

"Thanks again for the ride," I whisper at last.

"No problem. Thank you for inviting me in. Not sure what I would've done otherwise."

I swallow. "So . . . can I ask you something?"

"Sure."

"Why didn't you stay at Ella's?"

His shoulder slumps, and I sag farther against him. "It's complicated, but basically I don't feel welcome there. My sister-in-law's family . . . well, they don't like me very much. They think it's my fault that my brother . . . that he . . ."

Oh God. "I'm sorry," I whisper.

We're silent again. Questions swirl in my mind, but I can't bring myself to ask any more. He stares at his glass, then sets it down on the end table next to the couch. "Let's just say I would rather walk in a blizzard than stay there. But I'm sorry I messed up your plans."

I take a deep breath, catching a faint scent of a musky aftershave, and now I have to fight the urge to lean my head against his shoulder. "Believe me, you didn't. You *improved* my plans." I shrug it off, somehow not embarrassed by my forwardness. Thanks, wine.

Connor clears his throat. "So . . . can I ask *you* something?"

"Sure."

"What did your mom mean when she mentioned your doctor?"

I sit up straighter, hold my breath. It's not that nobody knows. Hell, Mom put me on the church's prayer chain, assuring that everyone within a fifty-mile radius now knows my business—including, clearly, nosy Mrs. Johnson. And yet, besides my awkward explanation at work of why I needed time off, *I* haven't actually told very many people about what I'm going through—I'm not sure how to explain it, to make someone else understand something I'm struggling to comprehend myself.

But when I glance at Connor, there's such earnestness in his face, and maybe it's the wine or the comfort of sitting here staring at the tree—or, probably, the fact that I will never see this nice man again—that draws the answer from my lips. "I might have multiple sclerosis."

"Oh." He pauses. "You *might?*"

I take a gulp of wine. "Yeah, it's not exactly easy to diagnose. I'm going to a specialist to be sure."

"Okay." He nods. "So, uh . . . what makes you think you might have it? I'm sorry if that's a dumb question."

I smile, shake my head. "No, it's fine. It started when my foot went numb last summer. The numbness kind of kept spreading, and I couldn't walk very well, and my doctor decided it was probably MS. But I'm feeling better now." I squeeze my eyes shut as if to hide from the sting of my own betrayal. I've just trivialized one of the scariest, most difficult times of my life. And yet even in the comfort of this moment, I can't bring myself to detail those terrifying memories of my leg locking up or those first few weeks when I didn't know if I was dying, or if it was all in my mind, or if I would ever have an answer at all.

And maybe it's also because this moment—with the warm light from the tree and the nearness of this handsome stranger—feels a little bit like magic, and I'm not ready to break the spell. I turn to him now with a guarded smile.

"I'm glad you're feeling better," Connor says. "So, when will you know for sure? When will you see the specialist, I mean?"

"My appointment is the day after Christmas." The answer is automatic—my focus is on his eyes, locked so intently on mine.

"Well, good luck." He smiles, and my attention can't help but shift to his lips.

I smile back, leaning forward ever so slightly. "Thank you," I whisper.

We're silent then, cocooned by the glow of the Christmas tree, and suddenly I'm nervous. *He is so handsome.* I fiddle with the collar of my dress.

Connor leans forward. "Ella was right about your dress. I like it, too."

I shrug awkwardly, and a lock of hair falls across my eyes. Slowly, he reaches toward me, his warm hand brushing my hair back, and his touch draws me toward him like a gravitational force. We're so close now—his lips are so near to mine that his breath warms my face. I close my eyes.

The basement stairs creak—a two-second warning that the door is about to open. Connor quickly pulls away from me and drapes his arm lazily along the back of the couch, and I sit stock straight, vibrating with discomfort. Emmett steps out of the basement, his eyes flitting from me to Connor and back again, and snorts. "Don't mind me. Just looking for some cookies."

I glare at my brother and point to the kitchen. When he's gone, I take a deep breath, not sure what to say. But when I turn to face Connor, he drops his gaze. "I, uh . . . I should let you get some sleep."

Ah, of course. I force a smile as I stand, wish him good night, then continue down my path. I don't know where it's leading, but it's sure to be long, uncertain.

It's sure to lead me away from him.

CHAPTER SIX

There's a certain melancholy in the days after Christmas, all the anticipation and promise leading up to the holiday now gone. It's a time of
loss—like yesterday, when I awoke Christmas morning to find Santa
had left me new books and comfy socks but had taken away the handsome stranger I'd nearly kissed the night before. Mean old bastard.

Of course, it wasn't Santa's sleigh, but the tow truck driver, who had
arrived super early and whisked Connor away.

Either way he's gone forever, and I'm sitting here now staring out
at the bleak gray Minneapolis skyline, dread lodged in my stomach.
Around me, the stark gray exam room feels heavy, with its muted
walls and posters of celebrities, their jarring smiles out of place as they
endorse the newest medication for their disease.

Our disease.

No one has said the words yet—so far I've told my story to the
nurse who ushered us in and the medical resident who examined me.
But I feel it, like another being in the room with us, heavy and dormant,
lying in wait for me to accept it at last.

This is my path.

Mom reaches across from her chair, squeezes my knee, and I manage a thin smile. Dad keeps his eyes out the window, working his jaw. I
want to say something—I should thank them for being here, for *always*

showing up, whether it was a school play or a piano recital, moving me to college or to my first job in Sioux Falls. I should thank them for the gift of knowing I will never be alone. But when I open my mouth, no words come.

The door clicks open, and the resident is back, leading an older man into the room, like a court jester announcing the king. "Good afternoon." His large hand shakes each of ours; then he settles into his chair and crosses his arms. "I'm Dr. Montgomery. How was your drive here?"

My dad is quick to respond; this is his territory. "Not bad. Highway 12 was nice and clear. Couple of rough spots, but nothin' too bad."

Dr. Montgomery nods politely but soon shifts his gaze to zero in on me. Small talk is over. "Simone, I've had the chance to review your files, and I concur with the suspected diagnosis of multiple sclerosis."

I blink in surprise—it's so quick, after all these months of doubt and uncertainty—then lean slowly back in my chair. My eyes stay focused on the doctor as he continues to speak, but I don't hear his words, like I've turned down the volume on the TV because I know how the story ends.

It's done. I have my answer.

I wait for tears but none come, like my body has reached its limit — my mind, too, and suddenly I'm so tired.

"Monie?" Mom asks, and I force myself to focus on her. "Do you have any questions?"

My mind is blank, and I shrug in helpless frustration. "I don't even know where to begin."

Dr. Montgomery clears his throat. "Have you given any thought to treatment?"

I shake my head, drop my eyes like I'm back in middle school, busted for not getting my homework done. But I couldn't bring myself to linger on the website my doctor in Sioux Falls provided, the medicines with names like Greek goddesses that I couldn't pronounce.

Dr. Montgomery nods. "That's understandable. There's a lot to think about, including not starting treatment at all, considering your past medical history."

I narrow my eyes in confusion as he clicks at his computer keyboard, but I'm sinking into utter exhaustion now. Luckily, my mom speaks up. "Ah, after college." She turns to me. "Your eyes. The headaches."

God, a lifetime ago—a bad reaction following a severe sinus infection, but I'd relied on my parents to deal with the scary, confusing words like *autoimmune* and *neurological*. Kind of like now.

"They did mention MS back then," Mom says. She continues to pepper Dr. Montgomery with questions, but it all fades to background noise as my eyes float to the door. I close them and picture myself walking out of here—a quiet coffee shop, a dimly lit bar—somewhere I don't have to think about this anymore, because it's all just too much.

"But it's your call, Simone."

My eyes fly open, and when I turn, everyone is watching me. I clear my throat. "Uh, what?"

Dr. Montgomery smiles, patient but detached. "I was saying that because you've been doing well since the initial onset and your mobility has returned, I feel comfortable recommending we monitor your condition with MRIs once a year, as long as no new attacks occur." He leans toward me. "But it's your call. There's no crystal ball, so I can't say with certainty how your disease will progress long term."

I barely register the disclaimer on this contract I didn't sign. I glance at my parents, both watching me expectantly, then look longingly at the doorway again. I just want this over. I want to go back to normal, as long as I can.

I meet Dr. Montgomery's gaze. "No treatment."

We're quiet as our car rolls back across the highway, city traffic thinning when we reach the open road of the wide prairie. Dad's old country music hums softly from the radio as he drives. From the passenger seat, Mom darts nervous eyes back at me every so often.

My phone buzzes. Nikki again—How did it go?—but I set my phone down. I'll call her once we're home. I lean my head against the cool window as snow-covered grass and trees rush by. For a moment, I catch my own reflection in the window, like a pale, sad ghost staring back at me, and it's like I'm roused awake, my shock giving way at last.

This is it for me. This is my path now.

I can't say with certainty how your disease will progress long term.

It hits me in a wave, a future I can no longer picture, a fear I can no longer contain. My face crumples, and Mom reaches a hand back, patting my leg.

"I'm scared," I say.

"I know, honey. But we're here, okay? Everything will be okay."

I'm not sure about that—not sure of anything anymore—but I nod, latching on to her calm reassurance as if it's my life raft through this storm.

Out the window, a truck rumbles past us. It looks vaguely like Connor's, and it disappears as quickly as he did. I lean back and let myself mourn one more loss, even though I know now that it was nothing more than a fairy tale. And there's no room in my life for fairy tales anymore.

PART TWO

FEAR

I hold my breath, cramped inside the cabinet like a caged animal, afraid to make a sound. But the footsteps recede, and I no longer hear the stranger's breathing. Relief washes over me like a wave of nausea.

The door clicks shut. My body shudders as I release my breath in one long rush. I push the cabinet door open a crack and scan the bathroom, but I can't make out any shapes in the inky blackness.

The shooter's gone. I'm sure of it.

And yet I'm trembling as I step out of the cabinet, blinking until my eyes adjust. Sink. Toilet. Mirror.

I am alone.

Still, my body remains tensed, ready to fight or flee. I stare at the door—he could be right outside, waiting. And I'm sure it is a *he*; it's almost always a man when you hear about terrifying stories like this—stories I never thought I'd be a part of. But now, one step out and he might shoot me—like in horror movies, when everyone knows the character should not go where the killer is, but they do anyway.

Not me—I will stand here as long as it takes. I shake my head in defiance, but the fear lingers, its oppressive tentacles tightly coiled within me.

Minutes roll by on a river of molasses, an eternity passing as I stand silently in the dark, calm enough to recite real prayers in my mind: *Our father who art in heaven hallowed be thy name thy kingdom come thy will be done . . .*

Thy will be done.

I ball my fists, the prayers in my head replaced with the sounds of violence I heard moments ago, on the other side of the thick wooden bathroom door. The terrifying crack of the first gunshot. Then the second. A woman's scream in the distance.

My hands fly to my mouth.

Nikki.

The prayers vanish now, and I fall back on my desperate plea.

Please God no please God no please God no.

That scream had to have been hers. That means she is out there now, alone. Injured. Or worse.

Panic consumes me—*I can't do it. I can't handle this*—and I curl down onto the cool tiled floor, hands wrapped around my legs.

My legs. I stare at them, at these limbs that have defied me, shaky and unreliable. I scratch my nails, listen to them rasp against my jeans. These legs work now—they can do this.

Nikki needs me. And I can get to her.

CHAPTER SEVEN

New Year's Eve, one year before

I need more sleep—or at least more coffee, since half of my first cup already splattered on my pants as I scrambled to make it to work on time. I open my office door, ready to cry or scream—I'm not sure. But when I step into the room, Nikki rushes toward me, wrapping me in a hug, and I sag into her.

I just need my best friend.

She pulls back but holds on to my hand. "I thought you were taking today off?"

I drop my purse onto my desk with a growl. "Stan texted last night to say they had to bump up the tour of the residence hall—scheduling conflicts or something. He promised the president we'd have updated photos to donors soon. I think he also told Admissions we'd promote it on social media."

"Sounds like he needs to stop making so many promises," Nikki says.

I nod, rubbing my face as if that'll slough off the exhaustion. I didn't get back to my apartment till almost midnight last night, so it's been a dry-shampoo, wear-whatever-is-clean type of morning. God, I wish I were back in bed.

But New Year's Eve is a quiet day on campus, which means it's perfect for getting things done—like posting updated photos of the fancy new residence hall we're building on campus, the first in twenty years. Social media is part of my job as the communications specialist, along with writing, editing, and media relations. And I do love my job . . . almost as much as I love a stable income and health insurance.

That means my reply to Stan's text was, of course: You bet, complete with a smiley-face emoji.

Nikki clears her throat. "Look, this is my gentle reminder that I'm waiting for you to talk first, okay?"

That was her vow after our post-appointment phone call, and a wave of gratitude hits me. "Okay," I say. "Maybe I'll just get a few things done first."

She retreats to her desk, and I plop down into my chair, eyeing the papers scattered about my desk from last week's unfinished projects—preholiday me deciding I could leave it for my postholiday self. God, preholiday me is a jerk on so many levels.

I sigh. Preholiday me had a lot on her mind.

A stack of mail balances precariously atop one pile of papers. I scan the first couple of envelopes—invitation to a local women's business empowerment conference, holiday postcard from the local blood bank that *really misses me*—but as I grab one, the pile topples, sending papers fluttering to the floor. I stare at the mess, which seems utterly insurmountable right now, then slowly lean my head down on my desk.

From Nikki's corner, I hear a snort, then soon her confident stride crossing the room. I peek one eye open as she stoops down, swoops up the pile, and returns it to my desk.

"Sorry," I mumble. "I think I just need more coffee before I can be fully functioning. At least I don't need to talk to any—"

"Happy New Year, bitches!"

The shrill greeting cuts me off, and an involuntary shiver rolls through my body. I turn toward the door with what I meant to be a smile but is surely a grimace that would put old Mr. Grinch himself to shame. "Hi, Hayley."

"God, girl, you look like hell." Hayley flips her sleekly straightened, expensively highlighted golden-blonde hair off her shoulder and smirks.

"Ease up, it's not even nine," Nikki scoffs.

A deep chuckle rings out from behind Hayley, and Raj's tall frame steps through the doorway. "Hey, guys." He flops his dark hair out of his eyes. "Have a good holiday?"

Should've known he was nearby—the two admissions counselors are inseparable. Nikki and I both want them to date already, but one of them always seems to be with someone else. They're both great work friends, but when it comes to early mornings, Raj is a lot easier to stomach—one of those laid-back, genuine guys. He's asked about our Christmases, for crying out loud, and he doesn't even celebrate it—his family is from India, and he's told us a lot about their Hindu customs.

I smile. "It was fine."

Nikki rakes her hand through her edgy platinum bob—her panicking-at-turning-thirty look, completely unnecessary because her big blue eyes and freckles make her look forever young. She looks at me, and my eyes plead with her. *Save me from them.*

She reads me and nods, a silent bestie exchange. "So, guys." She leans against the bookshelf that lines the wall by the door. "You won't *believe* how hungover my uncle was at church Christmas morning."

But Hayley's eyes don't leave my face—dammit, she's more perceptive than I give her credit for. "Are you sure Santa didn't leave *you* a hangover for Christmas?"

I squeeze my eyes shut, start a count to ten so I don't lash out. Nikki saves me again. "Nah, she just got back really late last night. Three gallons of coffee on an IV drip and she'll be just fine."

Raj laughs and I open my eyes, shooting another grateful glance at Nikki.

Hayley nods, eyes wide. "Ugh, I know *exactly* what you mean. My stupid cousin brought the stomach flu into our house at Christmas, and we all got sick. Then, right when we were getting better, my mom twisted her ankle, so of course I have to go help her out every night."

Raj clucks in sympathy, and I ball my fists until my nails dig into my palms, bile rising in my throat. *At least you don't have a devastating neurological disease for the rest of your life.*

I bite the words back, dropping my eyes when I feel Nikki's shrewd gaze on me.

"Anyway, sorry to bother you guys, but Chet asked us to drop off this flash drive for Stan." Raj peeks back down the hallway. "But his door is closed, so . . . is he out today?"

Nikki rolls her eyes. "We know he's coming in; we just don't know when."

"Chet is the same way," Raj says. "On his own schedule, but always on our asses if lunch goes five seconds over. Tries to pull that 'budgets are tight—you should all be proving yourselves every day' bullshit."

Hayley rolls her eyes. "It's totally a scare tactic. It's not like he'd ever actually fire anyone."

We all laugh, but it doesn't sit right with me even after they set off on their way. I look at Nikki, still leaning against the bookshelf by the door. She holds up a finger, then crosses the room back to her desk—specifically, her shelf behind it, which includes, among books and picture frames, a Keurig machine. I close my eyes, listening to the distinct gurgles and rush of the coffee maker, the heady scent of french roast wafting over me. Within minutes I hear a soft clink as she sets the steaming cup on my desk.

I open my eyes, force my body up. "You're a goddamned angel."

"I know." She plops down in the cushy green chair in front of my desk, directly in the path of the sunlight filtering in through the office window. "So, you gonna tell me, or what?"

I bristle. "But you just said you wouldn't bring it up."

"Right, but I want to know what happened on Christmas Eve." She leans forward, eyebrows raised. "Did you get your turkey stuffed or what?"

I choke on my coffee, cough-laughing as I wipe it off my chin. "Sheesh. No, of course not."

"Damn. That guy sounded hot. What was his name again?"

"Connor." I shrug away the thrill that ripples through me. "But I'm never going to see him again."

"Why?"

"He lives in Fargo."

I wince then because I know it's coming—the classic Nikki look. Sure enough, she crosses her arms, lowers her chin, shoots daggers at me with fire in her eyes. "Because Fargo is sooooo far from here, right? Three whole hours? No relationship could possibly withstand that kind of distance."

"Three and a *half*, actually." She leans forward to argue or smack me, I can't tell, but I hold up my hand. "But point taken. It's just . . . not the best time for me."

"Because?"

I blink. "I Imm, maybe because I was just diagnosed with multiple sclerosis?"

"So you intend to use your diagnosis as an excuse not to date ever again?"

Her voice is chiding, but my breath catches in my throat. I just can't right now—I didn't even want to talk about my diagnosis, and now here she is calling me out on this when things have been so damn hard. My tone is harsher than I mean it to be. "Dammit, Nik. You don't understand."

Several seconds tick by, the hum of my computer monitor the only sound to break the silence.

"Morning, ladies."

I look up, and our boss stands smiling in the doorway, the epitome of a TV sitcom father with gray hair and tie askew, one hand in his pocket, the other clutching a coffee mug of his own. And, like those clueless TV dads, he is completely unable to read the awkward tension in the room.

I force a smile. "Morning, Stan. How was your Christmas?"

He lets out a sigh. "Oh, it was fine, but there's always family drama when you have both sets of grandparents trying to spend time with the grandchild."

I nod sympathetically, eyes on Stan so I won't look at Nikki and risk bursting out laughing if she's making a face. She refers to Stan's new grandchild as "Baby Uggo." Perhaps he shouldn't have forwarded the poor kid's newborn picture around the office—but I thought the little kiddo was precious in that wrinkly, red-frowny-faced way.

"Anyway, back at it." Stan rubs his neck, then turns to me. "Thanks for coming with on the residence hall tour today. Construction is actually going faster than expected—I'm excited to see it, honestly."

I smile. "Me too. Meet you in your office in five?"

He nods and walks away, and the excruciating silence returns. I struggle to collect my thoughts, to phrase my feelings correctly, but Nikki speaks first. "You're right. I *don't* understand. But I care about you. And I'm trying to help."

"I know. I'm sorry."

"Have you decided if you're going to try that support group I texted you about?" Her eyes bore into mine.

"I haven't really had time to think about it." The truth is, I have made a conscious effort *not* to think about sitting in a roomful of strangers as I pour out my life story, but I leave that part out. I followed the link she sent me to the group's website, looked up the schedule, and then buried it among the exhaustive mental list of emotionally difficult things for future Simone to worry about.

"I know it's easier to bury your head in the sand, but you can't do that forever, you know." Her voice is so soft I can barely hear it.

I wince. "I know, okay? I know."

"When's the next meeting?"

"Tomorrow," I mumble. Her eyes are still on me, so I squeeze mine shut. Damn, that Nikki look. "Fine, yes. I'll go. But just once—to try it out."

"Good." Her smile is triumphant.

"But look, about dating." I cross my arms, stick out my chin. "I'm not ready, okay?"

She nods.

I stand and force a chuckle, but it's flat. "Anyway, I don't even know Connor's last name, so I it's not like I can even stalk him on Facebook or anything."

Nikki smiles. "Well, that is a damn shame."

A shame, indeed, I think as I walk away. But it's how it has to be.

CHAPTER EIGHT

Twisting puffs of our own breath against the crisp winter air lead the way for Stan and me on our hurried walk across campus. The walk isn't that far—our campus is small, with the cluster of residence halls situated just beyond the campus quad. But thankfully, it's too cold to talk.

"So, Simone, how are you feeling?"

Damn. Guess I was wrong. "Oh, fine, thanks."

"That's really great to hear." Stan's exaggerated cheeriness makes me cringe, though he's genuine in his own odd way. "So, no more . . . uh . . . trouble, then?"

I hesitate. Stan knows I've been having medical problems—that I've been going through the hell that is searching for a diagnosis—because of all the time off I've needed. But he doesn't know everything.

To him, in this moment, I don't have MS. I'm still just me.

I smile. "Nope." Technically true. I no longer fear my leg will lock up on the way to my car—muscle spasticity, I learned from Dr. Montgomery. He also told me it's normal for my knees to get weak and achy in the cold and isn't a sign of a new attack, so I push through the current flare in my left knee as we forge ahead.

Stan clears his throat. "Well, look, if you ever need anything, or need to take any more time off, don't hesitate to ask. Anything at all."

I glance over in surprise. "Thanks," I whisper.

We continue our walk in silence, feet crunching against the snow-packed walkways, passing a few small groups of parka-clad staff members hurrying between buildings.

When at last we near the construction site for the new hall, my stomach drops. The ground in front of the building is a sheet of ice. My damn lack of balance—even in my boots, I'm afraid I will fall. And along with the risk of injury and humiliation comes a fear that this is the first crack in my self-reliance—a tiny one, perhaps, but I don't know how fast and how far it will spread.

Stan is clueless, forging ahead across the ice toward the main entrance. Anxiety pulses through me, but I have to go on, so I try a shuffling, penguin-like approach—my feet don't leave the ground as I advance, one foot in front of the other, at a pace rivaling that of a turtle. At one point, my body jerks into an awkward version of an ice dance—where your foot slips and you flail your arms and jerk your whole body around, trying to right yourself.

But I don't go down.

I pray no eyes are on me, grateful the construction crew is working inside the building and that Stan doesn't turn around. When I reach the doorway, I allow myself a tiny fist pump of victory before following Stan inside, where we're greeted by wood-framed walls, the smell of sawdust, and the whirr of power drills. Music blares in the distance, and they're pumping heat throughout the building—it's so warm that sweat immediately begins to pool inside my thick wool coat.

Stan tugs off his stocking cap and wipes the sweat off his brow. "Chet said he was going to let the contractor know we were coming, so someone should be ready to show us around." Then he almost mutters to himself, "But Chet hasn't exactly been trustworthy lately, so who knows if he really did tell them."

I roll my eyes at that last part—Stan and Chet have a weird, competitive frenemy thing. As Stan pokes his head around the corner to look for our tour guide, I shrug out of my coat because I know getting too hot can make MS symptoms worse. I don't really know yet how hot is too hot, but I do know that I don't want to risk embarrassing myself around a bunch of strangers. I turn and drop my jacket in a corner by the door. I'd rather wash the sawdust off it later than lug it around the whole building.

"Ah, here he comes," Stan says. "Good morning."

"Morning. Ready to see the new building?"

My heart stops in recognition before I'm even fully turned back around. When we're face-to-face, it does an all-out back flip.

"Connor?"

CHAPTER NINE

"Simone?" Connor's eyes are as wide as his smile.

I blink at him. Stan looks from me to Connor and back again, confused. "You live in Fargo!" I blurt out.

Connor's brow furrows for a moment, but his smile remains. "Uh, well, my parents do. But I . . . uh . . . I live here in Sioux Falls."

"Oh." It's all I can manage, I am so goddamned flustered.

Connor removes his hard hat and runs a hand through his hair before sticking it out toward Stan. "Connor Davies."

Now I know his last name.

"Stan Lawson." He grips Connor's hand into a too-solid handshake—apparently a guy's need to appear manly in front of other dudes doesn't dissipate with age. He breaks the machismo to glance at me. "I guess you two already know each other?"

Heat creeps into my face and neck. The truth is, I've woken up every morning since Christmas thinking about Connor, even though I thought I'd never see him again.

And now he's here. At my workplace, where I need to remain poised and professional.

I nod and fix a smile on my face, prepared to masquerade myself with my communications persona. "Yes, we met at Christmas. Mutual car trouble."

Stan's face is confused, but Connor's eyes linger on mine, and I force myself to look away.

He clears his throat. "Uh, you guys might need one of these." He replaces his own yellow hard hat and reaches for two more on a nearby table.

I take one, careful not to brush his hand or even meet his eyes, but then I struggle as I try to smash the damn thing onto my apparently large head.

"You need some help?" I look up and Connor's mouth twitches.

My face is on fire, and it has nothing to do with the heat. "Um, no, thanks. I got it."

He nods, smiles, then pulls out a pair of hideously large plastic goggles. I wrinkle my nose, and he flashes his wide grin as he hands them to me. "Sorry, rules are rules."

I slip them onto my face and blink a few times—they're scratched and a bit foggy. But I have a clear view of Connor, whose eyes are once again fixed on me.

Stan steps up beside me then and, true to form, fails to read the room. "Well, I think we're ready." He gives his own hard hat a solid knock and chuckles. "Lead the way, Mr. Davies."

The tour commences, and somehow I manage to post on Twitter and Facebook—even string together a couple of short video clips and a Boomerang into a decent Instagram story—as we make our way through the semifinished building. This is a miracle, considering I spend the entire time trying not to stare at Connor. The way he folds his arms across his chest while he's talking. The way he laughs, soft and deep, at Stan's dumb jokes.

About a half hour in, he accidentally brushes my arm while pointing out a study alcove. That flash of warmth, skin against skin. The waft of a spicy cologne I didn't expect to remember.

I almost drop the goddamn phone.

Nearly a full hour of agony goes by and we're wrapping up the tour when Stan's phone rings. He takes off his goggles and squints down at it; then his jaw clenches as he raises it to his ear. "Hey, honey. Nope, not in the office—I'm on that tour I told you—" He stops abruptly, face reddening; then his eyes meet mine. "Louise," he mouths. "Sorry."

He shuffles down the hall a few feet, and it's not at all far enough for me to miss hearing the tension in his voice. Without thinking, I walk quickly through the nearest doorway, trying to ignore this weirdness—Louise has called his office plenty of times, but the calling has definitely increased lately. Tense calls, almost like she's checking up on him.

I'm preoccupied with this fact, and with the artsy way the sunlight filters through the window into this space—a future dorm room. Perfect: I haven't added anything to Snapchat yet. I flip through filters as I turn to the door, but when I look up, Connor is there, leaning against the doorway, smiling. "It's good to see you," he says softly.

My masquerade melts away. "You too."

He looks down, kicks at the floor, looks up again, and opens his mouth—but then stands up straight, smiling awkwardly as Stan steps up next to him. "Sorry about that." Stupid, clueless Stan. "Let's finish this, shall we?"

I stand as close to Connor as possible without seeming creepy, and when we return to the main entrance, I shrug into my sawdust-filled coat slowly. It feels too soon to have to leave him again.

But Stan already has the door open. "Thank you, Mr. Davies. We really appreciate the tour." He raises his eyebrows at me. "Ready, Simone?"

No. A blaze of bravery strikes and I turn back to Connor, but just then another construction worker rushes past in the hallway behind us. "Hey, Davies, we need you back here, man."

Connor squeezes his eyes shut. "Yeah, be right there." He tosses an apologetic smile over his shoulder as he walks away.

My shoulders slump. *Just as well.*

I step outside behind Stan, blinking into the blindingly white sky. His phone rings again, and he swears under his breath. "Sorry, gotta take this again. Seems like everyone's on my back lately. See you back at the office?"

He rushes ahead before I can reply—man, to be that confident on the ice.

I stare at my slippery nemesis, the frigid breeze stinging my nose as I take one step, then another. I square my shoulders. *Come on, Archer, you can do this.*

Behind me, the whoosh of a door, and I turn into a gust of warm air and sawdust. Connor steps outside. "Hey, sorry about that—crisis averted." He looks from me to the ice and back again. "It's pretty bad out here, huh?" He holds out his arm, and a puff of breath escapes me, emotions battling within, eyes blinking at rapid fire to keep the storm inside.

But his smile is easy, his arm steady, and I reach for it. We walk together across the ice, and this time with his warm, solid presence next to me, I have no fear of falling.

Back on the safety of the parking lot asphalt, I don't want to let go of his arm, but it's awkward now, so I slip my hand into my coat pocket, whisper, "Thank you."

"No problem." He glances back at the residence hall, then takes a deep breath. "Hey, so, what are you doing tonight? For, uh, for New Year's, I mean."

I bite back a scoff. *Oh, big plans—lying on my couch bingeing on ice cream and trying to stay up to watch the ball drop on TV.* I clear my throat. "Nothing major, really. How about you?" I pray my voice is casual, though my hand inside my pocket is trembling.

"I'm supposed to meet a few friends at a bar downtown around seven o'clock. Do you . . . I mean, would you want to come?" *Yes.* The word comes quick, the snap of a whip. I don't want to let him get away again.

But on the outside I hesitate. I meant what I told Nikki—I need time to adjust, to wrap my brain around my diagnosis. The thought of a first-date conversation now makes me cringe: *Hi, I'm Simone and I like going to the theater and reading books and talking about movies and by the way remember when I mentioned I might have a chronic neurological condition? Well, I sure do, and to be honest I don't know what it's going to do to me tomorrow let alone years from now but would you like to see me again?*

And yet despite everything, Connor is standing here in front of me, this handsome man I never thought I'd see again, smiling with so much hope. Maybe we wouldn't have to talk about it, not right away. Maybe we could just have fun.

Finally, the word pushes its way past my lips. "Yes."

We exchange numbers, say our goodbyes, and when I walk back across campus, my steps are lighter somehow, almost like I'm floating.

That evening, however, my stomach roils as if I'm adrift on a stormy sea, about to heave over the side of the ship. Christ, flipping through the clothes in my closet is like falling overboard into that murky seawater—nothing but boring neutrals I'm flinging one by one across the deep-blue comforter on my bed.

I'm supposed to meet Connor at the bar in an hour, and as I rake through the clothes hangers, my mind reels—there is absolutely no way tonight can go well and maybe he won't even show up and *holy shit what was I even thinking*—but when I shove a pair of gray yoga pants aside, a pop of shimmering gold emerges.

"Wait, what's *that* one?" Claudia clutches my arm, stopping my spiral, and yanks the dress from the closet—slinky and white with intricate golden designs that glisten as it moves. She sweeps her hand across the sparkly swirls and blinks her brown eyes at me. "This is *yours*?"

"I know, right? Got it at Goodwill during college." I turn to Nikki, who sits cross-legged on the bed. "We were going to go as an angel and a devil for Halloween, remember?"

Nikki snorts. "You chickened out and wore a white choir robe instead."

I cross my arms. "It was too cold." Plus, the flowing robe was much more forgiving than the form-fitting dress.

She shoots me the Nikki look; then it twists into a smirk. "Well, now's your chance to redeem yourself, kiddo."

"No way. It's still too cold!" And it would be even tighter now.

"Wear a coat."

"But . . ." I gesture at the dress. "*Look* at this thing. I'm going to be bulging out everywhere."

"That's what Spanx are for." Her singsong voice annoys me even more, and I glare at her. Her eyes burn back into mine. "You deserve this," she whispers.

I roll my eyes, frustrated. Claudia takes a deep breath, smooths a shiny lock of black hair behind her ear, then sits down by her girlfriend, putting a hand on her arm. They exchange a brief look; then Claudia turns to me with a gentle smile. "It'll be warm in the bar, Mone. How about you just try it on?"

I sigh, and my posture softens. Nikki's my best friend, but Claudia is definitely the voice of reason in their relationship. I huff and pull the dress off the hanger before slamming the bathroom door behind me and then setting to work squeezing myself into this garish costume of a dress. But it has more give than I expect as I pull it up over my hips—it's actually sort of comfortable.

I turn toward the mirror, run my hand down the contained curves of my stomach and hips. Well done, Spanx.

I open the door, and they're both still perched on the bed, waiting expectantly. When Claudia sees me, she gasps, then squeals. "You look so great! I've got some shimmering eye shadow that'll go great with it!"

Nikki smiles but doesn't rub it in—and that is why we're best friends. "Come on, let's work on your hair."

I nod, excitement finally replacing my anxiety. I mean, it *is* New Year's—maybe a little sparkle isn't a bad thing.

Maybe a little magic is possible.

CHAPTER TEN

At 6:57, Nikki pulls her forest-green crossover into a parking spot a half block from the bar. Tiny snowflakes start to fall onto downtown Sioux Falls and the holiday decorations that adorn Phillips Avenue, festive wreaths and twinkling white lights hung on each light pole. I open the door to the laughter and chatter of the bustling New Year's Eve crowd strolling along the sidewalks.

Through the windshield, Nikki eyes a group of stumbling dude bros who laugh and shove each other as they walk past, eventually entering O'Malley's. "This place, huh?"

Her voice is low and my stomach twists. Nikki and Claudia keep a mental list of bars and clubs they don't go to at night—a safety measure to avoid stupid, drunken bigots. But I didn't think O'Malley's—an odd, somewhat mismatched blend of a sports bar and an Irish pub—was one of them.

But Claudia elbows Nikki, shooting her another look. "We came here for lunch last week, remember? It was *nice*." She turns to me with a glowing smile. "Have *so* much fun, and tell us everything."

She turns to Nikki again, who offers a weak smile. "It was nice. And I know you'll have a great time."

I reach forward and squeeze her arm. "Thank you. Both of you."

My door is open and I'm climbing out of the back seat when Nikki clears her throat. "And remember, just text if you need a ride, okay?"

I nod, confident now as I shut the car door and stride toward O'Malley's, shoulders back, my perfectly curled head high. But the moment I open the thick wooden door and step into the loud, packed bar, my confidence shrivels like a popped balloon after a birthday party.

It's a truth universally acknowledged that no matter how hot you think you look before going out, you will get knocked down a peg upon arrival.

A sea of sparkly dresses surrounds me—not too different from my own, except they hug bodies much more toned than mine, their owners fitter, cuter, healthier. I fluff my hair and self-consciously suck in my gut, praying my Spanx hold out, as I scan the crowd for a familiar face.

Self-doubt floods back in. It's stuffy in this dimly lit pub, but I refuse to take off my coat and expose my inadequacies.

What the hell am I doing here?

You deserve this.

Do you really, though? The mean voice in my head drowns out Nikki's reassurance.

Then, a hand on my back. I stiffen in surprise, but it's gentle, steadying, and I look up into Connor's smile. "Sorry, it's so loud I couldn't get your attention." He points back the way he came from. "We're this way." He takes my hand, guiding me through the throng of people talking and dancing, and I don't even freak out about it—I savor how his hand feels in mine, warm and natural, like it's always been there. He shoulders past a drunk guy telling a loud, slurred story, and I stick close behind him—it's not easy being a short person crossing a crowded room, staring at backs and breathing recycled air.

At last, we emerge into a small opening next to a high wooden table with two open chairs. Connor gestures toward one, and as I sit down, he leans in close again. "You look beautiful."

My body floods with warmth and my confidence returns. I even slip out of my coat as I look around the table. A stocky man with a buzz cut and a thin woman with long, white-blonde hair are leaning together, talking. Connor sits in the other open chair and raises his voice over the music. "Simone, this is Harper and Jason. Guys, this is Simone."

"Ah, it's the damsel in distress." Jason laughs. "Did you get your car fixed?"

Harper elbows him, which gives me hope, but then her hawkish eyes dart to my low-cut dress in silent assessment. I turn the color of her modest rose-red turtleneck, and I fight the urge to pull my coat back on. "Nice to meet you," I mumble.

"So," Connor says to them, "what were you two talking about before? You were sick or something?" Harper starts to reply, but I have trouble listening at first—I'm too busy focusing on the fact that Connor's hand brushed my bare shoulder as he draped his arm across the back of my chair.

"Ugh," Harper moans. "This winter has been *so* bad—one sinus infection after another, and they really knock me out." She turns pained eyes from Jason to Connor. "You can't understand how hard that is."

Jason pats his wife's shoulder in comfort, and I stiffen.

But I keep the smile plastered on my face, and Jason turns his attention back to us.

"My turn to get this round." He stands, pointing to Connor, eyebrows raised.

Connor shakes his head. "Nah, I'm driving."

Jason turns to me. "Simone, what'll ya have?"

"Do they have good wine here?"

Harper's face lights up at last. "They do! Red or white?"

"Red."

"Try the house cab," she says sagely. "Surprisingly good for the price."

I flash a tentative smile. "Sounds great."

"Babe, another chardonnay?"

"Just one more," she warns. "We told my mom we wouldn't be out too late."

His shoulders slump, and he shuffles toward the bar.

"It's like he forgets we're parents, for Christ's sake," Harper mutters.

Connor chuckles, and I sit up straighter, clear my throat. "How old?"

She leans forward, lighting up in true mommy fashion at the chance to gush. "She's two." She holds up her phone. "Angelina."

I smile, swallowing a pang of guilt at my internal judgment as I gaze at the doe-eyed toddler on the screen. "She's beautiful."

Harper's eyes shine with pride, and when Jason returns with drinks, we raise our glasses for a toast.

"To a new year, and a new beginning." Harper smiles at me, and I blush as we clink our glasses together.

The silence that follows our inaugural sips is awkward—or maybe it's me. Either way, I feel the need to fill it. "So, uh, you know how Connor and I met." I tuck a lock of hair behind my ear. "How do you all know each other?"

"Connor and I played football together in college." Jason puffs out his chest.

"*Intramural* football."

I'm enjoying Harper's snark.

Her husband laughs. "Hey, it impressed you, didn't it?" She rolls her eyes but smiles when he kisses her cheek. "Anyway, we all used to hang out in college, sometimes double-date—you know."

The silence is definitely awkward, and they both dart wide eyes at Connor. He chuckles, though I notice a quick flash of pain in his eyes. "Guys, it's okay. I'm sure Simone won't be offended to learn I dated someone during college."

They laugh, too, and soon we're chattering again. Maybe it's the wine or the fact that Harper is hilarious now as she continues to rip on Jason, but I'm at ease.

When her wine is gone, they exchange a look and then stand. Jason claps his hands. "Well, Simone, it's been great. But my wife here has to get up tonight with a toddler who refuses to sleep through the night." Harper glares at him. "Okay, okay, *we* need to get up with her. Anyway, happy New Year."

"You too."

To my surprise, Harper squeezes my hand. "It really was great to meet you. Hope to see you again soon." Then she and Jason disappear into the throng of people.

The crowd thins the closer it gets to midnight. Turns out O'Malley's is not the kind of place hip young people ring in the New Year, but that's fine by me. The more people leave, the more Connor and I can hear each other talk.

"Favorite Star Wars movie?" he asks.

I take a sip of wine and set my glass down with a thud. "Wow, that's like asking parents to choose between children or something."

He laughs. "Well, my brother, Cam, loved *Rogue One*."

"Great movie." I nod. "But so sad. They were doomed from the beginning."

He shrugs. "Cam always said they fulfilled their mission. 'Without their sacrifice, the dark side would've won.' He thought it was the most meaningful, I guess."

Wine flushes my face and drives my hand forward as I squeeze his arm. "I'm sorry."

He flashes a crooked smile. "No worries." Then he clears his throat. "Hey, I was wondering, though, how everything, you know, was going."

I blink, pull my hand away, and tuck my hair behind my ear. "Um, fine, I guess. How about you?"

"I'm great," he says quickly. There's a beat of silence, and awkwardness starts to creep in. Then he cocks his head toward the dance floor and holds out his hand. "Dance with me?"

I smile, any awkwardness dissipating as I let him lead me to the dance floor. It's not as packed as before—only a few groups of friends dancing together under the kaleidoscopic light of a disco ball. The song is a fast, driving dance mix, and I lean toward Connor to speak above the music. "This is a bit different from last time!"

He winks down at me. "I guess no swing dancing tonight, huh?"

I laugh, and although being out on a dance floor like this would normally give me all kinds of social anxiety—since my sense of rhythm resembles that of a malfunctioning robot—tonight I just let go, my confidence fueled by the wine and Connor's smile, fixed on me.

I've finally found my groove when the music slows, falling back into an old ballad: "At Last." Connor places a hand on my waist, tentative but strong. He holds out his other hand and I take it, my other settling on his shoulder. Our bodies fold closer together as the music croons around us, smooth as silk, pulsing through the dance floor, through my entire body. Soon my arms are wrapped around his neck, while his surround my waist. My head leans in to his chest; his heart beats in my ear. I close my eyes, melt into this moment.

"Okay, everybody!" The muffled voice blares out of nowhere, and I crank my head around in surprise. The DJ with his goofy "Happy New Year" headband grins into his microphone, on the other side of the dance floor. "It's almost midnight."

The music cuts out, replaced by a drumroll as the DJ leads the crowd in a countdown from thirty. Connor and I have pulled apart, but he hasn't let go of my hand.

Twenty, nineteen, eighteen . . .

Should I kiss him, right here in the bar? I haven't thought this through. The drumroll continues around me, the seconds ticking by.

Ten, nine, eight . . .

No—it's too awkward to do it here, right? Our first kiss should be somewhere else, shouldn't it?

Five, four, three . . .

I mean, I want to kiss him, but what if he doesn't want to kiss me?

Two, one . . .

As the DJ booms "Happy New Year!" into the microphone, Connor leans down and plants a kiss on my lips, soft and quick.

Perfect.

The kisses we share in front of my apartment door are even better, and now my hands are on his neck; his are in my hair. I pull back to come up for air. "I had a wonderful time tonight."

"Me too." His voice is husky, and he leans forward for another kiss.

We're wrapped together for several more seconds, pressed up against my door, and the words float inside my head as if I'm trying them out. Seeing how they fit. *Why don't you come inside?*

He pulls back, leans an arm onto the drab tan wall of the hallway outside my apartment. "I suppose I should get going."

We stare at each other as a deep bass booms through the wall of an apartment down the hall, faint party chatter echoing within. Finally, the angel on my shoulder squashes out its counterpart—*Take it slow,* she advises—and I give a reluctant nod.

Connor clears his throat. "But I can walk you in. I mean, just get you inside or whatever."

I smirk, open the apartment door, and flick on the light in the entryway. "Did you want to check the place out, Officer?" I ask as we step inside.

He chuckles. "Sorry. Didn't seem right to leave before I knew you were safe inside." His face is beaming, and it's cute. An adorable gentleman. "So, can I see you again? Maybe a New Year's Day matinee?"

Tomorrow. I swallow, drop my eyes. "I can't. I'm sorry." Then I add quickly, "But maybe this weekend?"

His smile glows. "Great. I'll check out the movie times and text you?"

"Sounds perfect."

Connor leans down and kisses me again—soft and slow, his face lingering in front of mine afterward. "Happy New Year, Simone."

"Happy New Year, Connor."

The door clicks shut and I lean against it, dizzy from the wine and the kisses, my fingers warm where his hand was holding mine. I turn and catch my reflection in the silver wall mirror and can't help it—I flash myself a goofy grin. This night was perfect, and I'm seeing him again this weekend.

This weekend—but not tomorrow.

Tomorrow I'm going to my first MS support group meeting. I told Nikki I would, and I can't go back on my word.

I stare at myself in the mirror, my smile slowly fading—as if the woman staring back at me has drained all the elation from my body. As if she knows more than I do.

How long can this last? You don't know what's going to happen to you.

I don't like this dumb lady in the mirror.

So I use the rest of my wine buzz to stick my tongue out at the mirror and then skip off to bed, forcing the fear from sneaking into my gut, ignoring it when it inevitably does.

PART THREE

Determination

Monday, December 6, 9:42 a.m.

Fear cramps in my belly, but I rise from the floor, push gently against the bathroom door—the creak is deafening. I freeze, wait, but the room outside is silent. I risk another tiny push, then another, pausing each time, ready to leap back if the gun-wielding monster reappears. But he doesn't. At last, the door is open enough for me to slip out into the break room.

The fluorescents are garish, and I blink against them—oh God, what am I doing out here, exposed, with no plan. Last summer's active shooter training swirls through my mind—Alert, Lockdown, Inform, Counter, Evacuate. But I can't focus on that when Nikki is out there alone. She could be scared, injured.

She could be dying.

I press forward through the eerily calm break room, and it's surreal, like a diorama, not real life—a make-believe refrigerator, squat and humming; replica cherrywood cabinets, dulled by years of use. But I look down, and there's no more pretending. Charlene is so very real lying there on the floor, facedown, motionless. The snowmen on the back of her holiday-print turtleneck smile up at me as blood seeps into the faded brown carpeting.

I crouch next to her, whisper, "Charlene?" My trembling fingers find her wrist, search for a pulse, but I don't know if I'm doing it right. But I have to be sure. Deep breath now—one, two, three—I push up her shoulder so I can see her face, her chest.

My hands fly to my mouth, and she rolls back down—so much blood, its metallic scent mixing with my own nervous sweat and something else, something foul.

"Charlene." The word comes out an anguished whisper, and I squeeze my eyes shut—this can't be real, she can't be gone, not the woman with the infectious laugh and the face that lit up when she talked about her grandchildren.

Go, go, go!

The command rises from within me because I have to keep moving, I can't stay here. "I'm so sorry," I whisper to Charlene, then push myself up, stumble away.

But when I reach the doorway of the break room, I stop again. To the right, the corridor leads into the Student Union, to an exit. The commanding voice of our campus police officer rings in my head: *Get out, Archer!* Evacuating is the best option when possible, but I don't know what horrors await me in the Student Union. Students are gone for winter break, but there are staff members who work in that building—are they okay? Did the shooter stop there first?

The thought makes me shudder, and yet the real reason I won't go that way is because the other way leads to Nikki, and I won't leave her.

I stand up straight. *I'm coming, Nik.*

Holding my breath, I peek around the door—same empty corridor, more ominous than ever before. My hand throbs where my phone should be—dammit, I left it on my desk—but I step out anyway, crouching low. The stark white walls seem to close in around me as I creep forward, my own ragged breathing deafening in my ears.

With my next step, my left leg flares. I glare viciously down at it. *Don't you dare.* As if that could stop it. But I can't give up now. I push forward, trying to ignore the pins and needles in my leg.

Ahead on my left there's a doorway, and my pulse picks up. That door leads to a staircase—upstairs are Administrative offices, and downstairs is an exit. Freedom.

But instead I focus farther down the hall at a door on the other side—Stan's office, where we were supposed to meet. I cock my head. If Stan arrived when I was in the bathroom, Nikki would've come down here.

I try the knob, but it's locked. "Nik!" I whisper forcefully. "Stan?" I sneak a furtive look both ways down the hallway—still empty—then risk a soft knock. "It's Simone." Pressing my ear to the door, I hear nothing.

But just as I'm about to turn away, I hear it: a shuffle inside.

I freeze, eyes on the doorknob as it turns—slowly, the hand on the other side hesitant. As the door opens, I'm pleading within for it to be Nikki, for her to be okay.

But when a face peers out, I lurch back, eyes wide, because it's not Nikki at all.

CHAPTER ELEVEN

January 1, eleven months before

I peer out my apartment window, eyes squinting into this new year as it dawns, a vast gray procession of clouds across the sky. A misty fog shrouds downtown Sioux Falls, and as I sip my french roast, I try to pretend this is somehow a good omen.

I exhale long and slow, fuss with the row of green houseplants on the window ledge, their colorful pots lined up in rainbow order. But the knot in my stomach is relentless—and it's *not* an excited flutter from last night's perfect date. It's the burn of anxiety, the dread of what I've promised to do today.

The support group meeting.

As if on cue, my phone beeps. A text from Nikki.

Good luck today. Give it a chance—maybe they'll have some good advice.

The knot eases its grip. Nikki and Claudia are driving to Minneapolis today to see a musical and pick up Claudia's aunt, who's flying in from China—it'll be the first time Nikki meets her, and she's super nervous, yet she's still taking the time to send an encouraging text to her fragile best friend. Thanks, Nik. Good luck to you, too! I'll let you know how it goes. I end with some sparkle and smiley faces because nothing conveys lighthearted confidence like a well-placed emoji.

I pad across the wooden living room floor and onto the plush gray hall carpeting, but when I reach for my purse on the wall hook, my eyes land on the same mirror from last night. There's judgment in her eyes, and a pang of guilt strikes. The truth is, I probably would've had time to see a matinee with Connor today—the support group doesn't meet until five o'clock. But who wants to spend their second date trying to hide extreme anxiety?

You could've told him, she seems to say.

He seems to want to know, at least if I interpreted his awkward question at the bar correctly. *Hey, I was wondering, though, how every-thing, you know, was going.* But it was so vague and not even a question, technically. Maybe he wasn't even asking about it.

I stick out my chin. Maybe I'm not ready to answer, anyway. Maybe it's too soon to share the reality of my illness.

"Just let me live with the fairy tale, okay?" I whisper my plea out loud, but the lady in the mirror is silent.

I spend the day as one does when attempting to comfort oneself: curled up on my plump, faded brown couch, eating cereal from the box, fully engrossed in cheesy romantic comedies on Netflix. I'm about two and a half films in—woman returns to her small town, you know the rest—when I glance at my phone. It's almost four.

"Shit!" Frosted Flakes spray from my mouth, the box slipping to the floor. I jump up, throw the soft floral blanket off my shoulders, and race into the bathroom, stripping off my pajamas and hopping into the shower.

Dammit, I should've been writing down questions, picking a comfortable outfit, thinking of an appropriate excuse to leave early if necessary. Nikki's voice booms in my mind: *You can't keep burying your head in the sand.*

I sigh as I glob on some shampoo and lather up my hair. Well, too late now—and maybe it's better not to overthink or overprepare. After my shower, I move about the apartment in a flurry, finally grabbing my purse, shrugging into my coat, and dashing out to my car.

Traffic is forgivingly sparse on this holiday, and soon the massive steeple of the downtown Lutheran church looms before me. I have exactly nine minutes to sit in the parking lot and stare at the building, dark and hulking in the dwindling daylight, a warm amber glow emanating from its vast stained-glass windows.

My plan is to use every last one of those nine minutes, so I scroll through my phone. But I can't focus—I need to talk to somebody. I can't bother Nikki right now. I *won't*. So I do the next thing I think of.

Mom picks up after three rings, and I smile. "Happy New Year."

"Monie! Happy New Year to you!" She pauses and her voice is muffled. "Bob, it's Monie. I'm putting you on speaker, honey."

"Happy New Year!" Dad calls from across the room, and I smile, picturing him in his old gray recliner, beer in hand, eyes glued to a football game.

Mom clucks. "We had such a nice big meal, hon—so much leftover food! I wish you could've been here."

I roll my eyes out of habit, but the pang I feel surprises me. "I wish I could've been there, too, Mom," I say softly. "But I have to work tomorrow, and I, uh . . . I have this . . . you know, this meeting."

"Oh, the support group! Dad and I are so proud of you for going. Are there a lot of people there? Anyone your age?" Then she gasps, as if struck by a thought. "Anyone you know?"

God, I hope not. "Mom, I haven't even gone inside yet. I'll have to let you know, okay?"

"Oh, okay, hon."

We lull into silence, but the clock on the dash tells me I still have five minutes. "Hey, how's Grandma doing?"

There's a pause, then a catch in Mom's voice. "Oh, the same. She's fine, really. We're all good."

"Are you sure?"

"Yes, dear. Nothing you need to worry yourself with." I scrunch my nose, think about protesting, but she speaks again, her voice brighter. "Emmett has been talking to Kaley again."

"Really? That's great. Are they back together?"

"Oh, he won't tell us anything. You know how your brother is." Her chuckle is sad, but I join in anyway. The two of us are the same, talking without really saying anything. I don't know how long we've been this way, scratching the surface, hiding the pain in an attempt to protect each other from it.

I bite my hand, and the lump in my throat quells. The show must go on. "I suppose I should get in there, Mom." Then I glance at the clock again and gasp—two minutes. I need to move. But Mom drags out the goodbye in typical Midwestern fashion, reminding me I promised to come up for Memorial Day this year—*not that they don't want me home sooner, mind you.*

I cradle my cell phone between my ear and shoulder, uttering the appropriate number of mm-hmms and sures as I turn off the engine, toss my keys in my purse, drop the damn thing, bite back a curse word as I grab it off the floor, then open my car door, hitting the lock button as I step out. Out in the chilly evening air, I finally have to cut her off. "Okay, Mom, I *really* need to get in there now."

"Sure, hon. Let us know how it goes, okay? I love you." Her words are muffled. Then, my dad's voice in the distance: "Love you, Mone."

"Love you guys, too."

I end the call and stalk toward the church. A whirling flurry of snowflakes takes my breath away as I cross the parking lot, almost like a warning. I open the door anyway and step inside. The church is large, with a newer section added on to the original sanctuary that's more of a community center. In a room to my right, a choir rehearses a song, bright and peppy, about Jesus and love and with a lot of hallelujahs. I smile at the familiar hymn, like a security blanket from childhood.

Down the hall I spot a makeshift sign in front of another doorway: MULTIPLE SCLEROSIS SUPPORT GROUP—WELCOME!

Five more cautious steps and one shaky breath, and I'm in the room. Four long brown tables are pushed together into a square with an open center, as if a big crowd is expected, but there are only three people, clustered together on the side opposite from me. One spots me and leaps up with a wide smile. I clutch my purse in front of me as she approaches, hoping to God I'm smiling back.

"Hi there." She's about my mom's age and wears a similar flowery-musk perfume. I lower my purse slightly.

"Um, hi."

"Welcome! I'm Dora."

"Simone."

"Do you have a caregiver here with you, dear?" She glances behind me.

My fingers tighten around my purse, and the knot in my stomach flares. *Caregiver?*

Dora's smile doesn't falter. "The caregiver support group meeting is across the hall."

"Um, no, I don't." My eyes flick down. This was a mistake. "It's just me."

Dora puts an arm around my shoulder. "That's just fine. We're so happy to have you."

I lower my purse again and cross the room with her. Dora addresses the other two—both women. "Ladies, we have a newcomer! This is Simone." After a chorus of friendly hellos, she turns to me again. "Why don't you get settled—coffee and cookies are over there—and then we'll get started?"

Quiet conversation continues as I shrug out of my coat and set it down alongside my purse. I'm walking over to the refreshments just as another woman—a little older than me, with long dark hair—gets up from her chair and walks over as well. She smiles at me. "Hi. I'm Danielle."

"Simone." I smile back awkwardly, reaching for a cup to fill with coffee from the large silver carafe.

Danielle grabs a cookie, pauses, then grabs another one before turning to me, winking conspiratorially. "This is my only night out without the kids—usually we're driving them to all of their activities—so I'm taking *two* cookies. And I *might* even go to Target after the meeting."

I chuckle as she walks away, feeling lighter somehow, both from the perfectly normal exchange and the quaint family life she's described.

Nikki's words float into my mind—*Give it a chance*—and as I walk back to my seat, I finally feel ready to.

CHAPTER TWELVE

At my seat, I clutch the compact Styrofoam cup and dunk the soft sugar cookie into my coffee—so bland it's almost hot water and yet comforting, a reminder of the weak brew served at every church function, everywhere.

Dora stands. "Welcome, everyone." She laughs. "Well, all four of us. But that's okay—we always have a lighter turnout in the winter." She turns to me. "Some people travel, and for some it's harder to get around this time of year."

I nod, already more at ease with a smaller crowd.

"But since you're new, Simone, why don't we start with introductions." For confirmation Dora turns to the other women, who nod, then back to me, smoothing her light-blonde bob. "I'm Dora Baker. Diagnosed twelve years ago. I used to teach, but it got hard with fatigue—keeping up with little ones is no easy task! So now I work part-time at the library."

I smile, then turn to the woman sitting next to Dora—Danielle, whom I just met, and who I'm guessing is in her late thirties. "Hi again, I'm Danielle Sherman. And let's see . . . the first time I was diagnosed was almost fifteen years ago." She laughs at my raised eyebrows, flipping her long dark ponytail. "MS isn't the easiest disease to diagnose, as I'm sure you know."

Dora nods. "I think, looking back, most of us can think of symptoms we've had without even realizing it—we just dealt with them."

Everyone nods and I join in, remembering how Dr. Montgomery pointed out that my headaches and blurred vision were early clues.

Danielle continues. "Anyway, my *definitive* diagnosis came four years ago, after my youngest was born. I stay home with my kids, and they're a big help—my oldest always reminds me to rest." Her smile fades slightly. "It's not always easy, but we're making it."

Dora places a comforting hand on her arm. I turn my focus to the woman across from me, who offers a soft smile and a nod. "I'm Greta Nielsen." She's older than Dora, with thick glasses and short salt-and-pepper hair. "Diagnosed twenty-three years ago. I worked as an accountant, but you could say MS forced me into early retirement." Her smile widens, so I smile back.

They all face me now, expectant, and sticky sweat pools underneath my shirt as I shift in my seat. "Uh, it's nice to meet you all. I'm Simone Archer. My diagnosis . . . well, my doctor has suspected MS for a while, but the neurologist just confirmed it last week. I'm feeling pretty good, but the thing is . . . I don't really know what I'm doing. Or what I'm *supposed* to be doing—like on a daily basis, I mean—so I guess I wanted to come and try this out and meet you all, to understand it all, a little better."

My eyes are on the floor after the flurry of words, and when I look up, all three are leaning forward. "We're so glad you came, Simone," Dora says softly.

Danielle nods. "Yeah, it's great that you're educating yourself so soon. I think I was in a haze for the first few months."

A haze. I'd never thought to describe it that way. Maybe it's natural that I've been burying my head in the sand, as Nikki says—maybe it's part of the process.

"It's an overwhelming time," Dora adds, "but you've absolutely come to the right place."

My shoulders sag in relief, a glimmer of hope sparking somewhere deep within. Dora gestures to a table near the refreshments, where books, sheets of paper, and DVDs are stacked. "We have a lending library with about any topic you'd need—information on mobility aids and cooling packs, tips to beat fatigue, treatment comparisons. What treatment are you taking, by the way?"

"Um, I'm not taking anything."

Dora blinks but says nothing. For a moment, the room is silent. I grip my hands together under the table.

"What do you mean you're not taking anything?"

I turn toward the sharp voice—Greta stares at me, incredulous, and I deflate like a slit balloon. "I mean, I'm not on any medication for MS right now."

"But, why not, dear?" Dora's eyebrows are furrowed. Danielle's eyes drop to the floor.

My defenses shoot up, and I scramble to answer. "Well, my neurologist talked about options, and one option was to wait and monitor with annual MRIs. I mean, since I'm doing well right now." I catch myself rambling, and my voice finally trails off.

"Well, you got bad advice." Greta's bluntness is a punch to the gut, snuffing my spark of hope.

Dora forces a smile, eyes wide and earnest, and it's almost worse, like she's struggling to argue an obvious point with an irrational person. "The national standard is for everyone to start treatment immediately— that's how you get the best outcome, long term."

I want to run. I want to hide. I've been blindsided, and I don't have the knowledge or confidence to defend myself. "He said it was up to me. I guess . . . I guess I'm still thinking about it."

The room is silent, Greta's judging gaze boring into me. Finally, Dora clears her throat, politeness taking over. "Well, uh, Danielle, you wanted to start talking about this spring's Walk MS event, right?"

I can't force any more smiles, can't manage any more stiff nods. As Danielle begins talking, my legs lurch up as if on their own, and I'm upright, turning toward the door—but my foot catches the chair leg and I stumble, staggering a few steps forward. "Simone, is everything okay?" Dora calls.

I freeze, heat flushing my face. It's not even MS throwing me off balance—it's the unexpected attack of unwanted opinions, the rush to leave this judgment behind. My eyes dart around the room as if looking for an excuse—but careful to avoid the pale-blue pamphlets that whisper about depression; the bright-yellow flyer with taunting bold letters discussing intimacy issues and incontinence; the walker and wheelchair standing sentinel by the table.

Finally, I glance down at my phone, push the side button so the screen lights up, and give an exaggerated nod. "Oh, I'm fine, just got a text from my mom. I, uh . . . I forgot to pick her up." My smile is wide but forced. "So sorry, but I need to go. Thank you all very much."

Oldest trick in the book, and I have no idea if they actually fall for it or if they are just better at polite smiles than I am. I press forward, one foot in front of the other, feeling their eyes bore into my back as I cross the now-silent room. I'm almost out the door—clinging to my purse as if it were a life raft—when Danielle calls softly behind me. "Hope to see you again, Simone."

I wave without turning around. I don't want her to see me cry.

I burst through the church's double doors and then gulp at the cold air as if I'd been underwater. I tried this stupid support group, and it was not as bad as I expected it to be.

It was much, much worse.

I'm never going back. I'm going to bury my head in the sand, and no one can judge me ever again.

I trudge back across the parking lot, sucking in rapid breaths in a futile attempt to keep the fear at bay. But it's chasing me, nipping at my heels with fangs of doubt that are sharper than ever, now that I've been accused of not taking the right steps to manage my illness.

You got bad advice. The biting words echo in my brain.

Dr. Montgomery made so much sense—he said I didn't have to start treatment, and of course I jumped at the chance to put off feeling like a patient.

An ache in my gut now, sharp and accusing. *He also said there's no crystal ball.*

That means this might be the wrong choice. How will I ever know?

Maybe I should've asked more questions. But I just wanted it over. And once I'd decided, he shipped me off for a final meeting with the nurse—the last step of the appointment, a rushed visit where she piled me up with tips and brochures and ushered me out the door.

And now I am adrift in a sea of uncertainty.

I shiver at the bitter wind whipping across the parking lot and the brutal despair threatening to seep into my bones. But I have to get home. I can't stay here, and it's the thought of ice cream and Netflix—the perfect self-care to stave off the darkness—that gets me to take one shaky step, and then another. It's enough to get me to my car, but as I reach into my handbag, a flare of panic shoots through me.

My keys.

Where are they?

I dropped them into my purse before I went in—I'm *sure* of it—and yet my anxiety begins to crawl up out of my throat as I root through the purse and turn up nothing.

Frantic, I press my face against the driver's-side window and squint. An anguished cry escapes my mouth.

My keys, silver and shiny and attached to the key fob, are lying on the floor under the steering wheel.

CHAPTER THIRTEEN

The keys lie there, worthless, taunting me. *You think this day can't get worse—guess again!*

"No, no, no, this can't be happening."

I lean back against the door and zip up my jacket against the cold, biting back a sob, fighting off the feeling that the world is caving in on me—but no, I can't break down now.

Think, Simone, think.

I glance at the church, but I can't bring myself to go back in. I can't face them again; I can't take their judgment.

Nikki is out of town. My parents are more than three hours away and would freak out if they knew I was stranded.

A locksmith? Can AAA help with that? I cringe. Then I stand up straight. *Connor?*

Oh God. As much as I would love to see him, I'll have to explain what I'm doing here—I'll have to talk to him more deeply about my illness, my fears, and I'm not sure I'm ready to do that. But it's freezing, and I rub my hands together—my damn gloves are on the passenger seat—and rack my brain for a better solution.

I stare at my phone. My eyes flick back to the church again; my mind floats back to the meeting, the argument, my uncertain future. My shoulders sag.

My fingers fumble as I text—it's cold, and I don't know what to say without sounding incredibly stupid.

Hi! Are you busy?

He texts back within seconds, and I can't help but feel a thrill.

Hey, just working out. What's up?

I take a deep breath, go for it.

I'm kind of in trouble and need some help. I hit "Send" quickly—I don't want to lose my nerve. But then regret washes over me. I should've explained more. My phone rings before I can type any more. "Hey," I say sheepishly.

"What's wrong?"

There's worry in his voice, and I can't help it, dammit—my voice breaks. "I need a ride."

"Simone, are you okay?" Worry has leaped into alarm.

Deep breath—I force down the lump in my throat, force my voice to sound even. "Yes, I'm sorry—I'm fine, really. I just . . . I locked myself out of my car."

"Where are you?"

"At the big Lutheran church downtown—Dakota Avenue, near Twelfth Street?"

"Got it. My gym isn't too far away—I can be there in ten minutes. Just stay by your car, okay?"

"Okay." I end the call, stand in silence except for the rush of traffic in the distance. A bitter gust of winter wind whips by, and I shiver, hugging my arms around myself and leaning back against the car to steady my aching legs. A sob at the back of my throat is dangerously close to pushing its way out. But I close my eyes, steady my breathing.

Connor's on his way. Gratitude spreads its warmth over me. Maybe he isn't so easy to scare off.

Exactly eight minutes later, Connor's old Ford truck pulls up next to my car. He steps out and rushes over, eyes scanning the parking lot. I want to make a joke to hide my embarrassment, but his arms wrap around me, warm and solid, and I sag into him. Connor pulls back, touches my face. "Are you okay?"

I nod and he takes my hand as he leads me to his truck. We drive away in silence until I find my voice. "Thank you so much."

"No problem. Sorry I freaked out on the phone. Just kinda gave me a scare." He glances over, his eyes pained. "It was . . . sort of like when my sister-in-law texted me that night. I didn't think I'd react that way."

I gasp. "I'm so sorry," I whisper.

"Hey, don't apologize. I'm just glad you're okay." He reaches for my hand and brings it to his lips, kisses it softly, then doesn't let it go. We drive on, and as my body warms, fatigue seeps its insidious grip into my muscles. I lean back against the plush passenger seat and close my eyes, my hand still in his. Soon the car slows to a stop and the engine cuts out. I open my eyes and see the outline of my apartment building materialize into a solid structure as my vision focuses on the light flooding out from the glass doors of the main entryway. Connor speaks softly. "I'll take you back to your car tomorrow." I offer a weak smile in thanks, and he clears his throat. "So . . . why were you at the church? Do you want to talk about it?"

Not really. But I glance over, the ordeal of the meeting, the doubts and uncertainty swirling about in my mind. He dropped everything to pick me up—the least I can do is tell him the truth, for God's sake. I pull my hand from his to rub my face, then fix my stare out into the darkness of the parking lot. "I went to an MS support group meeting today for the first time. It didn't go well."

There's a beat of silence before he responds. "It's no longer a maybe, huh?"

I wince but meet his eyes. "I'm sorry I didn't tell you. It just . . . hasn't come up."

He reaches over and squeezes my hand. "It's okay. I figured you'd tell me when you were ready." He smiles, and I smile back. "So it didn't go well tonight?"

I sigh. "I didn't really expect it to, but I promised Nikki I'd try it. She thinks it'd be good for me to talk to other people going through the same thing as me."

"You don't agree?"

"It's just . . . with MS, *no one* is going through the exact same thing as me, you know?" I shake my head. "I don't expect you to know."

"You mean nobody's symptoms are exactly the same." I glance over in surprise, and he smiles. "I did try to read up on it. Just googled it, I mean, after we first met."

I smile back. He was thinking about me, too, after Christmas Eve. "That's right. And tonight I found out nobody's choices are the same, either. I told them I decided against starting treatment right away, and they told me I made a bad decision."

His eyes widen. "Wait, what do you mean you decided against treatment?"

I shake my head, shake away more words from the neurologist: *MS isn't fatal.* Except when it is. Damn internet and its unlimited information about progressive MS, about rare complications—severe infections, pneumonia. "MS is a chronic disease you live with. There are treatments available to lessen the likelihood of a relapse."

"You mean, to stop it from getting worse?"

"Sort of, yeah."

He nods slowly. "So why did you decide against treatment?"

Because the longer I stay off treatment, the longer I can ignore the fact that I have this disease. The words come fast and furious in my head, and I have to look away. My diagnosis was a terrible relief after months of the unknown. I couldn't take any more information; I couldn't take any more long conversations about it.

I draw a shaky breath, refuse to release those truths. "My neurologist said since I'm doing well right now and my earlier symptoms have resolved, we can wait and monitor my condition. That means I'll get an MRI every year, and if it shows any changes, or if I have any relapses before then, I'll need to start treatment." I swallow. "He said it's my choice."

I squeeze my eyes shut as the doubts over my decision pulse even stronger. Because it's all too clear now that I could have made the wrong choice. My brain could be betraying me right now, forming lesions without me even knowing it, succumbing to the progression of this relentless disease.

But treatment means injecting myself with expensive drugs three times a week—medicine that may or may not be covered by insurance, that may or may not make me feel nauseated, weaker than I'm already feeling. It might reduce relapses, may even delay disease progression in the long run. But with MS, there are no guarantees.

And dammit, I just want to feel normal for as long as I possibly can.

We sit in silence again, the distant blare of a train whistle the only sound, as if signaling a crossroads. I open my eyes and force myself to meet Connor's gaze, because this might be it, this might be too much, an ending before we've really begun.

But there's no judgment in his eyes, just a thoughtful intensity. "That makes sense to me. All you can do is keep making the choices that are right for you."

I let out a puff of breath, relief spreading its warmth through my body. "Yeah."

He gives my hand one more squeeze, flashes me his wide grin, then cocks his head toward my apartment building. "Come on. Let's head inside and take your mind off things, huh?"

My eyes are saucers now, and he laughs. "Whoa, I just meant maybe we could watch a movie or something."

"Right," I say quickly. "That sounds great."

I say a prayer of thanks as I peel off the spare key taped to the back of the HOME SWEET HOME sign hanging from my apartment door. Soon I'm curled up on my couch, tucked into a fluffy blanket and eyeing Connor, who has found the emergency supply of mint chocolate chip ice cream and stands in the kitchen in his gray hoodie and sweat pants. He looks up. "One scoop or two?" I grin slyly and he shakes his head. "What am I even saying?"

He walks over and hands me a bowl with two scoops and sits down next to me.

I smile as I take the first minty-sweet bite. "Do you want a drink or something? I think there's some beer in the fridge."

His jaw tenses. "Yeah, about that . . . I, uh, I don't drink."

"But you . . ." I stop, frown, think back . . . I never actually *saw* him drink from his glass on Christmas Eve. On New Year's Eve, he said he was driving. "Why didn't you tell me?"

He takes a deep breath. "I haven't had a drink since my brother, Cam, died." He rubs his neck, eyes on the floor. "It's something I decided that night, but I guess I haven't really told anyone yet. I'm sorry."

I reach for his hand. "Hey, it's okay."

He looks up and smiles. I give his hand a squeeze, then lean over for the remote and press play. The iconic *Star Wars* theme blares through my apartment.

"So which one are we starting with?" he asks.

"*Episode IV*," I say, snuggling up next to him.

Connor smiles as he wraps his arm around me. "*A New Hope.*"

PART FOUR

HOPE

Monday, December 6, 9:51 a.m.

"Hayley?" I sputter. For a moment, hope surges within me—there could be other people in Stan's office—but when I scan the room behind her, I find it's empty.

Hayley shrugs, grimacing. "Surprise."

I almost fly into a rage—it's just like her to be so goddamned flippant in a terrifying situation—but then I notice her trembling hands. "Are you okay?" I whisper.

"Yes." She squeezes her eyes shut before opening them again. "I mean no, not *really*, but physically, I am. What the hell is going on?"

My eyes implore hers. I whisper, "Do you have your phone?"

"No, I left it on my desk, and Stan's phone isn't working." She shakes her head, looking confused. "I just came over to ask for extra fact sheets for a high school visit next week—the door was unlocked, so I came in to wait, and then I heard gunshots and somebody ran past . . . he was . . . he had . . ."

I raise a finger to my lips—she's spiraling, and if I'm not careful, her panic will spread to me. "Did you see him? Did he see *you*?"

"I just saw a guy in a ski mask, but he ran by so fast, and the door was half-closed—I don't think he even noticed me." Her eyes grow wider. "I heard another gunshot after he ran by. And . . . a scream."

I wince. "Yeah. I'm going to get Nikki."

Her eyes widen. "You aren't getting out of here? You didn't . . . I thought you came here to . . . you know, rescue me."

A flare of anger again, but there's no time for that. "Consider yourself rescued, Hayley." I wrench my thumb toward the stairway exit across the hall. "It should be clear to go out this way. Go down those stairs and out the door—it'll take you past the food service loading zone and into the parking lot."

"You're not coming with me?"

I glare at her. "Find a phone and call 911 when you get out there."

Hayley stares back at me, and I can't read her face. But when she opens her mouth, something has changed, like the Grinch's heart growing three sizes. "Dammit, Simone. I can't just leave you here."

"You don't have to come with me."

She sighs. "I think I do."

All my judgment of her privilege, her ignorance, sweeps away, pushing me toward her for a quick hug. "Okay." I nod, grim. "Follow me."

"Wait!" She runs to Stan's desk and returns with an advertising award, a glass monstrosity from the days of old white men sitting around a table spouting their alleged brilliance. "This could be a weapon, right?"

I nod again, then sweep my eyes down the corridor. The office I share with Nikki is several more yards down the hall, but before I can take a step toward it, there's a crash from above—not a gunshot, but something heavy falling.

I whip around to face Hayley. "The shooter?" she breathes.

My mind races. It could be. Or it could be more survivors—or someone else hurt. My eyes flit down to my and Nikki's office, then back to the gray steel door to my right that leads to the staircase.

Strength in numbers. I have to check it out.

With a trembling hand I lean toward the door, push gently against the cool silver bar. The door eases open soundlessly, and I take a cautious step forward, my feet silent on the faded brown carpeting.

We listen, our heartbeats the only sound, until—there, a murmur, muffled but quick. Hayley gasps; she hears it, too.

Voices.

CHAPTER FOURTEEN

January 11, eleven months before

Nikki and I traipse out into the crisp morning air. A dazzling white frost blankets the trees on campus, a sparkling reminder that beauty exists even in the dead of winter. You can't ask for better winter marketing photos for a Midwest university—the perfect chance to paint the season as something to enjoy, not endure.

"So he stayed overnight." Nikki arches an eyebrow, then turns her attention to a frosty pillar in the middle of the campus green. "You guys getting serious?" Her voice is pinched, but it's her first day back from the trip to Minneapolis, so maybe she's just crabby.

I shrug. "We slept together, but we didn't *sleep together*. And I don't think it's been long enough to call it serious." But a smile tugs at my lips at the memory of his steamy kisses, the fact that he texts me good morning every day, calls me every night, and we've already had two coffee dates and have made plans for an official dinner-and-a-movie date this weekend.

Nikki frowns at an icy branch overhead. "Yeah, but serious enough that you called him before me." Her voice is hurt. "After the support group meeting last week, I mean. You know you can always call me, right? No matter what."

"I know." Her loyalty spreads its warmth all the way down to my toes. "But I don't want to always be such a drag of a friend . . . such a burden."

"You are *not* a burden. Okay?" I nod, and she drops her eyes. "I mean, you could cut the rest of us some slack once in a while." My brow furrows, but she scoffs, shaking her head. "I'm sorry the meeting sucked. What a bunch of assholes."

I wrap an arm around her shoulders. "Eh, I tried it, right? It's done. Now, do we have enough photos? It's cold out here, and it *is* Thursday morning."

Nikki grins. "Of course."

Arm in arm, we make our way across the twinkling campus into the Student Union, past a group of students playing pool in the gaming alcove, beyond rows of tables lined up with eager club representatives, and downstairs into the bustling student café.

I inhale deeply as the heady scent of brewed beans envelops us, welcoming us like an old friend. The line of backpacked students moves quickly, and soon, with coffees in hand, we sit down in our usual spot, a comfortable distance from the chatter of students and the grating sound of the milk steamer.

I sink down onto a plush mauve cushioned chair with a contented smile. When we first started working at Southeastern State University, this little gem gave us a way to keep part of our college lives going after graduation. Since sophomore year, Nikki and I have had Thursday-morning coffee dates—no matter how much homework we've had or how busy we've been juggling work-study jobs.

Now, it's grown into an even bigger occasion, with more of our work friends often joining us—like Raj and Hayley, or Charlene, the nice older lady who works on the floor above us in Administration. "Anybody else coming today?" I ask.

Nikki shakes her head. "Don't think so, which is a shame because I just overheard a couple of students waiting in line say something about two professors having an affair. Figured Charlene would have the scoop on that."

I roll my eyes. "Probably just a rumor. But *anyway*, I want to hear about the show!"

Nikki sighs and her face changes, her wistful smile reminding me of past Nikki, college Nikki, loud and proud and safe in the affirming environment of liberal arts college theater, free to be fully and completely herself. "Mone, it was *so* great. I mean, *Wicked* was fabulous, of course. But just . . . *being* there, you know? I didn't realize how much I missed the theater scene."

"Ugh, I don't miss opening-night jitters." My stomach twists at the memory. I tried out for that first production at Nikki's insistence, but despite my nerves, I had fun—and we banded together with the group of thespians into a tight-knit, boisterous troupe. But thinking of that terrifying moment before going onstage—standing in the darkness, waiting to step through the thick, velvety curtain and into the light— still sends shivers rippling through my core.

Nikki laughs. "Yeah, I loved the rush." Her eyes flick to mine. "Remember the plans we had? Living in the big city, working our way up?"

I snort. "I think it involved auditioning for Second City in Chicago, right?"

"Yeah, that would be epic. But I mean even working behind the scenes, in Minneapolis." She takes a breath, heavy and expectant. "We could still do it, you know."

I pause, coffee cup frozen midair. "What are you talking about?"

Her words come out in a rush, like she doesn't want to lose her nerve. "Claudia's clinic is opening a satellite in a suburb of Minneapolis. Burnsville. She's thinking about applying for a transfer."

I suck in a breath. "Wow, that sounds like a great opportunity."

Nikki nods, her eyes boring into mine. "Yes, we're thinking this could be a great long-term move for us. We're also thinking this might be my chance to try to get a job in set design, or a costume shop, even if I have to start at the bottom, you know? And you—you could look for a job, too. Theaters have marketing departments. Somebody has to write their press releases, right? We could still work together."

I set my cup down on the small wooden coffee table between our chairs. "I don't know, Nik . . . I'm not sure I can take that kind of leap anymore."

Nikki's eyes narrow. "Is this about your illness?"

Her words twist like a knife. "I'm just saying I can't give up a stable job with good health insurance." I swallow. "And I can't forever be your third wheel. Claudia doesn't deserve that, and neither do you."

She leans back as if I've struck her. "Neither of us think that. You *know* we don't."

My voice softens. "I know. I just . . . I don't want to hold you back."

She shakes her head in exasperation. "Hold me back? Dude, I'm trying to tell you that I'm ready to move forward."

"What do you mean?"

She sets her cup down, runs her hands through her hair, blows out a breath. "I've been meaning to talk to you about something."

My eyes widen. "What's wrong?"

Nikki rolls her eyes. "Nothing's wrong. But . . . do you remember that pact we made in college?"

I wrinkle my nose. "I tried pot brownies at your Halloween party a few years ago, remember? It made me so paranoid—please don't make me do that again."

Her mouth twitches into a smile. "Not that one."

My eyebrows shoot up. "Oh God. We need to hide a body? *Who?*"

Nikki sighs, pinching the bridge of her nose. "Look, remember junior year? You'd finally broken up with that asshole who thought he was so smart."

"Ugh, Chad." Then my eyes bulge. "You killed *Chad?*"

"Jesus Christ, Simone, nobody is dead." Nikki rubs her face before shooting me an exasperated look. "We got drunk that night and promised each other we would always be honest about the people we were dating—especially whenever we got serious about someone."

I nod. "Oh yeah. I remember."

"Like, if we got to the point where we wanted to . . . you know, marry someone, we would make sure the other one approved." She stops then, staring at me expectantly.

There's a beat of nodding, processing—then I gasp, beautiful realization washing over me, and I throw my arms around her neck. "Nikki!" It all makes sense—moving to Minneapolis for a better job opportunity is what you do when you settle down and get married. "Oh my God oh my God *oh my God*, you're going to marry Claudia!"

She pulls back, chuckling at the raised eyebrows of a group of students passing us. "Shh, yes, I mean, I *want* to. I've been saving up money."

I cover my mouth with my hands, then pull them back and shake them as my eyes start to well up. My Nikki—independent, carefree Nikki—is saving money to propose.

"Don't do that shit," Nikki chastises, but she's wiping her eyes, too. "So? I mean, it's going to be months before I can afford a ring, so please do not say *anything*. But . . . do I have your blessing or what?"

I level her with a look. "Are you kidding me? You know I love Claudia."

"I know, I just . . . want to be sure."

There's a vulnerability in her eyes that she usually doesn't let peek through, and I lean forward to take her hand. "Well, let me be absolutely clear: you ask that girl to marry you, or I will ask her myself."

Nikki bursts out laughing and we're hugging again; all is right with the world. But a wave of sadness, hot and quick, washes over me, scalding me with reality. Everything is changing. There's a bright, beautiful future ahead for Nikki and Claudia.

But what does my future hold?

I don't have an answer. The pain in my chest pulses, but I push it back, shove it down, hug my best friend tighter—because she is positively glowing with happiness. And in this moment I vow that no matter what the future holds for me, I will do everything in my power to make sure she gets the happily ever after she deserves.

CHAPTER FIFTEEN

We're on our way back to the office, discussing everything from dresses to DJs, when Nikki's phone buzzes. "Well, that's typical."

"What?" I ask.

"Stan. He's not going to make it to the blood drive. Called to a last-minute meeting with the president."

I wince. "That can't be good."

She shakes her head. "I got copied on an email from Chet the other day—God, he was pissed. Apparently Stan told them we were organizing a promotional video, so they got a bunch of students together, and no videographer showed up."

My eyes widen. "I didn't know anything about that. Did you?"

She laughs. "Stan tried to blame it on the company he contracted with, but I'd bet money that he never actually scheduled it. He and Chet went back and forth for about five more emails, pointing fingers. Chet was like, 'Is this even a good use of campus resources, if budgets are so tight?'"

"Yikes." I grimace. "You think that's what this meeting is about?"

She shakes her head. "Who knows? Could be that he screwed something else up."

My brow furrows, remembering the tense phone calls he took during the residence hall tour. "Does it seem like he's making more mistakes than usual lately? Like, is something going on with him at home?"

"Maybe . . . I have heard more angsty, dramatic sighs than usual coming from his office lately." I shoot Nikki a look and she chuckles. "Look, I know you like Stan—and it's not that I *don't* like him—but at some point he needs to actually be held accountable for his mistakes."

I sigh. "I know. But, I mean, we both agree that Stan is better than Chet, right? Chet kind of gives me the creeps."

"Ugh, yes, he's a sexist prick. But I say they are both equal when it comes to being entitled old white guys."

I laugh. "Well, either way, this means we need to go to the blood drive now. Somebody needs to take some pictures for Facebook."

Nikki groans. "Fine, but they are not sticking a fucking needle in my arm."

I smirk. "Don't worry, I'll protect you."

The squeak of the glossy wooden floor greets us as we step into the auxiliary gym, which today is set up with tables and chairs, white curtained partitions, and big red donation signs. At least two dozen students and staff members sit waiting in the folding chairs.

"Not a bad crowd, this soon after winter break," I say.

"Poor fools," Nikki grumbles.

I chuckle, then snap an overall shot with my phone and tweet out a reminder about the event: #StudentsSavingLives.

We make our way closer, and the woman at the registration desk looks up with a smile. "Are you two going to donate blood today?"

Nikki raises her camera and keeps clicking, walking away as if she hasn't heard the question. Clever. I turn back toward the woman's expectant face, and you know what—why not? "Sure. I haven't donated in a while—been meaning to set up an appointment."

"Excellent." She signs me in, then points me to the waiting area, which has already dwindled—they're moving folks along.

"Bunch of bloodsuckers." I jump at the creepy whisper in my ear, then elbow Nikki. One traumatic experience getting an IV put in when her appendix burst and now she nearly drives a stake through the heart of anyone coming near her with a needle. "I'm out. Can't stand this shit."

As Nikki walks away, an unfamiliar burn nags at my chest, an ugly thought forming unbidden. *Like anybody loves needles. Some of us don't have a choice.*

I put a hand to my mouth as if I've said it out loud. To my right, a white curtain whooshes open. A woman in dark-blue scrubs leans her head out. "Next."

I jump up and step around the curtain, and the woman smiles up at me, her round face a friendly beacon in this packed room. "Welcome." She nudges her trendy, black-framed glasses into place. "Have a seat."

I smile, my shoulders relaxing as I sit in the chair opposite her. She's young, with a purple-tipped cropped cut, and she oozes friendliness. "Have you donated with us before?"

"Yes. I'm Simone Archer."

"Thanks for coming in today, Simone." She keeps her smile but doesn't look up from the laptop as she clicks away at the keyboard. "Ah, here you are—yes, it's been long enough since your last donation. Your registration should be a breeze, then. As long as there are no changes since last time?"

Her words fly as fast as her fingers on the keyboard. I blink, registering. "Uh, what?"

She turns to me, still smiling, and I notice her name tag says Lucy. "Medically, I mean. No changes?"

My stomach drops. "Well, actually, no. I mean, *yes*, there's one change, but it probably doesn't matter." I clear my throat. "I was diagnosed with multiple sclerosis last month."

Shock flashes across her face, then a glimmer of confusion, and it's like I read her mind. *But you look fine.* Lucy recovers quickly, though, and gives me a sympathetic smile. "I'm sorry to hear that."

"Thanks." I tuck my hair behind my ear, fiddle with my necklace.

She leans in, lowers her voice. "Do you drink diet pop?"

My shoulders tense. "Um, no, I don't. Why?"

She lowers her chin, her look pointed. "My cousin read online that the effects of drinking too much aspartame can mimic MS. Might want to check into that."

I slouch forward. Oh God, she's one of those.

Hot, churning liquid boils within my chest, and I want to flip out a sarcastic *Well, I think I'll stick with the actual medical science of neurology, thank you very much.*

But Lucy is still smiling. She's nice, dammit—she's trying to help. Plus, I'm at work, so I need to at least be polite and professional. I force a smile. "Hmm, okay, thanks. But I suppose that's not really something that matters anyway? It's not like I'm contagious or anything." My laugh falls flat and her smile fades.

"Honestly, I don't know . . . this is my first week on the job." She turns back to her computer and squints at the screen. Her eyes flick to mine, and I catch a hint of guilt. "Just a second, okay, Simone? I'm going to check with my coworker real quick."

Lucy walks into the next booth, and I wait, heat creeping into my face and neck. My fingers squeeze around my necklace until they hurt as Lucy and her coworker begin to talk, their voices too low for me to catch their conversation. Finally, Lucy returns. She sighs as she sits back down and doesn't meet my eyes as she thrusts a pamphlet forward. "I'm sorry, but you can't donate today."

I blink. "Do I need to get a doctor's note or something?"

She shakes her head, meeting my eyes now. "We just . . . we aren't sure, honestly. My coworker hasn't had anyone come in with MS before, and our supervisor is out today." She holds the pamphlet out a little closer to me. "But this has an 800 number you can call, and they can tell you whether it's a permanent deferral."

My throat catches. "A what?"

"That's what it's called when you can't donate anymore."

I blink. "Like . . . *ever?*"

Lucy nods, and it occurs to me that I should say something, acknowledge that I understand, but all I can do is stand in bewildered silence until her eyes finally flit to the seats behind me. "So." She clears her throat. "Uh, thanks for coming in, though."

I nod at last, plaster a smile on my face, then stand and stumble back through the curtain. My eyes are on the floor as I walk toward the door, because now it feels like everyone is looking at me, wondering what's wrong with me, with my blood.

Permanent deferral?

The words, so confusing and so *final*, make my stomach hurt. I rush out the door and bump straight into our campus police officer. "Oh, I'm sorry."

"No worries, Archer." I look up into Officer Gemma Jackson's kind brown eyes. "Hey, thanks again for sending out that notice about the active shooter training."

I force a smile. "Of course. The session is coming up soon, right?" I've completed the online portion—at Stan's urging—learning about the devastatingly morbid scenarios of what other colleges have done wrong in the past. But to complete the training, I need to attend the live session, as terrifying as the whole topic is.

"No, unfortunately we had to reschedule." Officer Jackson smooths her crisp uniform, eyes darting to the side before resting on me again. "Between you and me, I had some trouble coordinating with the Admissions Office. I get the feeling it isn't exactly Chet's top priority."

I smile sympathetically. "I'm sorry."

"Anyway, we'll reschedule it during the summer—people aren't as busy with students gone."

I exhale, nodding. "I'll be there."

She looks past me, then into the blood-donation area, and sighs. "Guess I'd better get in there and get this over with."

I wince at the reminder, but she's already walking away, her confident walk the opposite of my own weak steps. As I push through the exit doors and walk back across campus to the Administration building, the frosty winter wonderland looks somehow garish now, and I'm chilled by the time I reach my office door.

From her desk, Nikki calls, "How'd it go?" and I slump across the office. She takes one look at me and leans back in her chair, hands folded behind her head. "Wow, did they take *all* your blood?"

"They didn't take any." I plop into a cushy brown chair next to her desk. "MS might be cause for a permanent deferral."

Her brow furrows. "*Might* be?"

"They didn't even know. Just gave me an 800 number to call."

"Well, then, let's call it." I scowl at her dogged positivity, but she snatches the pamphlet from my hand and is dialing the number before I can stop her. "Hi there, I'm Simone Archer and I have MS. Can I donate blood?"

She winks at me, and I let out an exasperated sigh. "Look, just forget it, okay? Hang up."

"Shh," she scolds. "I'm on hold."

I growl as I push up from the chair. I pace in front of her desk for what seems like forever before Nikki sits up straight. "Yes. Mm-hmm. Ah, that's great. No—" She glances up at me, and I stop in front of her desk. "I'll, uh, I'll call you back. Thanks."

She ends the call and sets the phone down, then folds her arms, leaning back in her chair. "Well, it took a while before they found someone who knew the answer, but you can totally donate."

I blink. "I can?"

She lifts her chin triumphantly. "Yep. So . . . do you want to go back over there?" I frown, and she chuckles. "I figured. But, good news, right?"

I say nothing as I sink back down in the chair in front of her desk. Nikki sighs. "So, this *isn't* good news?"

I grasp for the right words to describe the shock of it, the embarrassment at being turned away—and underneath it all, an unexpected shame, as if it's all my fault. I take a shuddering breath. "I just wasn't expecting it. And now I'm wondering how many more areas of my life MS is going to unexpectedly pop up in. Between the support group and now this, it's like . . . like I just don't feel like *me* anymore." Nikki says nothing, waits, and I scowl with frustration. "God, I'm sorry, I know I'm being dramatic, but I just want to feel like *I'm* in control of my life again. I want to decide to do something and just *do* it, you know?"

Nikki's brow furrows in thought. "So do it. Think of something you can do—some goal that's in your control and you can set for yourself—and accomplish it."

"Yeah." I nod thoughtfully, but the truth is, my mind is absolutely blank. Anything in my control seems so small and insignificant—like eating healthier, one of the generic recommendations from the neurologist's office. Big deal. And yet picking something too grand and unattainable would be setting myself up for failure.

There has to be *something*. My eyes scan the office—the Warhol painting on the wall behind Nikki's desk, the shelves with design and photo books. They finally land on the picture of Nikki and Claudia, arms around each other's shoulders, medals hanging from their necks, standing at the finish line of a half marathon they ran together last fall.

The words blurt out. "I want to run a race."

Nikki snorts, and I look up, glaring. "Sorry," she says quickly. "It's just . . . that doesn't seem like you."

I shrug. "It's something I've always admired other people for doing but always thought was out of reach."

She rubs the back of her neck. "You sure that's a good idea? With your legs and everything? I mean, maybe you should check with your neurologist."

I wave my hand dismissively. "They're the ones who told me to try and have healthier habits. If I'm supposed to exercise, why not try to run a race?" Honestly, I'm not sure if the neurologist's office would approve—and I'm not sure I could take it if they didn't. Nikki's still eyeing me, though, so I sigh. "If my legs start bothering me, I'll stop."

She nods slowly, as if allowing her mind to wrap itself around the idea. "A short race, right? Like a 5K?"

I have to bite back a chuckle—to a nonrunner, a 5K is anything but short. But it is the shortest possible race, and my mind is made up. My nod is confident.

Nikki nods back, cementing our plan. "Okay, then. You want to run a race, you'll run a race. I'm thinking the Turkey Day 5K on Thanksgiving weekend—it's the last local run this year, so we'll have plenty of time to train."

I scoff. "Gee, thanks for the vote of confidence."

She holds up a hand. "Hey, it's important to take things slow. But don't worry—I am going to train with you. Starting today. You're coming to the gym with me after work."

My phone buzzes—a text from Connor.

Hey, beautiful. Movie tonight? I'll bring pizza and The Empire Strikes Back.

Damn. My first test. A trifecta of temptation staring me right in the face—luscious food, one of my favorite films, and my hot new boyfriend.

A thrill shoots through me—*is* he my boyfriend?

No time to deliberate—Nikki reads my text and stares at me, a challenge in her eyes. I raise my chin, defiant, then text back:

I would love to, but I can't tonight—going to the gym with Nikki. Rain check?

Sure. Have fun.

I nod at Nikki. "Okay."

CHAPTER SIXTEEN

Two hours—*two full hours* of smelling stale sweat and humiliating myself on treadmills, ellipticals, and various other contraptions, each oddly resembling some ancient device of torture.

But thanks to Nikki, I did it.

Now, I'm dragging myself down the hall of my apartment building, soaked in sweat, arms and legs leaden, my feet shuffling across the faded gray carpeting because I'm drained of the energy necessary to lift them fully. And this is only the preshow. Tomorrow I'll be slugged with the main event: soreness so powerful that it'll hurt to move.

But dammit, it feels good somehow, like I've accomplished something.

I'm smiling to myself as I pass my neighbor's door, which clicks open a crack. "Everything all right, Simone?" Mrs. Wallace steps out, pushing up her thick glasses with one hand and clutching closed her powder-blue terry-cloth robe with the other.

I smile. "Oh yes, everything's fine."

The old woman's eyes widen, scanning me—my face flushed red from exertion, hair askew and matted with sweat. She scratches her soft white curls, puffs out her wrinkled brown cheeks. "You're sure you're okay?"

"Yep, just getting back from the gym." I shrug.

She looks confused but chuckles, then lifts up a finger for me to wait, disappears back behind the door, and returns with a pan of chocolate cupcakes. "I did it again."

They're fresh, and as the gooey sweet chocolate floods my nose, drool pools within my mouth. "Oh, those look amazing, Mrs. Wallace." I lean back against the tan wall, trying to distance myself from this temptation.

She beams. "You know I love to bake, but it's always way more than I can eat all by myself."

"Well, maybe I'll just take one . . ." She thrusts the entire pan toward me, holding it out until I take it. "Okay, twist my arm. Maybe I can bring them into work so I don't eat them all myself."

Mrs. Wallace crosses her arms, a twinkle in her eye. "Or, you could share some with that strapping young man I've seen you with."

She winks and turns back toward her apartment, the door shutting behind her with a soft click.

I stare down at the thickly frosted goodies in my hands, willpower sapping out of my weary bones. My stomach rumbles, struck by the intense hunger that comes after a workout. With a deep breath, I rush through my own apartment door, slamming it shut behind me, and stalk over to the fridge—I stick the cupcakes all the way in the back, behind the stale box of baking soda and last week's never-to-be-finished quinoa. "There." I nod, satisfied.

In my bathroom, I crank up a playlist on my phone so I can sing in the shower—off key but happy. Towel-clad, I pad to my bedroom afterward, toss my smelly heap of gym clothes in the hamper, and slip into the pajama set Mom gave me for Christmas—my coziest jammies, with fuzzy red pants and a top adorned in snowflakes.

My stomach calls to me again—*Feed me, oh cruel master*—threatening to gnaw away at my insides if I don't soon succumb to its demands.

Fuel your body, Nikki had advised.

You mean with pizza and wine?

She didn't find that response funny.

With the cupcakes safely stashed away, I'm confident I can make a healthier choice. All that stands between me and leftover chicken and veggies is a lingering chill, so I dig through my closet for a sweatshirt but come up with only short sleeves. My eyes flit to the heaping hamper, where I flung my workout clothes. Damn. Laundry day tomorrow, for sure.

Out in the living room, I scan with narrowed eyes until I spy a gray lump sticking out from under a throw pillow on the recliner. Bingo—score one for being a slob.

But when I pull it out, a goofy smile spreads across my face. It's Connor's sweatshirt, deep gray, with a purple Minnesota Vikings mascot head in the middle. I dart my eyes side to side as if someone will see me, then slip it on over my head. It's big and warm and blankets me in its safe, comforting embrace. I pull the neck up over my nose and inhale, hoping to catch a leftover trace of his musky cologne.

When my phone rings, I jump as if I've been busted creeping outside his window. A deep breath calms me for a moment, and I pull out my phone. My brow furrows at the name on the screen as I answer the call. "Emmett?"

"Heya, Mone."

"What's wrong?"

He snorts. "Why do you always assume something's wrong?"

"Because you have on numerous occasions informed me that phones are for texting, not calling."

"Touché."

"So?"

He sighs. "Now, promise you won't get mad . . ."

"I can't promise anything until you tell me what's going on."

He sighs. "I'm in Sioux Falls."

My eyes narrow. "Are Mom and Dad with you?"

"Not exactly."

"Emmett. It's a yes-or-no question."

"Okay, then, no. They're not."

Worry has turned to all-out alarm. "Do they know where you are?"

Pause. "Uh . . . not exactly."

"Emmett."

"Okay, that time it was true. They didn't know when I left, but I texted them when I stopped for gas in Watertown."

I ease down onto my plush green armchair, a hand-me-down from my parents, as my brain tries to process. "Em, did you run away?"

He snorts again. "Mone, I'm seventeen. I'm pretty sure I could legally live on my own if I wanted to."

"Then just tell me what's going on!" I yell the words louder than I intend to, dangerously close to flipping out.

"I'll tell you in about a minute."

"Emmett, I—"

A knock on my door cuts me off. I stare at the door, down at my phone, then back at the door. "Oh, for God's sake." I hit "End," march over to the door, and whip it open.

My brother stands on the other side, head bowed, smile apologetic. "Surprise," he murmurs.

PART FIVE

TREPIDATION

Monday, December 6, 9:56 a.m.

The lilting murmurs draw me forward like the Pied Piper's haunting melody. My entire body buzzes—I don't know if this is right or wrong, but some primal part of me needs to find out.

I motion for Hayley to hold the door, then crawl up the carpeted stairs, crouched like an animal, unsure whether I'm predator or prey.

All I have to do is get to the landing halfway up, where the staircase turns sharply and continues up the opposite way. I can peek around it, keeping most of myself hidden. If I see anything suspicious, we'll retreat. I can do this—I can stay safe.

Safe. I shudder.

At the landing, time seems to stand still as I hold my breath and peer around the corner, scanning frantically for danger above. At the top of the stairs, the doorway leading into the upstairs hallway is ajar, as if something is holding it open.

Oh God. It's a person. A human being is wedged in the doorway.

Sickness rises in my stomach—a man is lying there, hand outstretched as if reaching for help.

Covered in blood.

I puff out a terrified breath and pitch backward, stumbling down the stairs, where Hayley, thank God, is still holding the door open. I push her back into the hallway, easing the door closed so he doesn't hear it slam—because I know he's up there now.

The shooter is up there.

"What?" Hayley whispers, eyes wild. "What did you see?"

"Someone else . . . another . . ." I can't say the word, can't erase the vision in my head, another death. *How many more will there be?*

I need to find Nikki. I need to make sure this isn't her fate.

Without warning a wave of dizziness hits, and I sway, gripping the wall for support. I take deep breaths, reciting prayers, even though my mind is as jumbled and chaotic as the nightmarish scene around us. *I have to stay strong. I have to find her.*

When my head clears, I turn to Hayley, and she's trembling, fear etched on her face. I place my hand gently on her arm. "Go." I point back down the corridor, where a door leads into the Student Union. "It should be clear that way. You can get out—just be careful."

Seconds tick by as Hayley stares over her shoulder; then she turns back to me, drawing a shuddering breath. "No," she whispers. "Let's go find her. Together."

I nod, and without another word we walk toward the office I share with Nikki. Christmas music wafts faintly out the open door, the sugary-sweet notes chilling in this macabre scene. But the song changes as we reach the doorway, the melancholy notes of "Silent Night" now guiding us forward, and all does feel calm—eerily so.

I can see the entire expanse of our joint office, but my eyes are drawn to Nikki's chair, pushed way back from her desk, empty. She must've jumped up when she heard the first gunshot. Must've rushed toward the door. Must've clung to the string of white Christmas lights that line my bookshelf when the bullet took her down.

Because those lights are tangled in her outstretched hand.

Nikki is lying motionless on the floor.

CHAPTER SEVENTEEN

January 11, eleven months before

Outside my apartment door, my brother is standing before me. Then, behind him, a creak—Mrs. Wallace's door edges open, her small face peeks out, eyebrows raised. Oh God, that's all I need—my neighbor thinking I'm entertaining two young men. I wave, a smile plastered on my face. "Sorry for the noise—my brother is visiting."

My face is stern when I turn to Emmett. "Get in here, will you?" He shuffles in, and I shut the door behind him. "Okay, what the hell is going on?"

He holds up his hands. "Like I said, don't be mad, but . . ."

I raise my eyebrows. "But . . . ?"

He swallows. "But I kind of used your address for something."

My eyes narrow. "For what?"

"To . . . uh . . . to buy something."

"But why couldn't you just ship it home?"

He rubs his neck. "Because Mom and Dad wouldn't approve."

My hands fly to my mouth. "Oh God, Emmett, are you buying drugs?"

He rolls his eyes. "Ease up, sis. It's a snowmobile."

I blink. "You had a *snowmobile* shipped to my apartment?"

He laughs. "Nah, someone's meeting me here, in your parking lot, to drop it off."

"Someone who? Like a guy from a dealership or something?"

"Not exactly."

I cross my arms, leveling him with my fed-up-big-sister glare.

He sighs and slinks down onto the arm of the couch. "I bought it from a guy off Craigslist."

An alarm bell rings in my head, but I'm still busy figuring out the logistics of his plan. "How are you going to get a snowmobile back to Aberdeen?"

He looks down. "I . . . uh . . . I sort of borrowed Dad's truck."

I lean back against the entryway wall. "Holy shit, Em. Do you realize how much trouble you're in?" I bolt back upright before he can answer. "Oh God, you said you texted Mom and Dad from Watertown. Did they text back?"

"Yeah, like, a few times."

"I can't believe they haven't called me—"

My phone rings in my hand before I complete the thought. Emmett tries to laugh, but my glare cuts him off. I grimace as I bring the phone to my ear. "Hi, Mom."

"Simone, have you heard from Emmett?"

I ache at the fear in her voice, and my frown deepens at my brother until he drops his eyes. "He's standing right in front of me, Mom. He's at my place."

"Oh, thank God—Bob, he's with Simone." I can't understand my dad's reply, but his tone is biting. "Mone, can I talk to him?"

I hold the phone out to him, but he shakes his head. "Emmett," I whisper, but when he looks up, his eyes are pleading, and suddenly my little brother is five years old again, scared on his first day of kindergarten. Needing my protection. I sigh. "Mom, he's not up for talking right now. But he's okay—he's safe with me." It's true, but of course I've omitted the snowmobile purchase he's making from some rando. "I'll have him give you a call a little later?"

There's a muffled voice, some shuffling, then my dad booms into the phone, "You tell your brother it's fine if he doesn't want to talk to us now, but he is sure as hell going to talk to us when we get there."

I swallow. "You're coming here? Now?"

"Of course we are!" he roars. "He's already grounded until he's thirty, but if he doesn't have a damn good explanation for taking my truck, I'm going to call the police and report it stolen." Emmett is close enough to hear my dad over the phone, and his face pales. "Tell your brother he has about three hours until Judgment Day."

I say goodbye, then turn to Emmett. "They'll be here in three hours. I have so many questions for you, but right now I need to know two things. One, when is this snowmobile guy getting here?"

"In about forty-five minutes. He's going to text me when he's in the parking lot." He meets my eyes. "What's your other question?"

I stare at my brother as if noticing for the first time the sag in his shoulders, the droop of his eyelids, the way he's beaten down, too weathered for his young soul—the last leaf on a bare tree, ready to fall at any moment. "Are you okay?" I whisper.

He flinches but then quickly rolls his eyes. "I'm fine."

"Okay." I reach out and hug him, brief but fierce, then step back. He's not telling the full truth, but right now I'm in triage mode—there's a more pressing concern to deal with. "So this guy who's coming: What do you know about him?"

He shrugs. "Not much, I guess. He had a snowmobile I could afford."

I shake my head, my big-sister radar on full alert. "Craigslist, Emmett? Really? I swear to God the only time I hear about Craigslist is when someone gets murdered."

Emmett rolls his eyes. "It's not a big deal, Simone." I glare at him, and he changes tactic. "I mean, he's not coming inside or anything."

I want to inform my brother that murders can and probably do happen in parking lots every day, but he already seems to think I'm overreacting. Think, Simone, think. My phone beeps in my hand, and I look down.

Connor: How was your workout?

I look up at my brother, a glint in my eye. Emmett frowns. "What?"

I smile and look down at my phone again, typing out a text: Well, I won't be running any marathons soon, but it was okay.

I wait a few seconds, then: Hey, can I call you?

I swear less than a second goes by before his response appears: Sure.

As the phone rings, I find myself praying in my head—an absurd little habit when I'm nervous, like a holy antidote to stage fright and anxiety.

"Hey." His greeting is as warm as his sweatshirt—God, how can one word make your entire insides melt?

"Hi," I say. Emmett makes a face, and I wipe away my swooning smile, clear my throat. "So, random question, but, uh, what are you doing right now?"

"Oh, you know, something super important."

"Bingeing on Netflix and popcorn, huh?"

He laughs. "Busted. What's up?"

"My brother is here. Unexpectedly. He sort of bought a snowmobile on the internet and set it up to meet someone here to pick it up tonight."

"He did what?"

"Um, well, Emmett bought it on Craigslist, and the guy is apparently bringing it here to my place . . . tonight."

There's a pause. "So . . . a stranger your brother found on Craigslist is coming to your apartment?"

"Pretty much, yeah. Well, Emmett's supposed to meet him in the parking lot, but I guess that kind of makes me nervous. I mean, I'll totally go out there with him, of course, but I was just wondering, if, um . . . if you . . ." I trail off, suddenly afraid to say the words. Maybe this is a mistake. Once again, I'm asking him to drop everything to help me with a random minicrisis—not exactly the cool-girl vibe I'd like to project.

I open my mouth, prepared to backpedal, but Connor speaks gently. "Do you want me to come over?"

Relief floods through me. "Would you?"

"Of course. When is he coming?"

"In about forty minutes."

"I'll be there as soon as I can." He pauses. "But wait inside until I get there, even if the guy shows up before me. Please?"

"We will." I smile, glad I'm not the only one weirded out by this unexpected visitor. I end the call and turn to my brother. "Connor's on his way over."

But when I look at Emmett, he looks confused. "Connor from Christmas?" Then his eyes flash with anger. "You didn't need to do that. I'm not a child."

He's right about that—he's half a foot taller than I am—but I cross my arms. "I know you're not, but you're still my little brother, and apparently have questionable judgment."

We stare each other down, and my face reddens. I hate that we've both grown up and into a world where I can no longer be his protector. One more area of my life where I feel inadequate, helpless. I take a deep breath, try a softer approach. "Look, I was just thinking that a little backup isn't a bad thing, right?"

Emmett rolls his eyes, but he shrugs. "I guess." Then he smirks at me. "You and Mr. Blizzard, huh? Well, I hope he knows something about snowmobiles."

I nudge his arm with mine, and we sit together for a moment, silent, waiting. "So," I say finally. "Mom and Dad."

Emmett winces. "I'll handle it."

"You are seriously going to be grounded for the next decade."

He shrugs, then grins. "Guess I'll have plenty of time to work on my new snowmobile."

CHAPTER EIGHTEEN

Half an hour later, Connor knocks on the door. I take his hand, and he leans down and kisses me, soft and quick, as he steps in. It's so automatic, so comfortable.

Then he looks down at my chest quizzically and chuckles. "I was wondering where that went."

I cross my arms over his sweatshirt. Busted. But he kisses me again, a little longer this time, and I melt into him.

Emmett clears his throat and we pull apart. "Emmett." I smile awkwardly. "You remember Connor?"

Connor smiles, walks over to Emmett, and claps him on the back. "New snowmobile, huh?"

Emmett shrugs. "Do you ride?"

"Not much anymore, but my brother loved them." I wince, but Connor's smile hasn't faded. "Is this guy gonna let you take it for a spin around the parking lot to make sure it runs okay?"

Emmett drops his eyes. "Yeah, uh, it doesn't work."

"What?" I ask.

"I needed to get something cheap. The dude said the body is still in pretty good condition. It just needs a little work." He swallows. "Or, a lot."

Connor's eyes flick back and forth between us, apprehensive, and I sigh. "Why are you doing this, Em?"

"Don't call me that."

"Fine, sorry, *Emmett*." My eyes widen in realization, and I lean in closer. "Is this about you and Kaley?"

Emmett crosses his arms, casting his death glare upon me. "Don't worry about it, okay?"

Connor steps awkwardly back toward the kitchen, probably wishing he could sink into the floor, but I step toward my brother. "I'm just worried about *you*."

"Yeah, well, like I said, I'm *fine*."

I open my mouth, but his phone buzzes. He looks down. "He's here."

I walk to the window. Outside, a poison-green El Camino sits in the lot, parked across an entire row of empty spots. Hooked to its back hitch is a rusty old trailer carrying what I assume is my brother's new but nonworking snowmobile, concealed by a cloth cover. Emmett walks up and looks out, too. "Wow," I say. "Sweet ride."

Connor steps up behind us. "We're supposed to head down there?"

Emmett nods, his eyes a little nervous now. I nudge his arm with a wink. "Let's go get you a snowmobile."

Mr. El Camino turns out not to be a murderer but a jolly old gearhead—a collector of all things mechanical. He talks our ears off about Polaris and Yamaha as the four of us load the snowmobile from the trailer to the back of my dad's truck. Afterward, as we catch our breath, he starts babbling on about all these snowmobile competitions my brother will probably never enter. I stop listening after a while—instead I gaze up at the few stars that have pushed their glow through the light pollution of the city, trying not to think about how incredibly cold it is standing out here. Even Emmett seems to think the whole transaction takes way too long, but Connor seems to be in his element talking to this guy.

"So a bunch of you go out to the Black Hills every year?" His face is ruddy, but his eyes are bright, like a child listening to a bedtime story.

The old man—Pauly—chuckles. "Not for several years now, but my brothers and I used to make the trip every year."

There it is—the first flicker of sadness in Connor's eyes at the mention of brothers. I place my gloved hand in his, and he looks over and smiles. "Time to go in, huh?"

Pauly nods, turns to shake Emmett's hand. "Well, young man, have fun fixing up this old thing."

"Thank you, sir."

We wave as he drives away, but when the chug of the bright-green beast's engine fades into the night, I shudder and usher them both back into the building.

Upstairs, we shrug out of our coats, and Emmett pumps his fist in victory. "See, Mone? Told ya it was a good idea."

I roll my eyes and Connor laughs, then crosses his arms, leans back against the couch. "So, you ever rebuild something like that before?"

Emmett shrugs. "I figured I'd google it."

Connor raises his eyebrows. "Wait. Have you ever *driven* a snowmobile before?"

Emmett puffs out his chest, but there's pain in his eyes. "Of course I have."

I catch Connor's eye, give a slight shake of my head—the truth is, Emmett used to go snowmobiling with Kaley because her family is really into it. I am 100 percent certain that's why he's doing this—it's some sort of strange attempt to get her back. And yet my brother clearly does not want to talk about it, and I want to respect that. For now, at least.

Connor nods back at me, eases into his wide smile. "Well, it'll be an adventure, anyway. Honestly, I never have, either, but I used to hang out in the garage with my brother when he was working on them. Mostly just to drink beer, of course." Emmett smirks as Connor continues. "Hey, I could help you sometime. Even if it's just with questions."

Emmett keeps his indifferent expression, but his nod is quick. "Yeah, maybe that'd be cool. Thanks."

The unexpected rush of warmth within me at this brief moment of dude-bonding catches me off guard. I take a deep breath but can't keep the grin off my face. They both look over, so I turn toward the kitchen. "Hey, who wants hot chocolate?"

"Me." Emmett slides into the bench of my cute but tiny bare-wood kitchen nook, then pulls out his phone.

Connor joins me at the counter. "Cups up here?"

His arm brushes mine as he reaches to open it, and a thrill shoots through me. "Mm- hmm," I murmur, sneaking a glance at his chiseled profile.

Mugs in hand, we squeeze around the nook. With my hands wrapped around the warm cup—with Connor by my side, shoulder to shoulder—my anxiety ebbs. All is well.

Then—my landline rings. It's the shrill, clipped buzz telling me someone's ringing from the entryway, wanting to be let in.

"Oh shit." I turn, and Emmett's face is pale. "Mom and Dad."

Connor's arm freezes midair, mug in hand. "Your parents are here?"

I glance at him. "They came to get Emmett." I lean in close, voice low. "He kind of left without telling them."

"Mone, I can hear you," Emmett says.

"Uh, should I go?" Connor sets the mug down and rubs the back of his neck.

No. As much as I don't want him pulled into my family drama so soon, I'm not ready for him to leave quite yet.

Emmett scoffs. "No way, dude. You're the only chance of distracting them. Or at least lessening the blow." I narrow my eyes, and he grins mischievously. "Mom will have a million questions for your new boyfriend, Mone."

My stomach flips, and I'm sure my face is the same shade as my Christmas-red pants as I glower at my brother. But underneath the table, a warm, strong hand slips into mine. I look up and Connor is smiling. "I can handle that." He winks, and I return his grin, biting my lip. He leans down and nuzzles my neck, and I giggle.

"Gross," Emmett says. "But keep doing that shit when they get up here. That'll help for sure."

CHAPTER NINETEEN

Turns out no amount of new-boyfriend excitement is enough to help my brother. Beyond my mom's initial delighted smile and "Oh! *Hello*, Connor," the only thing his presence does is mute my dad.

If it were just us, he would've torn into Emmett, yelling and swearing the moment he got in the door. But in front of a nonfamily member, Dad's commands are clipped, his face red with the effort of holding back his anger. "What were you *thinking*, scaring your mother and me like that?" Emmett turns away from Dad, shrugging back into his coat. "*Answer* me, dammit."

"I'm *fine*, Dad. I can handle driving to Sioux Falls by myself. I'm not a child."

"But Em, what if you had an accident?" Mom is all worry and no anger, her hand on his arm. "And we had no idea where you were."

"He did text, Mom," I offer gently. "And he came here. It's not like he met the guy on his own."

Mom tsks. "But you don't need any extra stress in your life right now, Monie. You need to be thinking about taking care of yourself."

She turns to Emmett, already back to fretting over him, so my grimace goes unnoticed. Connor has retreated to the kitchen to provide space for the family argument, but in my peripheral vision I see his eyes on me.

"Let's go," Dad says. "We may have to drive slower if we have that damn thing in the back of the truck."

I frown. "You guys sure you want to drive back this late?"

"Oh, we're driving back, all right." Dad's eyes flash at Emmett. "*You* get to ride with me in the truck the whole way—*and* you're going to school in the morning. If you are one minute late, you're grounded even longer."

Emmett's shoulders slump, and I step forward to give him a hug. "It was good to see you, anyway."

His arms fold around me. "You too, Mone."

He looks up at Connor and waves. "Thanks again, man."

Connor nods. "You bet."

I hug my parents, and they promise to text when they've made it back safely. The door clicks behind them, the room is silent, and I walk to the window, watch as they drive away into the twinkling darkness of the city. Connor's arms wrap around me, warm and solid. "You've got a great family."

I smile, rubbing his arms. "We're . . . *interesting*, at least. Dad's pretty hard on Emmett. And Mom . . . she worries about us both. A lot." My voice catches and I clear my throat, grateful he's behind me.

Connor's arms slide back and his hands fall to my hips, spinning them around gently so we're facing each other, lifting my chin so we're eye to eye. "You're strong, you know." I scoff, roll my eyes, but swallow back a lump in my throat. "I mean it." Then he leans down and kisses me softly.

"Thank you," I whisper when he pulls back.

He kisses my forehead. "Well, tonight's been an adventure."

"You're leaving?"

He raises his eyebrows, shrugs. "I don't *have* to."

I twist my hands together. "I was thinking . . . since you're already here, maybe we could watch *The Empire Strikes Back*?"

"Sure, that would be great." With a grin, he walks over and plops down on the couch.

But I don't move. I wait until he looks up at me; then I smile and crane my head to the side. "I was thinking we could watch it in there."

Connor's eyes flit to the bedroom door, then back to mine.

"On the TV in my room," I explain.

He smiles a little too big; his words come a little too fast. "Okay, yeah." Then he leaps off the couch and follows me into the bedroom.

I gesture to the TV. "Want to get it ready? I'm going to use the bathroom quick." After crossing the plush gray carpeted floor, I shut the bathroom door behind me with a soft click. In front of the mirror, I scrutinize my face—scrubbed clean from the shower—and my eyes fall on my little pink makeup case, sitting dutifully on the smooth white countertop. Some mascara would open up my eyes more. Foundation, maybe, to even out my skin? Girl, at the very least you need some damn lip gloss.

But I take a deep breath. He's been looking at my bare face all night and hasn't run away screaming—clearly there's something he likes about it.

I fluff my hair, and my eyes float down to my body. None of my underwear is remotely sexy. My eyes focus on the baggy sweatshirt I'm wearing. *His* sweatshirt.

I cock my head to the side, raising my eyebrows at the woman in the mirror. *You up for this?*

The spark in her eye is the answer I need.

I strip down out of my pants, thanking the patron saint of shaved legs that I used my razor this morning. Then I tug the sweatshirt over my head, dropping it onto the floor so I can slip out of my pajama shirt before shrugging back into the bulky hoodie.

The chilled air as I step out of the bathroom sends goose bumps up my exposed legs. My hands brush my bare thighs—the sweatshirt covers the important parts but not much more, and I'm suddenly self-conscious.

But before me, Connor sits on the edge of my bed, facing the TV, and as I stare at his broad shoulders and back, his strong arms, my bravery returns. "Hey," I say softly.

He's turning toward me as he answers. "The movie's all cued—" His voice cuts off, and now he's the one staring.

I draw a shuddering breath, tucking my hair behind my ear. "Is this okay?"

His eyes float down my body, then back up, and they lock on to mine. "This is okay," he says. "This is very, very okay."

I smile as I walk toward him, climb onto the bed, and gently slide the remote out of his hand. "So, I sort of changed my mind about the movie."

He leans toward me, his voice husky. "Oh really?"

We're so close now that his breath warms my face. I close the distance, my lips lightly brushing his. "Will you stay tonight?" I whisper.

His strong hands cup my face, and he kisses me deeply, the answer I hoped for, and when he leans back, I'm breathless. I push myself up on my knees, all hesitation gone, replaced by the adoration in his eyes, and I pull the hoodie up over my head, drop it onto the floor behind me.

Connor rises up to his knees as well, eyes taking in my entire body. I reach for him, and it's like our bodies are drawn together—we're kissing without end, I'm pulling his shirt up over his head, running my hands down his warm chest and stomach. His hands find me, too, his lips trail down my neck, sending shivers of anticipation through me as we ease back onto the bed.

"Simone," he whispers, lips brushing my ear, "you are the most beautiful person I have ever known."

I exhale a soft puff of air as his lips find mine again, and I kiss him with all that is in me. My heart has melted away, exploded into a million particles of joy, nothing left but the blissful certainty that I have fallen completely in love with this man.

My eyes are closed but I'm smiling as I rest on Connor's warm chest, rising and falling in rhythm. Goose bumps prickle my bare shoulder, but he anticipates them, satisfies yet another need as he pulls the blanket higher up onto my shoulder.

"You comfortable?" he murmurs.

"Mm-hmm." I open my eyes. "Except . . ."

"Except?"

My stomach rumbles, the famished beast within weak now from hours of emptiness. "Except I'm starving."

Connor chuckles. "I could cook you something. I happen to make the best frozen pizza in the world."

I giggle, then gasp. "Oh, wait! My neighbor gave me a whole pan of chocolate cupcakes." I have earned those. My eyes light up, and I twist toward him. "We could watch the movie now. With a midnight snack?" Sleep be damned—I'll make my coffee extra strong tomorrow morning.

He kisses the tip of my nose. "Whatever you want."

I smile slyly and move in, kissing him slowly, savoring his taste on my lips. When I pull back, I whisper seductively in his ear, "Cupcakes and *Star Wars*, please."

"Yes, ma'am." Connor plants a soft kiss on my forehead before slipping out to the kitchen to retrieve the cupcakes.

I watch him walk away, lying in the warmth of the bed, already counting the moments until his arms are around me again.

PART SIX

Denial

Monday, December 6, 10:03 a.m.

I stare in horror at Nikki—my best friend in the world—lying on the floor, motionless.

I fall to my knees.

I can't do this.

All sounds stop. Time seems to stop. I shut my eyes, fade away, and suddenly it's like I'm back in our college theater. The smell of backstage, all dampness and dust and nervous sweat. The muted clip of the floorboards beneath my feet. The thick dark curtain, a sliver of light peeking underneath. The panic bubbling up within me until I'm sure I'm about to explode.

The gentle hand on my shoulder, calming me as always, turning darkness into light.

You can do this.

Nikki's whisper coats me with steel, thrusts me through that curtain and onto the stage.

I draw a shuddering breath, open my eyes. But it's not the stage that awaits me. It's something much more terrifying.

I force myself to crawl forward until I reach Nikki. Then I extend a trembling hand, trying desperately to hope, to pray, to believe that my best friend is still alive.

CHAPTER TWENTY

May 19, seven months before

No matter how desperately I hope and pray, jogging outside for the first time is so much harder than I imagined. We put it off as long as possible—a couple of late-season snowstorms helped—but now the snow is gone, and with it, any excuse to stay indoors. And yet no matter how brightly spring plays its melody on this crisp morning in Falls Park—the rush of the water, the laughter of children on end-of-the-school-year field trips—it's impossible to focus on the loveliness when you're drenched in sweat, panting out labored breaths with each step.

"Slogging" is a more accurate description of what I'm doing as I trudge along beside Nikki. I didn't expect it to be this damn hard. I've gotten up to a solid two miles on the treadmill, but she said running would be different outside—the terrain, wind, any number of factors.

My feet scrape on the pavement as we round a curve, and my knee twinges. *Damn, didn't expect that, either.* It technically started a few weeks ago, though at first I thought I'd simply pushed myself too hard that day—Connor had dropped me off, and we'd lingered in his car, hidden in the darkness of the YMCA parking lot. By the time I'd floated inside, I was already flying, ponytail and tank top disheveled, ready to rock that run.

But the pain kept coming back toward the end of each run, a sharp pull on the side of my kneecap.

"Feels good to be out here, doesn't it?" Nikki beams at me, and a grunt is all I can manage between heavy breaths.

I shrug, huff out, "How far have we gone?"

"Just passed a mile."

"Shit. This is demoralizing."

Nikki bursts out laughing. "That's a pretty big word. You can't be too tired." I glare at her and she smiles wider. "Aw, come on. It's tough, but trust me, your body will adjust. So will your mind—look around. The scenery's actually changing. At least we're going somewhere, you know? Moving forward. Not stuck on a treadmill."

Moving forward. I smile, pick up the pace as much as my knee will allow.

Nikki matches me easily, her shrewd eyes narrowing. "Hey, how's the knee?"

I squint up into the sun so I don't have to look at her, the pain throbbing now as if responding to being called out. "Fine."

She sighs, slows to a walk. "Let's skip to the cooldown, okay?" I match her pace, grateful. She clears her throat. "What did the neurologist say?"

I swallow. "Well . . ."

"Simone." Nikki throws her hands up, exasperated.

"At my appointment, the nurse said to only let them know if a symptom persists, otherwise just work with my primary doctor." Plus I didn't feel comfortable calling the nurse who had brushed me aside and rushed me out the door back in December.

"So define 'persists.' How long do you let it go before you call them?"

The truth is, after months of vague symptoms that ebbed and flowed unpredictably until I questioned whether I was imagining them, having an answer was a goddamned victory. And afterward, when Dr. Montgomery said I didn't have to go on treatment if I didn't want to, it was like freedom, like I hadn't lost control of my life after all.

It was all a mirage.

Because it turns out there is no way to go back to living your life the way it was before your diagnosis. Not with the albatross of chronic illness around your neck. I know that now.

So I've gotten good at pretending.

I glance at Nikki at last. "I don't know."

She sighs. "Don't you think you should feel comfortable asking your neurologist questions? Have you ever thought about going to someone else?"

I have absolutely thought of that, and the idea is as frightening as it is exhausting. Pretending is easier. It's less scary than making the effort to dig deeper into my illness, into what my uncertain future might bring.

Like with Connor.

Meeting him was like magic. With him, I can pretend there's nothing wrong with me and there never will be. I can pretend everything is perfect.

But searching for a new neurologist would mean once again gathering my medical records, scheduling appointments, going over the details of my history of symptoms. Starting over with someone new who might be just as distant as my current one.

It would mean I couldn't pretend anymore, and I'm not sure I'm ready for that. Not yet. I don't respond, instead placing my hands on my hips as we walk, so Nikki presses on. "Mone, I know it's hard, but you can't keep putting things off forever." Her voice is low, but her words sting. "You can't keep burying your head in the sand. This is your *life*."

I wince, chest flaring its resistance. And yet I'm weakened from the run, from Nikki's penetrating gaze. "*Fine*, I'll call. And I've got my annual exam coming up soon with my primary doctor, too, so that covers all the bases."

Nikki eyes me for several more seconds before nodding. "Good. And you need to start stretching more after our runs. Come to yoga with Claudia and me like you used to."

I groan. "But my balance . . ."

Nikki eyes me pointedly. "Just try. Okay? We'll both be there with you."

I sigh in defeat, then smirk at her. "Damn, running *and* yoga? Our college selves would hate us so much right now. They'd tell us to get drunk and eat pizza instead."

Nikki laughs. "Growing up is a bitch, isn't it?"

It is indeed, I think the next day as I sit cross-legged on my couch, stomach rolling with nerves as I tap out the number for Dr. Montgomery's office. I make my way through the automated menu, and the soothing-grating hold music kicks in.

The music cuts off abruptly. "Hello, can I help you?"

"Uh, yes." I clear my throat. "I have a question for Dr. Montgomery's nurse." I give her my name and date of birth, and her doubtful voice tells me she'll check if the nurse is in, but I might have to leave a message. When the crooning saxophone blares into my ear again, I'm filled with relief—I tried. If I leave a message and she doesn't get back to me, then I've done what I could.

I've barely finished the thought before the hold music comes to another screeching halt. "Yes?"

I blink, scramble for words. "Uh . . . is this . . . is this Dr. Montgomery's nurse?"

An impatient sigh, barely audible. "Yes, this is Kris. Can I help you, Miss Archer?"

My moment has come—all the questions that have been rolling around in my head can finally come out. And yet I freeze, can barely manage the one reason I called. "Uh, yes. I . . . um . . . I started running—well, jogging, really. And my knee started hurting. So I thought I should check in . . . you know, to make sure it's not the start of another attack?"

Her voice is crisp. "How long did you say it's been going on?"

"A month or so, I guess?"

"Is it constant, steadily worsening, or does it come and go?"

"It comes and goes." I swallow. "Depending on how long I run."

"Then it sounds like a running-related injury to me. Have you talked to your primary doctor about this?" I open my mouth, but she continues before I can answer. "Because we encourage patients to work with their primary doctor as much as possible on these sorts of questions." She's barely hiding her annoyance. "Is there anything else I can help you with?"

"Well, um . . ." For a second I falter, regret and embarrassment flooding me. And yet I've *finally* made this damn call; I better make it count. "Well, I guess I was wondering about flu shots. I mean, I know it's not until fall, but am I supposed to get one?"

"Definitely. You need to avoid the live virus, though, so get the shot, not the nasal spray."

"So that *is* a question I should direct to you guys, then." The triumphant words come out before I can stop them.

She pauses again. "We encourage our patients to work with their primary doctors as much as possible when appropriate."

"But what if I don't know when it's appropriate?"

"Start with your primary, and if they recommend you call us, then do so." She sighs. "If that's all, I can transfer you back to the scheduling desk if needed."

I pause. "No, thank you."

I end the call and throw my phone down onto the couch, punch a pillow, then look around my empty living room.

The silence is suddenly all consuming, and I sit, frustrated.

Alone.

CHAPTER TWENTY-ONE

May 24, seven months before

The next week, I sit in the sterile exam room, my foot tapping to the rhythm of my nervous heartbeat as I wait. It's not that I've ever loved going to the doctor—who does, honestly? But now, doctor visits will never be the same. I will always expect bad news or anticipate the need for a painful test of some sort.

But the instant the thick door whooshes open and I'm greeted by Dr. Reynolds's smiling face, my shoulders relax.

"Ah, Simone, so good to see you."

"You too." It's not entirely a lie; I might hate coming in, but she's been my doctor since I first moved to Sioux Falls, and her common sense and calm demeanor have been a blessing, especially during the months leading up to my diagnosis.

She sits down and runs a hand through her graying brown hair, then folds her arms across her lap, leaning toward me. "Simone, I have to say right away that I received the complete report from the neurologist's office, and it's very promising that they feel they can monitor your condition for now without treatment."

I nod, her validation washing over me like a cleansing bath.

"Now, how *are* you?"

I open my mouth to say something positive—*I'm fine I'm great thank you very much*—but instead I'm overcome, swiping at mascara-smudged eyes. Dr. Reynolds hands me a tissue, her kind smile not wavering. At last, I compose myself enough to take a deep breath. "Sorry, everything is okay, really; it's just that I don't know what I'm doing or what's going to happen, and when I called the neurologist, they weren't exactly help-ful, and it's just *so* frustrating."

She nods sagely. "Everything you're feeling is completely normal."

More words I needed to hear. "But what do I *do*?"

She glances at my chart. "You keep doing everything you've been doing. You get enough rest, you exercise, you try to avoid stress, keep your habits as healthy as possible."

I nod, wiping at my eyes again. "I started running. But, well, my knee has been bothering me. I think it's related to that, but I do worry it could be MS related."

"Hmm. How long has it been going on?"

"A month or so, I suppose? Maybe longer."

"And it seems to happen only when you run—it doesn't happen at other times, or steadily worsen?"

"No, just with running."

She narrows her eyes, assessing. "Sounds like it's running related to me, but I'll take a closer look during your exam today, and I definitely want you to keep me posted—start logging any symptoms and how long they last."

I nod, soaking in her advice like a plant facing the sun, and she cocks her head to the side. "Simone, did you ask the neurologist's office these questions?"

My stomach twists. "Yes, but it didn't go very well."

"It might take a while to develop a rapport with the nurses."

"How long?"

"It depends." She narrows her eyes. "But honestly, if you feel uncomfortable at any point and decide to follow up with someone else, we'll gladly refer you. Just say the word."

I could hug her—I want to, but that might be a step too far in the doctor-patient relationship. Instead I beam my gratitude, and she turns back to my chart. "Now, anything else to update since last time? Anything new?"

The blush comes without warning. "Well, I mean, I don't know if this is relevant, but . . . I met someone."

Her eyebrows raise. "Oh, that's wonderful!"

"Thanks." My blush deepens. "He's pretty great."

"How long?"

"Almost five months now."

Another sage nod. "Do we need to discuss any birth control changes?"

I giggle like a teenager—God, I'm a dork. "Uh, nope. Same old pill is working fine."

She smiles. "I have to ask." Then she clears her throat. "I also should ask, since it's been five months: Does he know about your MS?"

My giddiness fades. "Um, yes."

"Good. Does he have any questions?"

I blink. "Uh, I guess I don't know. I mean, we haven't really talked about it much. I did tell him, though." A defensive edge creeps into my voice.

She leans forward. "That's okay, Simone. There's no right or wrong way to do any of this. I just thought I'd bring it up. If you two are getting serious, he might want to learn how best he can partner in your diagnosis long term. It might be something to discuss at some point."

I bristle. The image of Connor partnering in my diagnosis is a hell of a buzzkill after the sexy scenes that flashed through my mind after the birth control question. I force a smile and nod, and Dr. Reynolds moves on to more mundane questions—how I've been sleeping, when I last performed a self–breast exam—but I'm fixated on her earlier words, now blending with Nikki's in my mind.

Maybe I shouldn't bury my head in the sand. Maybe I should talk to Connor.

But doubts swim through my mind. He and I talked, back when I told him I wasn't starting treatment. That was enough.

Wasn't it?

The truth is, I'm not sure I want to talk with him about it. The only time I'm not thinking about having MS is when I'm with him. And I don't want to risk shattering this perfect distraction.

CHAPTER TWENTY-TWO

May 25, seven months before

My doubts followed me home from the doctor's appointment, stinging like a wound that wouldn't scab over, and they continued to fester that evening and as I got ready for work the next morning.

And they continued earlier today, while I sat at my desk going through morning emails. The sting has only now finally faded to the background during our staff meeting as we sit around Stan's conference table.

"Okay." He claps his hands, then rests them on the faux-cherry-wood table. "What do we have this week?"

I flip open my yellow-lined notebook and consult my list. "Let's see. I'm finishing up the story about the alum who biked across the country to raise money for cancer research. That should be good for our next issue of the alumni magazine. For social, there's a vocal-jazz camp for high school students on campus this week."

Stan nods. "Were you thinking Facebook?"

"Yeah, a few pictures that their parents can like. But it also might be fun for Snapchat."

"That is where the kids are these days, huh?" Stan chuckles. "Make sure you bring release forms."

I jot down a note as he turns to Nikki, who launches into an update about the graduate-studies brochure, a seemingly never-ending project already on round seven of revisions. Poor Nik. But I've heard this story before, so as she speaks I let my eyes gaze out the window, let my mind wander, and let my doubts creep back in.

"Sounds like you need a plan."

Stan's voice catches me off guard, and I turn to him in surprise. "What?"

His brow furrows. "Oh, I was just saying to Nikki that it might help next time when working with difficult departments to discuss a plan up front." He turns back to Nikki. "And I can help facilitate a meeting, if needed."

They continue talking, but my mind is buzzing now. A plan. Of course.

I'll make a plan of my own. I will pay attention to how my knee reacts to outdoor running and log my symptoms, as Dr. Reynolds suggested. I'll also start researching different neurologists. My one-year follow-up MRI is this fall, and Dr. Reynolds's office will send the results—and all my medical records—to whichever neurologist I choose to follow up with. So I really just need to make a decision before I get the MRI results. That means I have plenty of time, considering I don't even need to think about getting the MRI scheduled until summer is over.

Come to think of it, end of summer would also be a great deadline to give myself to have a talk with Connor about my illness. If we're getting serious, I should be able to talk to him—about my frustrations with my neurologist, my fears regarding my illness long term. End of summer will put us well past the six-month mark, which somehow seems like a big deal and is not at all a stalling tactic.

I'm satisfied now with my successful adulting, and when the meeting ends, I bounce back to my office and throw my focus into the story about the bicycling alum—hmm, better ask her to email me a high-res picture. My fingers fly over the keys, and I don't notice the figure lurking in my office doorway until a throat clears. I look up in surprise. "Oh. Hi, Louise."

"Hello, Simone. How *are* you?"

The tone, the emphasis—they're nails on a chalkboard, and yet I keep my smile. "I'm fine, thanks." Stan's wife is a nice lady—she is—and yet there's something about her that's hard to pinpoint. It's like she goes through the motions of being friendly, checks off all the boxes required to be a polite person, but it seems false somehow, like the boxes are empty. "How are you?"

She sighs, tucks a lock of her graying blonde hair behind her ear. "Can't complain." Her eyes dart back and forth across the office before resting on me again. "Is Stan around, by any chance? He's not answering his cell, so maybe he's in a meeting?"

I click over to our shared calendars, scan his column. "Hmm . . . nothing scheduled, but something might've come up. Do you want me to try emailing him? Sometimes it's easier to respond to emails in a meeting than a phone call."

"No," she says quickly, then pauses, composes herself. "It's not important. You don't even need to tell him I was here."

There's a twinge to her voice now, a crack in her smile, but I nod. "Okay."

She smiles a moment longer. "Stan said you've started dating someone?"

I blush, silently cursing myself for not just ignoring Stan last week when he asked, *Say, whatever happened to that young man from the construction tour?* "Um, yeah," I say now to Louise. "A few months ago."

There's no denying the sadness in her smile. "Ah, so new. Enjoy it." Then she's gone, as if she were an apparition I'd simply imagined.

I shake my head, pop back into Microsoft Word, and try to type again, but my fingers lag and I stare at the doorway where Louise had stood. There's something strange going on with those two. Distracted now, I click open Facebook for some good old-fashioned social media stalking.

I'm a week back on Stan's profile page when another figure looms, clears his throat. I look up, automatically clicking back into Word.

Chet raises his eyebrows. "Didn't mean to interrupt your busy schedule."

My face blazes, but I straighten my shoulders, trying to hide my embarrassment from the admissions director. "Uh, hi. Can I help you with something?"

A smile slides across Chet's face, and yet somehow that only makes me more uneasy. "Do you know where Stan is?" His voice is quiet, yet there's a heaviness behind it, like something's simmering beneath the surface.

"His wife was just here looking for him, too. He must be out, because I just checked for her, and there's nothing on his calendar this afternoon."

Chet runs a hand through his perfectly clipped dark hair, peering at me like he's calculating, then finally sighs. "I just don't understand how you have *no idea* where your boss is in the middle of a workday."

My defenses shoot up. "Well, I mean, I think he had a video to work on, so maybe he's out shooting some footage with the videographer." I scrunch up my face, thinking. "Or that might be tomorrow . . ."

Chet raises his eyebrows for a full two seconds before his lips curl up, his smile crueler than before. "So you don't know anything?"

I ball my fists. "Last time I checked, it wasn't part of my job description to keep tabs on my boss. We're a little too busy over here to do that."

He throws a pointed glance at my computer screen before his icy eyes cut back to me. "Yeah, it sure looked that way. Perhaps you can find the time to give Stan a message for me?" I fight to keep my face blank, fuming inside, as he continues. "I came over here to tell your boss that Joel over in Financial Aid has been let go."

My eyes widen. "Why?" I don't really know Joel, but he's always seemed friendly. Nikki said he has two daughters in high school he likes to brag about.

"Used up his FMLA." Chet shrugs, indifferent. "Rules are rules. Weakness doesn't give you a pass."

I shrink back from the sting of this callous dismissal. But Chet is oblivious—or maybe that's part of his game, a cat toying with his mouse before he destroys it. "Fortunately, his duties were absorbed by the rest of his department, but if someone in your office could find time in your *extremely* busy schedules to update the website accordingly, that would be—" Suddenly he turns, a look of irritation quickly replaced by a tight smile. "Can I help you?"

Connor steps into view, arms crossed, stony gaze on Chet, who takes a step back. "I'm here to see Simone." Connor's voice is one step above a growl, and I've never loved him more.

"Ah, well. We were just finishing up." Chet's face is red now as he turns to me. "Have Stan call me when he comes back from wherever he is." His eyes flit to Connor, then back to me. "Please."

He walks away and Connor glowers after him. "Who was that?" He turns to look at me. "You okay?"

I take a deep breath, flash a brave smile. "He's nobody important."

"I'll say." Connor glares down the hallway in the direction Chet left, then turns back to me with a smile. "Well, I'm on a late lunch break and wanted to stop over to say hi." He walks to my desk, and I stand, lean over, and meet him halfway for a soft kiss. When I pull back, he grins. "And to let you know I'm all packed."

"Already?" I raise my eyebrows. "It's Tuesday."

We're planning on leaving Thursday night to beat the Memorial Day traffic, and I intend to wait until the very last minute to pack. And to prepare for yet another extended gathering of family and friends at my parents' annual barbecue.

Connor shrugs. "I might be a little excited for our first trip together."

"Me too." I reach up and pull his face down toward mine for a kiss, and suddenly all of Louise's awkwardness, all of Chet's assholery, melt away.

Suddenly the weekend can't come fast enough.

CHAPTER TWENTY-THREE

May 27, seven months before

Connor and I reach Aberdeen as the sun is dipping low. As we pull onto my parents' street, I immediately see that the driveway seems to have turned into a used-car lot. My nose wrinkles. "Why are there so many cars here?"

"Is the barbecue tonight?" Connor asks.

I groan. "Mom said something about maybe needing to change the date, but I never checked back with her."

Connor shrugs and steps out to walk to the trunk for our bags, and I flip down the rearview mirror. "Yikes." I comb through my hair with my fingers, reapply my lip gloss, rub off the excess mascara smudged under my eyes—evidence of a car nap.

I step out and grab the smaller bags from the back seat, but Connor takes them from me, looping them over the handle of my suitcase, which he's pulling behind him. He lugs his own duffel bag over his shoulder and smiles. "Ready?"

Before I have a chance to answer, the front door creaks open. "Ah, you're here!"

I turn and smile. "Hi, Mom. Sorry, I didn't realize the party is tonight."

"Oh, this is just the pre-party," she says. "We'll be having family fun together all weekend long."

My eyes flit to Connor, who smirks. "Sounds great," I say with as much enthusiasm as I can muster.

We near the door, and a woman steps out behind Mom. I squint into the dusky haze, but her squeal reveals her identity. "Mon-*ieee*!" My aunt Kit rushes down the steps and races toward me. "I haven't seen you in ages, girl. You look great."

Aunt Kit is not really my aunt but an old friend of my mom's, super fun and clinging to her youth with vigor—ever since a very nasty divorce from Uncle Dean (who actually can no longer be called "uncle" and in fact whose name shall never again be uttered in our household). Kit has dyed all traces of gray from her hair, hired a personal trainer, and let a touch of Botox even out the rest. These days she usually has a much younger boyfriend on her arm, but tonight the only thing in her hand is a red Solo cup, which she now raises toward Connor—along with her eyebrows—before leaning back to me with an approving nod. "Speaking of looking great . . ."

"Kit," I whisper, and Connor blushes. She flashes a toothy smile. "Sorry. Where are my manners? You must be Connor."

He recovers brilliantly, flashing his own wide smile. "Yes, ma'am."

Her eyes flit to the bags he's carrying. "You sure are . . . *handy* to have around." She turns her smirk toward me. "You got another one of these for your favorite auntie? Maybe he's got a brother or something?"

There's an awkward silence and I wince, my eyes darting to Connor, but Mom swoops in and saves the day. "Kit, for God's sake, let these kids get inside, will you?"

She giggles and embraces me again, pulling Connor in as well. "I'm only kidding. So happy for both of you." She steps back, puts her hand gently on my face. "And so glad you're doing well. You really do look great."

By "great," she means "healthy," but I don't bristle. It's Kit, and I'm happy for the compliment. "Thanks," I whisper, and we walk inside together arm in arm.

Backyards on a summer evening are a glorious thing. The citronella candles and bonfire keep the mosquitoes at bay, the scent of grilled meats lingers in the air, the soft breeze carries laughter and chatter and the cracking of beer-can tabs. From my comfortable patio chair—parked out on the lawn because this party is sprawling—I have a great view of the sunset, its smudges of oranges and purples brilliant against the blue-back sky.

Kit walks over and refills my glass of moscato. "One should really be my limit," I say, but she only winks and pours a little more. I sigh, shoving the stern faces of the neurology nurse and Dr. Montgomery out of my mind—*be as healthy as possible.* Exercise, low-fat diet, don't drink *too much.* Such a subjective term, really. I look down at my full wineglass and the empty dish of ice cream on the ground next to my chair, then shrug. "Special occasion, I guess."

"Attagirl." Kit plops down in the chair next to mine with a flourish, crosses her tanned legs, and tips the wide-brimmed hat covering her blonde highlights toward me. "I won't tell anyone." She raises her own glass in a toast. "May all of life be a special occasion."

I smile. "Here, here."

We sip in silence, surveying the yard games and conversations around us, until she lets out a dramatic sigh, bringing a hand to her forehead. "Are you okay?" I ask.

"Oh, fine, really, but I . . ." She drops her hand, bites her lip, pauses a bit too long. "I don't know if your mom told you, but I've been diagnosed with low blood sugar."

I blink. "What?"

She nods, pulling out a granola bar from her bedazzled purse. "I'm okay, really, just need to keep it in mind when I'm planning the day."

My chest constricts, and I try to paint a sympathetic smile on my face. "Oh, wow, I'm sorry, that's tough." I take a swig from my glass, drowning out the vicious thoughts within: *At least it's not MS.* This is Aunt Kit, the woman who came to all my piano recitals, the woman who talked my mom into letting me pierce my ears when I was eight. I care about her, about her well-being.

And yet the stabbing in my chest burns out all the sympathy; the cruel comparison to my disease erases empathy for anyone else who might be struggling, telling me their suffering can't possibly match mine. I take one more gulp of wine to push it back, but it's there, nibbling at me from the inside.

Kit turns to me, and for a moment I fear my pettiness is transparent. But she places a hand on mine. "You know, we have an opening at the library this summer."

I smile. Kit is the director of the Aberdeen Public Library, and ever since I interned one summer in high school, helping out with children's events, she's been trying to lure me back. "I'm happy where I am, but thank you." My smile falters. "Besides . . ."

She turns to me. "Besides what?"

I swallow. "I have really good health insurance right now. Probably wouldn't be wise of me to give that up."

"The city has excellent insurance as well."

I draw a shuddering breath, my mind flashing to Joel—poor, jobless Joel from Financial Aid. Perhaps having a backup job offer wouldn't be such a bad idea. "But would they . . . I mean, what if they . . . denied me?"

She sets her glass down and leans in, a flash in her eye. "Simone, do you know how many people live with a preexisting condition?" She scoffs. "Shit, being a woman seems to be a preexisting condition these days. But they've never denied anyone yet, and I'd sure raise holy hell if they tried to start with you."

My throat burns with shame and gratitude for this woman who'd stand up for me even when I've secretly judged her. "Thank you so much," I whisper. "And thank you for the job offer. I'm flattered, but I'm not looking to move back to Aberdeen anytime soon."

"I can see why." She winks. "Where did your hot guy run off to, by the way?"

I blush involuntarily and look around. "You know, I'm not sure." Then I cringe. "I'd better go make sure our neighbor Dave doesn't corner him and find out he's a Democrat." She giggles and I shake my head.

Kit waves me off, and I walk around the yard, saying hellos and scanning crowds—wow, there are a lot of people here; Mom and Dad sure know how to throw a party. But no Connor. I turn to walk up the steps of the back deck and almost run into someone. "Oh, sorry." I look up and blink. "Walter?"

His smile is sheepish, and he raises his red Solo cup in salute. "Surprise."

"I didn't realize you were coming back for Memorial Day."

"My parents needed help with some remodeling work, and you know my mom—she said it *had* to be this weekend." He rolls his eyes and I laugh. Then he clears his throat. "I flew into Minneapolis to see an old friend and, uh, check out some houses."

I raise my eyebrows. "You're moving?"

"My parents aren't getting any younger. Figure it's time to be closer to home."

"Well." I nod. "Good for you."

He clears his throat again. "Say, Simone, I wanted to mention something." His tone is off, forced—oh God, please don't ask me out. I search for an escape route, but there's no way to bolt without being a total jerk, so I stand still, a smile frozen on my face. "I have a good friend in Minneapolis who is . . . well, she knows a lot about your disease."

Slow blink—man, did I misread the situation. "Oh yeah?" My voice is flat. Walter was so cool about it last time. I hope he hasn't turned into one of those people whose flaky friend has read on Facebook that all I have to do is pray more—like getting MS is my fault, the result of some sort of moral failing.

He nods. "She's young, but she's already really well respected in the field of neurology."

Hold up now. "Wow," I say, and I mean it.

"Yeah. My mom—again, I'm sorry, but you *know* how she is—she heard from *your* mom that you weren't . . . entirely pleased with your neurologist. Amira is phenomenal. She really listens to her patients."

I smile, cock my head. "Amira?"

He blushes. "Sorry. Dr. Amira Bukhari. We did our undergrad together, and we've . . . kept in touch over the years." Suddenly it all makes sense—flying into Minneapolis to see an old friend. Maybe he's moving back for more than his parents. He fishes in his pocket and pulls out a business card, then hands it to me. "Anyway, I don't mean to be presumptuous, but she's really great. I wanted to mention it in case you ever want to try a new neurologist."

I take the card with a shaky hand. This is so unexpected and kind—and something actually useful. Plus I'm happy for Walter. Without thinking, I lean forward and wrap my arms around him for a hug. He seems surprised at first, and I'm pretty sure I slosh out some of his keg beer, but eventually he hugs me back. "Thank you," I whisper when I pull back.

He smiles. "It's what friends are for."

"Good luck. With the move and everything, I mean." He blushes again, nods, and we continue on our separate paths.

CHAPTER TWENTY-FOUR

When I find Connor at last, my heart fills even more—he's in the garage with Emmett, tinkering on that old piece of junk snowmobile. They're laughing and joking when I come in; then I hear another voice. A third man stands up from a crouched position in front of the snowmobile, and I freeze.

"Dad?" I don't even try to hide the incredulity in my voice.

All three look toward me, and Dad shrugs. "What? Your mom thought it would be good bonding time." Emmett smirks and Dad smirks back. "He's *still* grounded."

I smile and shake my head. "Well, I think it's great." I meet Connor's gaze, and he smiles back, but not as fully as I expect. I walk up and step on my tiptoes to kiss him, but I catch a whiff and narrow my eyes. That's when I finally notice the red cup in his hand. "You're drinking?"

Dad and Emmett exchange a look. "What, is he not twenty-one?" Dad asks. "Should I have carded him?"

I roll my eyes. "Very funny. Can you give us a minute, please?" They turn away, and I take Connor's hand, pulling him over to the corner. "What's going on?"

He shrugs. "I decided to have a beer." His voice is defensive, and there's a challenge in his eyes. "I didn't realize it would matter."

"It doesn't matter to me. I mean, it *does*, but only because it's your own rule—I thought you didn't want to drink anymore."

His laugh is bitter. "Of course I do. I just wish I could go back to when it was fun and didn't remind me of the worst day of my life."

"So if it's not fun, why are you doing it?" I ask gently.

He looks down, his jaw set. "It's just . . . being here with all your family is harder than I thought it would be. It makes me miss my brother even more, especially with the anniversary coming up . . ."

Oh God. "The anniversary is coming up?"

He squeezes his eyes shut. "It'll be a year next week."

My hand flies to my mouth. "Babe, I'm so sorry." I reach my hand out to touch his arm, and he stiffens. "Is something else wrong? I mean, did *I* do something wrong?"

He takes a swig of his beer, his face red like his cup. "How's Walter?"

I blink in surprise. "Why do you ask?"

He won't meet my eyes, but I can see the flash of pain in his. "That was quite a hug."

I cross my arms and look at him with my eyebrows raised. "You're seriously mad because I *hugged* Walter?"

"Well, it wasn't exactly the highlight of my evening." His eyes flick up and then down again. "I was already feeling shitty, and that just wasn't what I expected to see when I went out to grab your dad's toolbox from his truck."

I take a deep breath, bite back my annoyance—he's hurting—then reach up and place my hands on the sides of his face, pulling him down for a deep kiss until my dad clears his throat and my brother calls, "Really, Mone? Gross."

I ignore them, and when I pull back, Connor finally meets my eyes. "You have absolutely nothing to worry about. From Walter, or anyone. Okay?"

172

He nods, his shoulders relaxing.

"I'm sorry you're having a bad night. It looks like you're having fun in here, though."

He smiles, but it's sad. "Working on this stuff still reminds me of hanging out with Cam, but in a good way at least." He takes my hand, brings it up to his mouth, and kisses it. "And you're having fun? Besides your boyfriend being a jealous bastard, I mean?"

A giggle escapes my throat. "I am. I got a job offer from Aunt Kit. Told her thanks but no thanks. And the thing with Walter—the reason for the hug—is this." I reach in my pocket and pull out the card. "He knows a really good neurologist in Minneapolis, who I actually think might be his girlfriend. She sounds great, and honestly I might consider it. At least looking her up online, I mean."

Connor looks down at the card and back up at me. "That's wonderful. Really." He squeezes his eyes shut, shakes his head. "Now I really feel like an asshole. I'm sorry."

I wrap my arms around him. "Hey, it's okay. I think that qualifies as our first fight, so that's a milestone, right?"

There's a spark in his eye, and he leans down, whispers in my ear, "You know what we're supposed to do to make up after a fight, right?"

My entire body tingles. My moment has arrived. "Well, thank God we have a hotel room for tonight," I whisper.

"We do?" Connor keeps his face even. His eyes cut to where my dad and brother are working away, but he can't stop his eyebrows from raising, a kid who knows he's getting the shiny new bike for his birthday but is trying to play it cool.

"Mm-hmm. Mom promised my cousin she and her kids could stay here, so she offered to pay for us to stay at one of our nation's finest establishments, the Holiday Inn."

"Well, what a coincidence." Connor's smile is mischievous. "That happens to be my new favorite hotel chain."

The family fun goes later than expected, though, with lawn games and card games and board games galore, like a party store exploded on my parents' property. We finally say our goodbyes, trying desperately not to drag it out Midwest-style as we fight our way toward the doorway. Soon the wine and the long drive earlier that day converge into a cocoon of sleepiness.

At the hotel, the moment I step into the room, any remaining ounce of energy saps out of me. When Connor leaves to haul up the rest of our bags, I flop down onto the massive bed, snuggle up onto a cozy white pillow, and rest my eyes.

Suddenly I startle at the sound of the door clamping shut. I'm facing away, but I hear Connor's footsteps cross the carpeting; then the bed dips as he lies down behind me, wrapping his strong arm around me.

"Was I sleeping?" I'm flustered, head fuzzy as I struggle to wake fully. "Sorry, I didn't mean to fall asleep."

"Hey, it's okay," Connor says softly. "But are *you* okay?"

I squeeze my eyes shut, embarrassed at this new level of vulnerability. We're not discussing a theoretical symptom—he's actually witnessing it. "I'm just . . . so tired." I don't know how to describe it, how this fatigue is beyond normal exhaustion, how it fills up my insides until my limbs are so heavy and my body refuses to function any further, like a computer shutting down. Connor slips his hand into mine, and I turn to face him at last. "I know this isn't how you wanted tonight to go," I say softly.

But he just smiles. "Tonight's seemed pretty perfect to me." He pulls my hand to his lips, and I'm flooded with warmth, with relief. "Do you want to just go back to sleep?"

"Mm, maybe we can talk?" I say, but my eyes are already closed again.

I hear his soft chuckle, feel it in his chest as he wraps his arms around me again. We lie together in silence, but scenes from tonight dance in my mind until one pops forward, waking me enough to speak. "Can I ask you something?"

"Sure."

"You said the anniversary is coming up. When?"

"June tenth."

"Would you like to . . . honor it in some way?"

Connor sighs. "My family wants to do something when we're all together over the Fourth of July. But that day, I just want to be as normal as possible. Just get through it." He squeezes my hand. "I miss him every day; the anniversary will be no different."

I smile. "Tell me about him."

"He was the charmer. Also the wiseass, but his charm could get him out of trouble." I feel his laughter against me again. "He always wanted to open his own bar. We actually talked about opening one together."

"Ah, your business-management degree."

There's a pause. "I *majored* in business management. Never actually finished. Things, uh . . . well, things kinda went to hell my senior year."

I peek an eye open. "What happened?"

Connor sighs. "Long story. I mean, ultimately it was my own fault—I'm the one who chose to skip class, party . . . I fell behind a semester. Then I got a job one summer working construction. I enjoyed it; the money was good. So that was it, I guess. I just didn't go back to school."

I hesitate for a moment, unsure what to say. "You could always go back. Get your degree. Or open a bar like you guys planned."

"Hmm. Maybe."

The silence is heavy, waking me fully. "Can I ask another question?"

He chuckles. "You don't have to keep asking if you can ask a question."

"Okay . . . well, I guess you never told me what happened?" I add quickly, "If you don't want to, I understand."

This time the pause lasts so long that I fear I've crossed a line.

But at last Connor sighs again. "Cam and I used to go out. A lot. We slowed down a bit after he and Arielle got married, slowed down even more after Ella was born. But we didn't slow down enough." I wait, lulled by the rhythm of our breathing, the murmur of the television, the weight of expectation, of a secret he's about to reveal. "One night he drove when he shouldn't have."

I force myself to push through the fatigue, propping up on my elbow. But he's staring at some point on the wall, pained eyes focused on the past, watching a movie that must play over and over in his mind.

"I wasn't there," he says quietly, almost to himself.

I reach for his hand. "Do you really think you could have stopped him?"

"We always closed down the bar together, and I was the one who called the cab, or Lyft, or whatever. But I left with someone that night." Connor stops again, and the room is heavier. He looks at me as if he's forcing himself to, punishment that's self-inflicted. He's begun his confession and needs to see it through. "After Diana and I broke up, I didn't date anyone for a long time," he says, and the name jolts me—it's the first time I've ever heard it. "Then when I tried to date again, it was terrible. One shitty date after another. So I kind of gave up, and stuck to"—he clears his throat—"more short-term commitments."

We're silent again, and I will myself to be supportive—I can't seriously hold something against Connor from before I even knew him. And yet the selfish pang of jealousy persists—and I realize now that their breakup is surely the reason everything went to hell his senior year.

But I push through it, squeeze his hand, wait out the storm. And when he opens his eyes, they're the same clear, true eyes I've been staring into all these months.

"Then I met you," he says softly. "And it was like . . . a miracle."

My breath catches and I smile. "Really?"

"Of course. Suddenly, in the middle of a snowstorm"—he smiles—"there's this kind, smart, beautiful woman who is somehow into me." His smile quickly fades. "But with Cam, I should've called a cab; I should've made sure he had cash for a ride. I should've been there. It's why I haven't had a drink since." He winces. "Until tonight."

"Connor, it wasn't your fault," I whisper.

His chuckle is bitter. "Well, you are about the only one who thinks that. Everybody else—my sister-in-law; her family; even my parents, to some degree, I think, at least the way they look at me sometimes. Everybody knows I screwed up."

I reach for his face, gently turn it toward me. "And what do you think your brother would say?" Connor's brow furrows, and I hold my breath—I didn't know Cam at all and have no idea where this question has come from, but it seems right.

He stares at me for a moment, pained eyes glistening, then finally shakes his head with a sad smile. "He would probably tell me to stop feeling so damn sorry for myself."

We chuckle together and I lean forward, kissing him softly, and he folds me into his embrace. After a few moments, I pull back, force a bright smile. "I did pack my laptop. We could watch a movie, if you want."

He smiles. "*Return of the Jedi*?"

"Absolutely." I snuggle back under the covers. "I might watch it with my eyes closed, though."

He laughs, then gets up to find the laptop. When he returns with it, he sits next to me on the bed again, one hand in mine as the opening theme starts to play. As I drift off he leans close, kisses my cheek, whispers in my ear: "I love you."

A shiver of electricity, a jolt of happiness, pure warmth and joy. The theme song blares bold and confident, and I smile. "I know."

PART SEVEN

REVELATION

Pure terror courses through me as I place a trembling hand on Nikki's chest. But it rises, then falls. A sob escapes my lips.

She's alive.

On my computer, "It's the Most Wonderful Time of the Year" starts blasting from my cheap old speakers—it sure as hell is *not* wonderful, but the lively tune spurs me into motion. I jump up, pull Hayley from the doorframe (where she stands frozen), then slam the door shut and press in the silver lock. I'm finally following active shooter protocol: *If you can't get out, find somewhere safe, lock the door, and barricade it.*

In my mind, Officer Jackson's voice lectures me from our training exercise: *Everyone has better odds if you get out, get yourself somewhere safe, and call for help.*

But this isn't a training exercise. This is real.

This is my best friend's life on the line.

"Help me!" I bark, and Hayley finally tears her eyes away from Nikki. Together we grab my bookshelf and wrench it in front of the door. Then I turn to my desk, eyes landing on my phone.

A moan creeps up from the floor, and Hayley gasps as she scrambles into the corner, but I rush to Nikki and drop to my knees. "Nik!" I need to stop the bleeding—but I still haven't called for help. I'm failing on so many levels, but I can't get my mind to slow down and focus. My legs flare, pins and needles all up and down, and a wave of dizziness hits.

No. Not now.

I have to get through this. Please, God, just let me save her.

I draw in a deep breath and look down at my legs. "I'm ignoring you." An absurd placebo of the mind, but I'm barely hanging on. From the corner, a whimper—Hayley, hand covering her mouth. "I need your help." Hayley obeys, too shell-shocked to argue, and I kneel next to Nikki again. "I'm going to turn you over so I can put pressure on your wound, okay?" She murmurs something, and as we turn her over, she cries out in pain. "I'm sorry!" But even when Hayley shrinks back, I don't stop.

Nikki's chest glistens a deep, almost blackish red, but it's not the sight of it that gets me—I've seen bullet wounds so often on TV that it's almost surreal. It's the rusty-sweet smell, the squish of the warm liquid through my fingers as I press down on her wound, that makes me shudder. Nikki groans but I don't ease up—I have no idea what I'm doing, but this is my chance to stop the bleeding, or at least slow it until help arrives.

Help.

I whip my head to my desk, where both my cell phone and cordless landline sit. "Hayley, I need you to get both of my phones for me, okay?" She crawls forward, grabs them, then hands them out to me. I take the receiver with one hand but keep my other on Nikki's midsection. "Open the university's Twitter on my cell—we have to let people know."

Hayley's face is ashen. "What . . . what do I say?"

"Just—shooter on campus." Her eyes widen. "*Do it*, Hayley."

She starts tapping at my phone, and I dial 9 on the receiver—then Nikki moans again. "Gmmph." Her voice is thick, slurred.

"Shh," I say, dialing 1.

"Go," Nikki says clearly. "You . . . need . . . to . . . go." Her face twists in pain with the effort.

"The hell we will." I meet Hayley's eyes—daring her or absolving her, I'm not sure—but she says nothing.

"Get . . . help," Nikki says.

"I won't leave you." My voice catches, hand hovering over the 1.

"Please." A tear escapes her eye. "Tell Claudia I love her."

I shake my head, spit out my reply through gritted teeth. "You tell her yourself." I hit the second 1 and cradle the phone to my ear, the shrill ring seeming to stretch on forever.

Then I hear another sound.

A creak just outside the office door, followed by another.

Footsteps.

CHAPTER TWENTY-FIVE

July 1, five months before

Footsteps pad across the grass, and I look up, smiling through squinting eyes as Nikki plops down next to me on the quad. It's a gorgeous summer day on campus, the sun beating down on lush green grass and a gentle breeze rustling the leaves of the stately elms that surround us. We found some shade, so I don't even have to worry about the heat sensitivity the stern neuro nurse has warned me about.

Besides, right now I'm holding the best summer cooling measure ever: a chocolate ice cream cone. Compliments of Stan, "For making it through another academic year." It's also the end of the fiscal year—July always brings a sigh of relief across campus, when budgets are fresh, contracts renewed. Every department gets a clean slate. If only life worked that way.

Today, our department is enjoying this impromptu ice cream break on the campus green—even if hanging out with your boss can be awkward sometimes.

Stan flashes a cheery smile. "Now that it's July, we can start making our wish list for the year again."

"Does that mean we can attend that higher education marketing conference in Orlando I mentioned last month?" Nikki is the picture of sincerity, but I know she's messing with him.

Stan chuckles nervously. "Uh, budgets are still a little tight for that. I was thinking more along the lines of office supplies—I need a new phone, for instance, since mine seems to be on the fritz. So if you need anything like that, just let me know."

I nod. "Will do."

Stan's smile returns. "Anyone have exciting Fourth of July plans?" He's dropped a glob of ice cream on his yellow polo without realizing it, so it's hard to make eye contact without my gaze being drawn to the stain.

Nikki shrugs. "Claudia's cousin has a place on Lake Poinsett, so we might head up there."

I take a deep breath. "Connor and I are going to spend the day with his family. They have a cabin on a lake outside of Fargo."

Stan raises his eyebrows. "First time meeting the family?" I blush and he beams. "So glad you two have hit it off so well."

"Thanks," I say as Nikki rolls her eyes out of Stan's view. For some reason he's taken credit for us meeting because of the construction tour, which we've decided is a whole new level of mansplaining.

But the knot pulsing in my gut has nothing to do with Stan and everything to do with meeting Connor's family. It's not just social anxiety—it's the realization after our Memorial Day trip that his family hasn't met any other women since Diana.

They might not like me—I could be a big disappointment.

A drip of melting chocolate dribbles down my finger, and I quickly lick it off. At least we're not staying overnight—Connor needs to work this weekend, and I have to be back at work the day after the holiday, so we're driving up early the morning of the Fourth and coming back that night. As Nikki said, "If they're terrible, at least you'll be with them for less than twenty-four hours."

"So what are your plans, Stan?" Nikki asks now.

"Oh, Louise and I invited a few people out to the lake—the president, some members of the cabinet." Stan's chest puffs out, and he's using his booming name-dropping voice, but his face reddens when he realizes he's misread the theoretical room. "I—uh—I was going to invite you both, but I figured you'd have plans."

I smile. "And we do, so it's all good. Hope you guys have fun."

Nikki's eyes are narrowed, but then she smirks, nodding past Stan. "Did you invite Mr. Personality?"

We both look up to see Chet walking across campus, and even though he's wearing sunglasses, it's obvious he sees us, too—it's in the way his head jerks away and he fumbles with his phone to look busy, the way he's careful to pass by far enough from where we're sitting that he can pretend he *doesn't* see us.

Stan's eyes are nervous. "No. We, uh . . . we don't exactly see eye to eye." He chuckles and it's awkward, but then I notice that, shortly behind Chet, Raj and Hayley are walking toward us, waving enthusiastically.

"You guys are already on holiday mode, huh?" Raj runs a hand through his dark hair, his eyes darting to Hayley, who giggles as expected and flops down on the grass next to us.

Nikki smirks. "Isn't Chet going to wonder why you two aren't following him back to the Admissions Office adoringly?"

Hayley scoffs, gathering up her blonde locks into a loose bun on the top of her head. "We weren't going to the same place—we're heading to the Financial Aid Office for some scholarship flyers to take on the road. Mr. Big Man has a meeting with the president."

Stan sits up straight. "What about?"

Raj and Hayley exchange an uncomfortable glance, and Raj clears his throat. "Uh, he said they're going to discuss strategic recruitment and marketing strategies for next year."

Stan's face reddens and he stands, crumpling the napkin in his hand. "If you'll all excuse me." He's gone before any of us can answer.

Nikki shakes her head. "What is up with him? He just told us he and Louise invited people out to the lake this weekend, but Louise and I have mutual friends on Facebook, and I swear I saw her tagged in some sort of girls' camping trip photo."

I shrug. "Hmm. Maybe she's coming back tonight or something."

But something doesn't sit quite right, and suddenly the ice cream doesn't taste so sweet.

Hayley shudders. "I don't know about Stan, but Chet is going through some shit, that's for sure."

My brow furrows. "What do you mean?"

She and Raj exchange another look, and he nods. "Okay, you did *not* hear this from me," Hayley says, "but Chet's been charged with domestic assault against his ex. Apparently he showed up at her house, and things got ugly. She had to call the cops on him."

"Holy shit," Nikki says. "How do you know?"

"My sister told me—her boyfriend's aunt is a clerk at the courthouse. I guess Chet tried to act all repentant and charm the judge into dropping the charge down to disorderly conduct, but she wasn't having it, so he flipped out, started yelling and swearing." Hayley rips a fistful of grass out of the ground and shakes her head. "So we're pretty sure the *real* reason he's talking to the president is to beg to keep his job."

"Or ours," Raj says, chuckling mirthlessly. "You know, with all the talk of layoffs and everything."

My stomach churns, my ice cream losing all its appeal. "Layoffs?" I thought with the end of the year we'd made it into the safe zone.

Hayley releases the grass in her hand, a flurry of green blades fluttering on the breeze. "Did you guys hear about Joel?"

The ache in my gut pulses, and Nikki speaks quickly. "Yeah, we know."

Raj sighs. "Marcus over in his office said it's a tough break for the poor old guy, but it actually relieved some pressure for their department."

I frown. "What does that mean?"

"It means they won't need to lay anybody off now. He heard every department had to slash their budgets by a certain percentage this fiscal year. A lot of departments aren't filling open positions right now. Layoffs could be next."

Nikki's eyes dart to me, then she scoffs. "Well, it's July—new fiscal year—so obviously that was only a rumor."

He nods. "Right, everybody made it—*this* time. But if things don't turn around, the cuts will be even bigger next time, and there will be no way to avoid letting people go."

There's an uncomfortable pause. My insides roil with fear and doubt; then Hayley harrumphs. "You know what? Screw it. We can't control any of it, right?" She's so breezy about it, and even though a part of me knows she's right, mostly my chest burns because it's so easy to blow that fear off when you're young and healthy. "So what are you two doing for the Fourth?" Hayley doesn't pause for us to answer—she launches into her own story, which is just as well, because I'm still reeling from all this cryptic news. "I'm heading home to my parents' house . . . they're having the whole family over. And my cousin Shelley is going to bring her new *boyfriend*."

She wrinkles her nose, and Raj smirks. "I take it you don't like him?"

"I just can't wait to see what's wrong with the poor schmuck." She rolls her eyes. "My cousin always goes for guys that have some sort of problem she needs to solve. We call her a fixer."

The knot in my gut tightens. "What?"

Hayley takes a deep breath—she's relishing her captive audience now. "In high school, Shelley dated the captain of the football team—but only after he broke his femur. Spent his entire senior year on crutches, and she had to help him. No big deal, right? Well, in *college*, she dates a guy who's recently been in a horrible car accident. Spends months driving him to and from PT. Last year, she brought her new boyfriend to Christmas, and he seemed ordinary enough . . . then, when they're leaving, she says they have to stop by to check in with his parole officer. Turns out he's done time for meth."

Raj frowns. "So you're saying she can't have actual feelings for these people because they have flaws?" I blink at his uncharacteristic criticism of Hayley in all her cute blondeness.

Hayley's eyes widen. "Oh God, no. It's not *them*, it's her. Like, is she actually genuine, or does she just get a rush out of helping them? Because she always seems to be looking for her next cause, you know?" She shrugs. "Like I said, she's a fixer."

Something about the word makes the ice cream threaten to make a reappearance, and I scramble to my feet. "I, uh . . . forgot I have to email a reporter back about an interview next week." I stride away before any of them can question me.

It's all too much—people getting let go at the worst times of their lives because they've used up their sick leave. People getting let go for no reason at all, with no notice. Dating someone who is sick or injured in order to feel good about themselves.

Inside, my fingers fumble to unlock my office door, and I end up dropping the keys onto the faded brown carpeting. "Dammit."

"I got it." Nikki swoops in and saves the day, as best friends do. She unlocks the door and lets me go in first; then she follows me inside and turns to me, arms crossed. We stare at each other for a long time, until finally she speaks. "Fuck them."

It's so unexpected, and I'm a bit punch drunk from sugar and sadness, so a laugh blurts out.

"I'm serious, Mone." She's smiling, though, as she reaches over to hand me the napkin she's brought in from outside. "What the hell do they know about a plan for layoffs?"

I wipe at my eyes and nod.

She nods back. "Repeat after me: I, Simone Archer, am going to go home and drink a big ol' glass of wine, finish packing, and then I'm going to go on a super-fun vacation with my big hot boyfriend and have lots of sex and alcohol."

I'm shaking with laughter now, but her Nikki look is fierce. "Say it."

"I mean, that was a lot of words."

"*Say* it, Simone."

"I'm going to do all those things."

"And I'm not going to worry about what a bunch of jerks say."

I smile. "And I am *not* going to worry about what a bunch of jerks say."

"Okay, then."

Behind me, a throat clears. I whip around, and Connor is in the doorway. "Oh God," I say, "you didn't hear any of that, right?"

A smile twitches at his lips. "No, of course not . . . but I mean, if I *did*, I would say that Nikki gives *excellent* advice."

Heat creeps into my face and across my neck, but Nikki bursts out laughing. Connor winks and walks over, puts his arm around me, and kisses the top of my head. "So," he says to Nikki, who is finally reining in her laughter, "when are we gonna do a poker night again? I want to beat Claudia this time."

Nikki snorts. "Um, yeah, good luck with that, buddy. Nobody ever beats her."

"Damn, I know, I'm a big talker." He sighs, then turns to face me. "I didn't mean to interrupt or anything—just wanted to stop by and remind you I'll be over bright and early Sunday morning to pick you up, okay?"

I nod, and he plants a soft kiss on my lips, then turns back to Nikki. "Seriously, though, game night—let's make it happen. Even if I lose all my money again." They high-five and I beam. There's something about your boyfriend and best friend actually liking each other—being able to double-date—that is so glorious.

He walks out and Nikki turns to me. "You feeling better?"

I answer with an attack hug, hanging on tight, not wanting to let her go.

CHAPTER TWENTY-SIX

July 4, five months before

There's something beautiful about the open prairie stretching before you, all waving fields of gold and rolling hills of green capped by a wispy-clouded blue sky, full of promise. Or maybe it's because Connor is next to me. Whenever he's by my side, the sun shines brighter and I feel strong.

I sip the mocha Connor brought me bright and early this Fourth of July morning, basking in the blue sky and sunshine streaming through the passenger window. In a surge of good spirits, I pull out my phone to call my mom and wish her a happy Independence Day. Her voice is filled with surprise—and exhaustion.

"You and Dad up late partying last night?" I joke.

She chuckles, but it's forced. "Oh, your grandma was up again."

My stomach drops. "What?"

There's a pause. "I thought we'd told you. She gets up at night sometimes. Wanders around the house." Mom sighs. "It's not so bad this time of year, but in the winter it's scary . . . you know, if she were to get outside."

Oh God. My hand goes to my mouth involuntarily. Out of the corner of my eye, I see Connor sneaking a glance at me, and I meet his eyes and force a smile. "I'm sorry, Mom. Have you . . . have you guys thought any more about finding somewhere permanent for Grandma?" I saw the brochures on the table over Memorial Day—now it makes sense.

"Now, Mone, you don't need to be worried about this, okay? You've got enough on your plate already." Mom's voice is stern. "That's for me and Dad to talk about."

A surge of frustration hits, and yet I'm the one who's been sulking, measuring everyone else's troubles against my own. "Well, I'm here if you need me, Mom. Please let me know if there's anything I can do." Such an empty phrase, and it leaves me empty, too.

"Okay, hon." Then Mom's voice brightens. "Hey, you kids have a great time. Big day, huh? First time meeting Connor's family?"

She's trying so hard to gush, to share this moment with me, that I can't help but chuckle. "Yeah, pretty exciting."

"You two are getting serious, aren't you?" Her voice is still cheerful, but it's a little forced now. Something else is coming in this line of questioning.

"I guess so," I say slowly.

"Have you talked about . . . you know, your MS? I mean, does he know about it?"

I scoff. "Of course he knows about it." Connor glances over again, and I roll my eyes at him.

"Good. But have you talked about the future?" There's a pause, and she quickly adds, "I just want to make sure you're thinking about it, honey."

Only every second of every day. "I am, Mom." My voice is quieter—there's an edge to it—and when Connor glances over, I don't meet his eyes. The truth is, we haven't had much of a conversation about my illness since he picked me up from the support group meeting that night months ago.

But I still have plenty of summer left, still within the timeline of the plan, so I leave that conversation to future Simone. For now, I'd much rather talk about *Star Wars* and mint chocolate chip ice cream and Chris Stapleton's music and everything else we have in common—I want to talk about all the things that normal couples do. I want to pretend that I am normal, that there's nothing wrong with me—why burst this perfect new bubble of love?

Mom sighs. "We just want the best for you, honey. You know we're always here for you."

"I know." She means well—she didn't intend to plant the shaky seed of doubt in my gut, but it's there now, and I take a deep breath, try not to let it sprout. "Thanks, Mom. You guys have a great Fourth, okay?" I force a laugh. "And tell Dad and Emmett to be careful with those fireworks, for crying out loud."

Connor taps my arm. "I want to talk to Emmett," he whispers when I look over.

I narrow my eyes in confusion. "Uh, Mom? Is Emmett around? Connor wants to talk to him."

"Sure, Monie—he's standing right here. Take care now and have fun. Love you."

"Love you, too, Mom."

I hand the phone to Connor, who takes it with a grin. "Hey, Emmett, what's up? How'd everything go?"

I lean in, unable to hear my brother but trying to decipher this one-sided conversation. But it involves a lot of "uh-huhs" and "okays" from Connor, so I'm not getting anywhere. "Just remember what I told you," he says at last. "It'll all work out."

I lean back, arms crossed, as Connor ends the call. "So . . . what was that about?"

"Oh, you know. Guy stuff."

He smirks out the windshield, but when he turns toward me, he sees the look I'm giving him and his smirk vanishes. "Okay, well, I gave him some advice."

I raise my eyebrows. "About the snowmobile?"

"About Kaley."

"You did? When?"

"In the garage that night when we were up for Memorial Day." He gives me a sly smile. "Before you came barging in during guy time."

I glare at him; then my eyes widen. "Wait. Do you know what happened between them? Why they broke up, I mean?"

He shoots me a puzzled look. "You don't?"

"No, he hasn't told any of us."

I ignore the puff of pride in Connor's chest and wait for him to speak. "Well, apparently they'd been arguing a lot, and then at a party, she kissed another guy to make him mad."

"Oh God. Poor guy."

"Yeah." Connor looks down, his eyes more pained than I expect them to be. "They broke up that night, but he said he's been thinking a lot and realizing he's partly to blame, too—he was spending so much time with gaming and stuff that he didn't realize she was unhappy."

"Wow." I'm sad for my little brother but proud of his maturity, too. "So . . . what was your advice?"

He sighs. "I told him if he still cares about her, he should tell her. No sense holding it in. Sometimes you have to stand up and say how you feel—fight for what you want, even if you end up looking like a fool. But then, you know, back off. All you can do is be honest and hope for the best. If she doesn't feel the same, then you need to respect that and let her go."

I blink. "Wow. That's . . . some pretty extensive advice."

He shrugs. "I have some experience in that whole area."

A twinge of jealousy, but mostly pain as I think about someone hurting him. I keep my voice light. "Standing up and fighting for what you want?"

He smiles. "Mostly the 'looking like a fool' part." I reach for his hand, and he squeezes mine. "Ancient history, though. Things turned out the way they were meant to."

Suddenly nothing else matters.

He's right. Things have indeed turned out the way they were meant to.

And maybe things will keep turning out.

CHAPTER TWENTY-SEVEN

The lake is gorgeous, its rippling waves sparkling in the glow of the sun. The breeze carries the scent of summer—of sunscreen and sweat, charcoal and citronella—and also the laughter and chatter of family as we approach. It reminds me of my childhood, of visiting family in Minnesota, chasing Emmett around the beach, laughing as Dad tried to water-ski like he did in his "glory days."

The thought is so pleasant it puts me at ease, until I remember it's not *my* family gathered in the backyard overlooking the lake. It's Connor's family.

It's a large group of people I have never met, who may not like me at all.

My stomach flip-flops, and I find myself subconsciously (okay, very consciously) slowing as we round the side of the brown wood-stained cabin. We step out into the open, and I blink into the sun, God's flashlight, my eyes flitting from person to person—this sea of red faces and red cups, brightly colored swimsuits and festive summer decor. Party conversation stops, heads turn toward us, and in this moment of silence, I consider bolting. But Connor squeezes my hand, and an older woman flips her graying brown hair, eyes lighting up. "You made it!"

"Hi, Mom." He releases my hand to walk forward and hug her. Other people turn and wave, shout a greeting, or walk over to hug him or clap him on the back.

Connor extracts himself from a fierce-looking bear hug from a barrel-chested, middle-aged man with a face reddened either by the sun or some good old-fashioned day drinking—probably a little of both. "Guys, this is Simone." He grins and motions me over. "Come on over so I can introduce you to everyone."

Before I can take a step, an excited little shriek belts out across the lawn. "Simone!" A tiny body shoots forward and plows straight into me.

"Ella!" I crouch down so I can return her hug fully, so happy to not only know someone, but that she's excited to see me. "You remember me?"

She rolls her big blue eyes and brushes her dark hair back off her bronzed shoulder. "Of course I *totally* remember you."

I laugh, and so does everyone around us. They're now watching with approving smiles, and I straighten my shoulders a little more. I stand, and Connor squeezes my hand, leans in. "She's usually super shy, but she really likes you." The adoration in his eyes melts away my anxieties.

"Miss Ella's new favorite word is 'totally.'" I turn, and a young woman is walking toward us with a dimpled smirk. "She's, like, *totally* six going on sixteen."

"Mo-*om*," Ella laments, adding another eye roll.

I chuckle. "Well, I feel pretty special that she remembers me."

"From the way I understand it, Connor thinks you're pretty special, too." I blush and she laughs. "I'm Arielle, by the way—Ella's mom."

She pushes her large sunglasses back, brown eyes twinkling as she sticks out her hand. I shake it, feeling even more at ease. "Very nice to meet you."

Connor's mom steps forward, extending her hand as well—then, seemingly thinking better of it, she pulls it back. "Oh, let's get right to it, shall we?" And she leans forward and wraps her arms around me. I freeze, but only for a moment, then hug her back. She pulls away and beams at me with the same disarming smile as Connor has. "I'm Irene. We are *so* glad you could make it, Simone."

The barrel-chested man steps up and puts his arm around her, his thick white hair mussed up, eyes swimmy but full of emotion. I'm pretty sure the buttons on his hawaiian shirt are off. "Now, it's a party. Somebody get these two a drink."

Connor clears his throat, leans in. "Not for me, Dad. I'll just grab a water."

They stare at each other a split second too long—their expressions reveal nothing, yet something makes me uneasy. I slip my hand into Connor's as his mom claps her hands. "Well, you heard him, Bert. One water, and . . ." She turns to me. "How about you, dear? Arielle made some sort of . . . oh, an adult lemonade, I guess you could call it. Would you like to try it?"

Arielle raises her eyebrows, smiling expectantly. God, one of those effortlessly pretty and confident women, and suddenly I'm back in middle school and just want her to like me. I smile as the sun beats down on us. "I'd love to."

Morning rolls into afternoon, the breeze from the lake fluttering my hair as I rest on the cool lawn chair. After surviving the initial get-to-know-you questions—*Where are you from? What do you do? How long have you two lovebirds been dating? How did you meet?*—somehow I've managed to people watch without having to say too much else.

Surely the drink has helped—the sweet, cold liquid sliding easily down my throat on this hot summer day. I look up and Connor is by my side, leaning down to kiss me. "I'm going to walk to the lake and try out Dad's new Jet Ski. Wanna come?"

I wrinkle my nose before I can help it, and a tinkling laugh rings out. "I know, right?" Arielle plops down next to me and shoos Connor away. "Go do your sporty shit—we're going to keep drinking and sunning ourselves."

I nod triumphantly, though while she's wearing a bikini and cutoffs, chair positioned in the blazing sun, I've got my three-quarter-length red shirt and dark denim bermuda shorts on, chair strategically in the shade of one of the large trees that frame the cabin. Connor shrugs. "Suit yourselves." He flashes a grin. "I'll be back soon."

I watch him walk away, then close my eyes again as the breeze picks up. I lay my head against the back of the chair. A bird calls in the distance, adding to my personal realm of tranquility. *Why was I worried about this?*

Another giggle erupts next to me, and I open my eyes to Ella's face, flushed and excited, inches from mine. "Simone, do you want to come catch butterflies with me?"

I smile as she holds up two green nets. How can I turn down that hopeful little face? Plus, her timing is impeccable—I spot Connor's mom walking toward us with another couple who's arrived, so playing with Ella will save me from a fresh round of questioning.

"Sure." I take one of the nets and jump up, then quickly reach my hand down to steady myself—head rush. After taking a beat to gather myself, I trot after Ella.

It's warmer than I expect out in the sun, but I press forward. Ella has her eye on a bright-orange monarch in her grandma's flower garden, and I'm her dutiful sidekick along for the ride. I make a show of grandly sweeping my net at a ladybug, and Ella giggles uncontrollably until we lose sight of the monarch. She's disappointed until she spots a dragonfly and decides it's now a dragonfly hunt.

That goes on for several minutes, and by the time I sprint after her toward a grove of trees, I'm breathing heavily, the sun blazing down on my back. Ella doubles back toward the flower garden and plops down among the flowers, disappointed. When I catch her, I drop down, too, wiping my slick face and trying to catch my breath. It's like any stamina I've gained from all the workouts with Nikki is no match for this heat. My throat is dry, but I croak out, "What's wrong?"

She pouts. "I can't catch anything."

"Maybe we could find more ladybugs?"

Her face lights up, and she springs to her feet. "Come on!"

I smile, wishing I had half her energy, and push myself up. But as I stand my head swims, my eyes blur. I take a deep breath, but a flash of nausea hits—the final blow—and when I reach out to steady myself, there's nothing to grab on to. My hand flails, and I stumble forward onto one knee.

Ella leaps back, her little eyes widening. "Simone?"

I want to stand up and laugh it off, show her there's nothing to fear, but the exhaustion is too strong, it's too damn hot, and I need to focus on my breathing until the nausea subsides. I roll back to a sitting position, press a shaky hand to my burning cheeks in a feeble attempt to part the fog in my head. "Ella, can you please get Connor?" But in the distance I can hear the roar of the Jet Ski.

"Mom!" Ella yells, and I want so badly to tell her no, please don't call attention to me, but the sun is blazing down, relentless. So I stay silent as I sit and wait, powerless.

CHAPTER TWENTY-EIGHT

Arielle rushes over and crouches in front of me, followed closely by Irene and the other couple—two people I've never met before. *Perfect.*

I focus on my breathing, slow and steady, but I don't miss the stage whisper of the man behind Irene. "Is she drunk?" At least his wife has the decency to elbow him.

Arielle rolls her eyes. "Irene, why don't you take the Fritzes and wave down Connor? They're not that far from shore."

She watches them go, cursing at them under her breath, then turns to me. "How can I help, Simone?"

She hands me a water bottle, and I take a cautious sip, then force a smile. "I'm sorry, it's just so hot."

"Do you need to go inside?"

I nod weakly. " I just . . . don't want to . . ." I glance around at the party, where people are still mingling in their respective areas but also sneaking furtive glances in our direction. I swallow back the lump in my throat. *I don't want to humiliate myself in front of a big group of strangers.*

Arielle pshaws. "I wouldn't worry about these people. Half of them are already drunk." She sits down next to me, wrapping up her long black curls into a loose bun, and we're quiet for a few moments before she speaks again. "The first time I met Cam's family, we stayed up late playing drinking games, and I puked all over their table."

"It happens," I say sympathetically.

"All over the giant white-lace doily Irene used as a tablecloth."

"Oof."

"Yep. Her grandmother made it."

My cringe deepens. "I mean, was it really a wise choice to have it out there in the first place?"

"Right? That's what I thought, too." We share a smile, and I am grateful. Ella walks over, and Arielle scoops her into her lap, braiding her daughter's hair as we sit in silence, together.

Within moments, Connor rushes up to us, kneeling in front of me with worried eyes. "Simone, what happened?" His hand strokes gently across my flushed face.

I flash a wan smile. "It's the heat. It's not good . . . for . . ."

"MS." His eyes soften in understanding.

"I'm sorry. It's just . . . this hasn't happened before."

"Hey, don't apologize," he says softly as he takes my arm. "Come on, let's get you inside."

With him next to me, strong and solid, I rise to my feet easily, though another head rush rocks me as I stand. He wraps an arm around my shoulder, but as his other arm circles around me, I shake my head. "You don't need to carry me. I can walk."

"Are you sure?"

"I don't . . ." My eyes dart around again. "I'm already embarrassed enough."

"You have nothing to be embarrassed about," Arielle says as she and Ella stand.

But I turn pleading eyes to Connor. "Please." He nods, and we walk slowly together toward the house.

Inside, the air-conditioning wraps me in its cool embrace, and I ease down on the sofa.

"I'll be right back," Connor says. He returns within moments with a glass of ice water and a fan, which he points directly at my face, then sits down next to me and leans in, voice low. "Do you need to go to the doctor?"

I shake my head slowly, not wanting any more dizziness. "I'll be fine, really. I just need to rest."

He looks doubtful, though, as Arielle and Ella settle across from us on the opposite couch. "Hey, let's watch a movie," Arielle says brightly.

"*The Last Jedi*!" Ella cries.

Arielle's eyes darken briefly, but she smiles, her voice light. "You've watched that, like, a million times already, El. Let's watch something else."

Ella sighs dramatically. "Okay, *fine. Beauty and the Beast.*"

The movie begins, and it's just the four of us—no one else is looking at me, no one judging—and yet I can't shake it. The knot in my gut. The shame and the helplessness. The fear, taunting me.

This will keep happening. Things will only get worse.

But Connor circles his arm around me, and I lean in to him, warm and solid. He is here, and everything is okay. That's all that matters right now. I close my eyes and try to let my body rest, drifting off with the murmur of the movie in the background.

After a few minutes, Irene sticks her head in, her chipper voice waking me. "Hey, guys, Davey and Mick are here."

Arielle scrunches her nose when Irene isn't looking, but Connor's face lights up. "Oh yeah? I didn't know they were coming."

"They'd like to see all of you. I told them Ella is getting so big. They're waiting by the keg, of course." Irene rolls her eyes, then adds wryly, "Don't worry, your father is keeping them company."

Connor turns to me. "They're a couple of buddies from high school."

Irene fixes her expectant smile on Arielle, whose face is expressionless as she pauses the movie. Ella whines, but Arielle gets her up and outside with the promise of another freezie pop. As they breeze stoically by, I marvel at Arielle's strength, how every moment here with Cam's family and friends must be a reminder of all that she's lost.

I turn to Connor. "Aren't you going out to say hi?"

He shakes his head, grabs the remote. "Nah, I'm good."

"Connor." I stare at him until he meets my eyes. "I'm fine. *Go.*"

"You're sure?" I nod, so he leans in and kisses my forehead, then jumps up. "I'll be back in a few minutes, okay?"

I smile as I watch him go, and so does his mom. At least I think she's watching him, but when I turn toward her, I realize she's watching me, her smile at the dangerous crossroads between sympathy and pity. I brace myself.

She clucks, hand to her chest. "He's always been *such* a good boy— so loyal and dependable."

"That's great," I say cautiously.

"He's my little fixer."

My stomach lurches. "Your what?"

"You know, just always there to help people who need it—his friends, his family, people who are, you know, struggling. Less fortunate." She beams at me. "And it's just so *nice* that now you have him to help *you*."

It's like a punch to the gut. She sighs, a wistful little puff, and then flits away still wearing her proud-mama smile.

But her words linger behind. And I sit with them in the silence, alone.

PART EIGHT

Concealment

Monday, December 6, 10:11 a.m.

I freeze, silent, as another footstep creaks outside the office door—then terror courses through me when the handle jiggles.

"911, what's your emergency?"

It's locked and barricaded, I remind myself. *He can't get in.*

"Hello? 911. Is someone there?" I want to answer the woman on the phone, but I can't take my focus off the door handle. There's a scrape of metal on metal, one and then another, the handle jiggling each time but not giving.

As if the person has a set of keys, trying each one.

Hayley whimpers and Nikki clutches my hand, her fingers cold and clammy. It's the jolt I need—this is real, and time is running out.

And I'll be damned if we sit here in the open, defenseless.

"There's a shooter on campus at Southeastern State University," I hiss into the phone. "Herald Hall 120."

I drop the receiver and turn to Hayley. "Closet." The word is barely a whisper, but she leaps up, rushes across the office, and pulls open the closet door.

I wrap my arms under Nikki and lift, the rush of self-preservation on my side as I carry her across the room, legs aflame with pins and needles with every step. Her breaths are rough and I know she's in pain, she's losing so much blood, but we have to hide—nothing will matter if we don't get to that goddamn closet.

Inside the long, narrow closet, I lay Nikki down as gently as possible as Hayley eases the door shut behind us. Nikki is shaking now—*I think she's going into shock?*—so I whip off my cardigan and drape it over her.

My arms tremble as I press down on her wound again. She'll be okay. We'll stay here in the dark until help arrives. Police response time is minutes—Officer Jackson might even be on campus right now.

Or she might be dead.

Before the thought fully forms, a loud bang shatters the silence. My eyes whip frantically to Hayley, who stares back at me wide eyed, crouched in the corner of the closet.

But it isn't a gunshot—it's the office door, slamming against the bookshelf.

Another bang rings out, then another, like a relentless beating drum, but suddenly it stops. A deathly silence hums around us, seconds ticking by excruciatingly slowly, and then I hear a sound even more terrifying.

The creak of footsteps inside the office.

CHAPTER TWENTY-NINE

July 4, five months before

Fixer. The word repeats itself inside my head, a relentless beating drum, but I don't have long to wallow before Arielle and Ella return, the former muttering obscenities under her breath. Gratitude fills me—at least we can sit in our misery together. Surely the low point of the day is over. Once we're out of here, I can try to process Connor's mom's statement and how it made me feel—for now, I need to get through the rest of this visit.

Thankfully, I get to hide here in this blessedly cool room with two members of Connor's family I truly like.

I'm getting hungry, but I'll be damned if I'll risk talking to anyone else to go out to the buffet table and make a plate. I glance at my phone—almost eight o'clock. We'd planned to be on the road by nine. I can hold out for another hour; then maybe we can stop for food on the way home.

Connor bounds into the room then and sets a plate on my lap triumphantly. I catch a whiff of nacho-cheesy goodness before I even look down. "I wasn't sure if you wanted a burger or a brat, so I thought

I would bring you Doritos for an appetizer." He grins at all three of us, and when Ella jumps up, he scoops her up. "Come on, guys, grab a plate. They're about to start."

"About to start what?" Arielle's eyes narrow.

"The slideshow." Connor's grin broadens, and it strikes me that his enthusiasm is fake, the Doritos a delicious bribe to stay later than our agreed-upon departure time.

"Slideshow?" I ask softly.

"God dammit." Arielle doesn't mutter, and Connor's jaw tenses.

"Mommy!" Ella claps a hand to her mouth.

Arielle forces a smile. "Sorry, baby. I'll put a quarter in the swear jar when we get home."

Connor turns to me, his eyes questioning. "You feeling up to it?"

His mom's words—*my little fixer*—slice through me, and I nod, pushing myself to my feet. I shove some Doritos into my mouth and follow them down the fluffy carpeted stairs into the basement great room, unsure exactly what it is we're walking into.

Apparently it's an annual family tradition to stuff their sweaty, tipsy bodies downstairs to watch a slideshow of their family adventures throughout the years. I'm hanging out in the back, leaning against the wall, giggling as I watch Connor with his awkward preteen mullet flexing for pictures with his cousins, or Connor the chubby little toddler wearing his He-Man Halloween costume.

But as the pictures press on—well past nine o'clock—through the relentless procession of time, Arielle's face grows paler. Connor is growing closer to adulthood—and so is his brother. Sure enough, photos begin to pop up of Arielle and Cam—at prom, graduation, and finally, their wedding day.

Ella is loving it, sitting on her grandma's lap, eyes glued to the large flat-screen on the wall in front of her, but I catch Arielle swiping at her eyes as she sneaks silently up the stairs.

Then another couple fills the screen, and my heart leaps to my throat.

It's Connor, a bit younger, with a strikingly beautiful redhead.

Well, it's nice to finally meet you, Diana.

I was wrong. I hadn't yet reached the night's low point—or maybe I had, but somehow we've now sunk *beyond* the low point and into the second level of hell.

And is it my imagination, or has an awkward hush fallen over the room—are eyes darting to me? It's certainly quieter, voices not as boisterous now. Next to me, Connor visibly tenses, his eyes flitting apologetically to mine as the screen shows Connor and Diana dancing at Cam and Arielle's wedding, Connor and Diana wearing matching sweaters at Christmastime, Connor and Diana cuddled together on a ski lift.

Finally, he rubs his forehead. "Mom."

A few uncomfortable snickers burst out around the room, and Irene shrugs. "Sorry—we add on to the same old slideshow every year. We'll be past these soon, Simone."

I am horrified at the callout and the laughter that follows. I shrink into myself but still can't stop watching as the photos continue. Connor and Diana running a marathon—a *marathon*? I glance at him, and he smiles sheepishly, shrugs. He has never mentioned this, and I am humiliated when I realize why—because I'm struggling to even run a 5K, and he didn't want to embarrass me.

Of course not—he wants to help me. I'm the girlfriend he needs to help.

Next—as if the universe really wants to drive home the stark contrasts between us—is a rock-climbing selfie. Shit, she's even one of those women who looks beautifully put together when she sweats.

Then the room goes silent. Connor jumps up, mutters "God dammit," and bolts forward to manually skip the slideshow forward, but not before I see it. Diana, smiling big as life, Connor kissing her demurely.

Her hand thrust forward, displaying her bright, shiny diamond ring.

My breath leaves me.

They were engaged?

I fight not to react. I know all eyes are on me, but as Connor and his mom argue and fumble with the projector, I slip up the stairs as quickly as possible, not looking back.

CHAPTER THIRTY

Up in the silent kitchen, my hands shake as I take out my phone and type out a text to Nikki.

I am in hell.

My phone buzzes with her response within moments.

Well, you are in North Dakota.

I scoff. Very funny. Seriously, this is terrible.

You're meeting the in-laws. What do you expect?

The in-laws. The phrase jolts me. Before today I could picture it. I've *been* picturing it since we met, if I'm honest. The fantasy of it.

But now the reality doesn't seem as possible. Now I've seen a glimpse of Connor's past life with Diana—healthy, adventurous Diana. I try to reconcile it with his life with me—needy, fragile me.

More ugly words swirl about my mind, taunting me. Telling me I'm fooling myself to think this could work. Even a fixer has limits when the burden is too great.

Burden. The word strikes me hard and fast, a white-hot poker straight to my core.

A sob wells up in my throat, threatening to escape, and I clamp my hand over my mouth.

"Oh God, honey, are you getting sick?"

I whip my head to the right, and I see Arielle standing on the other side of the screened-in patio. I shake my head, lowering my hand.

"You can't take any more of that shit downstairs, either, huh?" My shoulders sag, and as she slides open the screen door, I catch a pungent whiff from the cigarette in her hand. "Well, come on. It's a hell of a lot better out here."

I step out and gasp at the grand canopy of stars that lights up the black sky. The water is still, and the stars are mirrored in the lake so you can't tell where the sky ends and the water begins. My feelings, too, are a mixed-up jumble inside me. I love Connor and he loves me.

He *loves* me. I'm *sure* he does. But when does love become obligation?

I sigh, leaning forward against the railing of the deck, wishing I had the answer.

"Does the smoke bother you?" Arielle asks.

"No," I say. "Just . . . tired."

She nods without looking over. "So when were you diagnosed?"

I pause, unsure for a moment, then give in. "About eight months ago."

"How long have you known you had it, though?"

I glance at her in surprise, but she keeps her eyes on the stars. Then I sigh. "The first signs were about nine years ago—bad headaches; my eyes wouldn't focus. The funny thing is, I'd almost forgotten about it. Isn't that stupid?"

"It's not stupid to try not to think about the bad stuff," Arielle says softly. "So when did you know for sure?"

"This time around, my foot went numb, and then I had some muscle spasticity. That's how I was eventually diagnosed." I narrow my eyes, turn toward her. "Do you know someone with MS?"

"My aunt."

I swallow. "How is she?" *Please be okay. Please be okay.*

She shrugs. "Same old feisty Aunt Maria."

She meets my eyes and smiles. I smile back, my shoulders sagging in relief. Arielle is definitely my favorite in this family.

We stare out at the stars again until I clear my throat. "I'm really sorry, by the way. About Cam."

"Thank you."

"Is it . . . is it hard being around them all the time?" I motion back toward the house.

She sighs. "Oh yeah. Especially with this shit. I thought they weren't going to do it anymore, but Irene is a stickler for tradition. But it's her way of dealing with it, so I get it." She drops her cigarette and crushes it underfoot. "Sometimes I wish I could just go, you know? Just me and Ella, and nobody else. We don't *need* anybody else, you know?"

I nod vigorously.

Arielle laughs bitterly. "But who am I kidding? Ella does need them." She stares at the stars again, her voice so soft I almost don't hear it. "Maybe I do, too." She gives her shoulders a little shake and then turns back to me. "I do need a change, though. Something different. Christ, even just a new piercing, or blue hair—or maybe another tattoo. Anything to show *I'm* still here, you know. I'm alive and I'm still in control of my own goddamned life."

I want to hug her, to comfort her, to thank her, this woman I just met who is making so much sense—who has experienced an entirely different tragedy and yet endures the same emotions I can't seem to express. But she turns toward me and abruptly changes the subject. "Let me guess: you're out here because they got to the 'Connor and Diana Montage of Love.'"

She says it in such a mocking, sickeningly sweet tone that I have to laugh. But it quickly fades. "I . . . he never told me they were engaged."

Her eyes widen. "God dammit, Connor." I say nothing, and she sighs. "I'm sure it's because it's painful to talk about, you know? It all ended pretty abruptly. I mean, she called from her internship in Boston to say she wanted to break up. Pretty sure she was already with somebody else."

I'm not sure how many more surprises I can take. "So, do you . . . do you think he's over her?"

"Oh yeah, totally." Arielle doesn't hesitate, which should be more of a comfort than it is. "Don't let that shitty slideshow fool you. Diana was the queen of looking perfect, and maybe she was, sort of, but she was a little *too* perfect, if you ask me. You know what I mean?"

I don't know, but I nod anyway because I desperately want her to be right. I need the nagging doubt planted in my mind to stop growing.

We stare into the stars again, and I wish they could tell me my future. Whether I'm making the right choices about my health, my relationship. Whether delaying treatment will be worse for me in the end.

And whether delaying the inevitable conversation with Connor will only make things hurt more in the long run.

CHAPTER
THIRTY-ONE

We're on our way home at last, and in the darkness of the truck I make a point to stare out the window, refusing to make eye contact with Connor. We don't speak at all for the first thirty miles, but he doesn't seem to notice until about mile twenty. I can tell that he notices because he starts to fidget with the music, ask random questions. I'm able to respond with one-word answers, so I can prolong my silence.

"*Need to make a bathroom stop?*"

"No."

"*Should we stop for gas at the truck stop in Summit?*"

"*Sure.*"

Finally, after forty-five minutes, he sighs. "Look, since you're not talking to me, can I tell you about something?"

I frown but I'm curious, so I look over. His eyes are twinkling. "Uh, sure."

Connor takes a deep breath. "I've been thinking about what you said, about how I could still finish my degree, even open up a bar, and I was kind of coming around to the idea, and, well, I was talking to Dr. Fritz today—did you meet him?"

He was the jerk who thought I was drunk. I nod, biting back the sarcasm.

"He's a professor at a private college in Saint Paul, and he was telling me about their online business degree. He convinced me to apply."

I suck in a breath. "Wow."

"I know. It'll mean that I'll be really busy between work and homework and everything, but we'll make it work, right?" He doesn't stop to let me answer, his mind buzzing. "Everything is online, but they do require an on-campus visit one week during the summer, for orientation." He stops, glances over. "It's next week."

My eyes widen. "Next week?"

"I know, it's so soon—obviously they can't process my application that quickly, so I'm not *technically* enrolled yet, but Dr. Fritz said I could sit in on this current session. It'll give me a head start, help me make some contacts for possible internships—get my foot in the door."

His eyes are pleading, and God, he is *glowing* with excitement. I can't help but smile. "That's amazing, Connor."

He beams and reaches for my hand, but then he sighs, his smile fading. "Look, I am so sorry about the stupid slideshow."

"You never told me you were engaged."

His head whips over. "What?"

I meet his gaze. "Why didn't you tell me?"

He looks away, shrugs, but his face is red. "You never asked," he says quietly.

"How would I have known to specifically ask that?" My voice rises, and he flinches. "It seems like something you would've volunteered."

"I just . . . didn't think it was important. Not anymore. Ancient history." He looks over again, his eyes sincere, but I wait for those magic words. "I'm sorry."

My shoulders relax and I nod. He reaches for my hand. "Honestly, I forgot about that part of the slideshow because I haven't watched it in years. Cam and I would usually skip out and keep drinking. But I have to say, it was really nice seeing all those old pictures of him."

I squeeze his hand. "You were pretty cute when you were a kid."

"Right? I mean, overall it wasn't too bad, was it?"

"Oh no, I truly enjoyed the 'Connor and Diana Montage of Love.'"

He sighs. "Look, I asked Mom to take those pictures out of the slideshow. Next year will be better, okay?"

Next year. I try to cover my apprehension with a strained smile.

He narrows his eyes. "Okay, what else did I screw up?"

I take a deep breath, but I can't do it—I can't bring myself to repeat what his mom said. How she made me fear he is with me out of some sort of obligation, out of some need to help, to be a fixer.

I'm also afraid of the answer, of seeing the truth in his eyes.

"I'm just tired." I turn toward the window and stare into the darkness.

Soon the bright lights of Sioux Falls twinkle ahead of us. When Connor pulls into the parking lot of my apartment building and shuts the engine off, I clear my throat, stare up at the tan three-story building, aging but sturdy. "You don't need to come in."

He looks over in surprise. "Oh. I thought I would stay tonight?"

I shrug, but it's stiff. "It's late. We both have to work in the morning."

His eyes are hurt now, and somewhere deep down I want to comfort him, but I fight it.

"I was thinking we could watch *The Phantom Menace*," he says. I wrinkle my nose, and he quickly continues. "Okay, we can skip to *The Force Awakens*, if you don't want to watch those episodes—"

"Connor," I say, cutting him off. "It's late, and I'm tired." The truth, but not the whole truth. Without meeting his gaze, I step out into the darkness, the rush of the cool night breeze tickling my face, and walk to the back of the truck. Connor meets me there, eases open the back, and reaches underneath the truck-bed cover for the extra-large beach bag I packed for the day. "I got it." My voice is sharper than I intended, and he stiffens.

The bag is heavy—I'm a chronic overpacker, dammit—and it takes effort to lug it out and onto my shoulder.

I look up at him, and he's eyeing me. "I can carry that up for you, you know."

I raise my chin, my insides churning with ugly words. *Fixer. Burden.* "I can do it myself."

He blinks, nods, then leans over to give me a quick kiss. I don't stop him, but I don't return it. "Okay then." His voice is flat. "I'll call you tomorrow, I guess."

I don't say anything, don't turn to wave as I walk inside. Instead I drag my exhausted body up to my apartment, straight into bed, and try to drown out the sound of his mother's voice in my head, try to quell the doubts swimming through my mind, the knot of fear lodged in my gut.

I try to pretend everything is going to turn out okay.

PART NINE

REALIZATION

Monday, December 6, 10:14 a.m.

Everything will be okay. It has to be. I'm willing myself to believe this even as I listen to the footsteps of the shooter approaching the closet.

Another footstep, then another. My heart beats in my ears—it's fight-or-flight time, and I blink around the darkness until I see a small plastic tray on a shelf that contains extra office supplies.

"Hayley," I whisper, pointing, and she sees it and grabs the large pair of scissors on top. Then we both wait here in our hiding place, cramped and covered in blood, fearful eyes on the door.

The footsteps stop and I hold my breath. Suddenly the door bangs against the bookshelf again, and a second set of footsteps scuffs in. Hope surges within me—someone else is here, maybe to save us. But there's no commotion, only the sound of two voices now, speaking softly to each other.

My stomach drops. They're not here to help. They're working with the shooter.

This person's sound is different, though, their feet clomping around the room rather than taking measured footsteps like their counterpart—one voice murmuring at a near-frantic pace, the other clipped and contained. Their voices get louder, and I lean forward, straining to hear. It's two men.

Then the calmer of the two voices rises, and the hairs on my arms prickle.

"I had to start sooner than expected because you didn't secure upstairs like you were supposed to."

My eyes meet Hayley's in the darkness, and I wonder if she feels it, too—the icy shiver of recognition and dread.

Because it's her boss out there. Chet is the shooter.

The picture solidifies in my mind now, a puzzle coming together. The smug little man who craved control, whose calm facade hid a monster all this time. An entitled, violent monster.

"Did you really think we were just going to *scare* them?" Chet asks now, his voice even louder, crueler. The clomping pacing stops, but the other voice stays low, and I can't hear their response. Chet screams again. "You weren't even going to fire the gun, were you? I swear to God, if I hadn't come up there, they would've overpowered you and it would all be over. *Pathetic.*"

His words slice through the air like razor blades, and the room falls silent, the air heavy with a terrible expectancy.

At last the other shooter speaks up, and it's as if his words steal my breath, pierce right through me.

Because I recognize the second voice, too.

CHAPTER
THIRTY-TWO

July 12, five months before

The next week is a whirlwind for Connor—I recognize that and play the dutiful girlfriend as he rushes to pack, to beg out of work by promising to take extra shifts when he returns. I smile and wish him luck when he leaves for his week of orientation in the Twin Cities, but the echoes of fear and doubt still reverberate within me from our strained argument after his family gathering on the Fourth—and from the words his mother said that I can't get out of my mind.

"So he's gone all week?" Nikki asks as we walk together down the long hallway toward the Student Union for the—finally scheduled—active shooter training session.

I nod. "It's required, plus it's an incredible opportunity for the professor to introduce him to some contacts."

She scrunches her face. "Why did you say that so weird? Like, your voice got all high and fakey."

"What do you mean?" I squeak.

She smirks and I bristle. I haven't told her about any of the tension between Connor and me yet—the slideshow, his mom's "fixer" comment, the way I brushed him off when we got back. I'm putting off telling Nikki about it because I know what she'll say: talk to Connor. And she'd be right—we need to talk about a lot—and I'm approaching my promised deadline of discussing my illness, the future, our future.

But now more than ever, I am afraid to.

I'm saved now by my phone buzzing, and I glance down. Connor. "Do I have time to take this?"

Nikki waves a hand. "Yeah, I'll save you a seat."

I plop down on a cushy mauve sofa outside the conference room, where coworkers from various departments are already filing in for the training. "Hello?"

"Hey, beautiful."

The connection is scratchy, but somehow hearing his voice manages to push back the fear and doubt for now, and I can't help but smile. "Hey, yourself. Are you counting down the days until Friday?" There's a pause, and at first I think I've lost the call. "Connor? Are you there?"

He groans. "Well, that's why I called. I just found out I need to stay a few more days."

"Why?"

"Dr. Fritz set up another meeting this weekend—I might be able to get an internship with a major liquor distributor next year, and it would be great to see that side of the business."

I pause, the fear creeping back in. "Oh."

"Oh, what?"

His voice is scratchy, and it's more than just the connection—I'm not used to hearing an edge of tension in his voice. I swallow. "I just . . . I thought you were going to be here Friday is all."

"I know, I'm sorry. I'm figuring things out as I go here." Connor sighs. "It's all kind of overwhelming, honestly."

A surge of guilt hits—he's stressed. I should be supportive. "I understand. So when do you expect to be home?"

"Sunday. And then I promise we'll spend some—"

His voice stops abruptly. I stare at the phone, screen dark and silent in my hand, until I'm sure that I've lost him.

"Is everything all right, dear?"

I look up in surprise into a kind smile and worried eyes behind thick glasses. "Charlene, you're back!" I shove my phone into my pocket and return her smile. "Everything's fine—just dropped a call. How was your vacation?"

"Oh, it was wonderful." She pats her cheek and chuckles. "I even got some sun."

I cluck my tongue. "I'm so jealous. The weather was good for the wedding, then?"

She gives a relieved nod—Nikki and I heard all about Charlene's concerns about her daughter's outdoor wedding venue at coffee a couple of weeks ago. "Yes, thank heavens. And the reception was beautiful—so much space for the grandkids to run around and work off all that sugar." She chuckles. "Isn't it funny how something that seems all wrong can actually be just right?"

Her words jolt me, but I keep my smile. "So true." I stand. "Well, I'd better get in there. Are you going to the active shooter training?"

Charlene shudders. "No, I'll be sure to read up on it afterward, though. Your office usually posts a summary, right?" I nod and she smiles. "You take care now."

We part ways, and as I walk toward the training room, I remember her words—and I hope that even though things seem wrong with Connor right now, everything will be just right after all.

I scramble into the training session at the last minute, apologizing as I bump into people's knees as I make my way to the seat Nikki saved for me. My eyes scan the room, and I frown. "Where's Stan?" I whisper.

Nikki shakes her head. "He was here, but then Louise called, and he stepped out."

As Officer Jackson begins the session by firing up a PowerPoint and welcoming everyone, my thoughts begin to drift between Stan's mysterious behavior and my own problems. I stare out the window at the sky, squinting to blur the grayness, to blur my thoughts.

"Archer?"

I blink, whip my head around to face the front.

Officer Jackson's hands are on her hips. "Do you remember what ALICE stands for?"

"Uh, yes." My voice is a squeak, so I clear my throat, square my shoulders. "ALICE. Alert, Lockdown, Inform, Counter, Evacuate."

Her nod is firm. "Excellent." She directs her attention back to the PowerPoint, and I narrow my eyes in concentration as she continues. "Now, ALICE isn't necessarily meant to be performed in any sort of order. It's an options-based training method—meaning you do whatever you have to do to survive in the scenario you're facing. Today is going to be about practicing some of those scenarios." She nods to Chet, the admissions director. "And I think we're ready to start. But before we do, does anyone have any questions?"

Nikki raises a hand, and I turn to her in surprise. "Yeah, I get why we're training, but shouldn't we also be focusing on the root of the problem?" Officer Jackson furrows her brow in confusion. "Commonsense gun reform. This shit should not keep happening."

The room is silent, and I bite back a smile of pride. Nikki is such a badass.

From the back of the room, an annoyed sigh—I turn, and Chet is shaking his head, frowning—but when I turn back, Officer Jackson is nodding at Nikki, unfazed. "I appreciate your comment, Ms. Donovan. It's a topic I've spoken on before." That's right—last year I wrote a feature about how Officer Jackson speaks at law enforcement forums around the Upper Midwest, and that's in addition to her job, her role as adviser to the university's Black Student Union, and instructor at a community self-defense course. "I'd be happy to discuss that with you another time," she continues, "but since today's focus is specifically on the ALICE method, I'd like to limit questions to that topic." She turns to address the rest of the room. "Any other questions?"

In front of us, Hayley's hand goes up, and Officer Jackson nods for her to speak. "Yeah, you said we're supposed to get out if at all possible, right? But, I mean, what if there's, like, a shooter out in the Student Union and I'm fleeing, but I come upon someone who's been shot?" She elbows Raj next to her, who rolls his eyes. "Do I just leave him there?"

"Yes." Hayley flinches and so do I, but Officer Jackson remains stoic in her response. "Your number one priority is getting out so you can call 911, and letting campus security and law enforcement do our jobs."

Raj leans forward. "But what if I die before you can get there?"

"The faster we can get there, the more people we can save." Officer Jackson hadn't exactly answered the question, but I'm not about to call her on it. "Response time is only minutes—after we've been alerted. Response times slow drastically when people don't call 911 right away. That's why getting out and calling for help immediately is so crucial."

"But not all shooters have the same motive, right?" Raj's eyes are on Officer Jackson, intense. "I mean, there's a difference between a shooter who's looking to take hostages and one who's just looking to kill as many people as possible. Some of those guys are going in there planning to die, with nothing to lose, but some actually have demands they hope will be met."

Hayley turns to Raj with a glaring WTF look, but Officer Jackson nods solemnly. "Yes, that's true. But my advice to you is the same."

"Really?"

"Really. If you have a chance to get out, take it—regardless of what you believe the shooter's motive to be."

"But—" Hayley elbows Raj to cut him off, but he asks, "What? I just want to prove there's a scenario where you shouldn't leave me bleeding to death on the floor."

I shake my head, laughing at his macabre humor. From the back of the room, Chet clears his throat loudly. "Can we get to the scenarios soon, please? We're on a tight schedule, and I know all of these *valuable* employees have work they need to get back to."

Next to me, Nikki mouths, "Jackass," and I roll my eyes. But we get up and follow the crowd into the Admissions Office.

"Okay, if you work here, go to your normal work station," Officer Jackson commands. "If this isn't your department, pretend you're visiting."

Hayley loops her arms through mine and Nikki's. "Come on, losers. We can all visit in Raj's office."

We follow her in. Raj is already sitting with his feet up on his desk, and we plop into chairs around the small office. Nikki grins. "Did you get all your burning questions answered?"

"Hey, it's important to be an engaged participant in these types of sessions." He smirks. "Plus, I could see it was pissing Chet off, so I was planning on asking any and every question I could think of."

They laugh, but I'm busy scanning the room. "Okay, there isn't a secondary exit here. So when they yell 'Gun,' we're going to have to lock and barricade the door, and I suppose hide behind the desk?"

No one answers, so I turn, and they're all looking at me in surprise. "Listen to you, Miss Commander." Raj runs a hand through his floppy black hair. "I hope you're around in a real crisis. Otherwise we're stuck with the leadership of Mr. Arrogant Asshole."

Nikki smirks. "Yeah, and he and Stan will probably be so busy arguing over who's in charge of leading us to safety that we'll all be dead."

Hayley laughs and flips her blonde hair while reaching for a handful of M&M's out of a dish on Raj's desk, popping them into her mouth.

"By the way, I caught Stan yelling at the president's sweet old secretary the other day."

I recoil. "Stan yelled at Charlene? I just saw her, and she didn't say anything—she just got back from vacation, for crying out loud."

"This was before she left, I think," Hayley says. "I could hear it from the hallway passing by—he claimed he had a meeting with the president, but apparently it wasn't on the calendar and he flipped."

"God, I can't *believe* him," Nikki says.

I nod but look down, my chest burning with a weird sense of loyalty—and yet of conflict—as I picture Charlene's kind face from earlier as well as Louise's sad face in my doorway.

"Right?" Hayley shakes her head. Then she shoots a look at Raj, who raises his eyebrows. She turns back to us. "Hey, has Stan said anything weird about budget stuff?"

I frown. "No. Why?"

"We think Chet's in trouble." Raj blurts it out like he couldn't wait to tell us. "He's charged way too many questionable trips to the university—conferences that he really didn't need to be at."

"Or that didn't even exist," Hayley adds.

"You're sure?" I ask.

"Eh, it's a rumor floating around, anyway." Raj shrugs. "But knowing Chet, it's probably true. And considering budgets are already tight—he's gotta be in some serious shit."

Nikki's eyes narrow. "Stan went to some of the same conferences, I think."

Hayley shakes her head. "God, one minute it seems like they can't stand each other, the next they're BFFs."

Nikki and I exchange a look. "BFFs?" I say.

Hayley shrugs. "Okay, maybe not quite, but they have a weird . . . camaraderie maybe?"

"That's a big word," Raj teases.

She smacks him before continuing. "Well, the two of them were huddled in front of his computer the other day when I stopped over to get a signature for something, and they got all flustered when I walked in. Chet looked pissed, but Stan's face was so red I felt kinda bad for interrupting." But she giggles, which means she really didn't feel that bad.

Raj groans. "Dude, they were totally looking at porn."

"You think *everyone's* looking at porn."

"What the hell else do you think two frustrated, middle-aged white guys would be doing in that situation?"

Hayley considers. "I mean, it's a plausible theory."

Raj whistles. "Wow, Hayley, more big words."

We all laugh, but I catch Nikki's eye. Something isn't right about this.

"Gun!"

The cry from the outer information desk sets us into motion, and we lockdown and barricade. As we crouch together behind the desk, I'm scared—even though it's a drill, it's still creepy. And sitting there, in the darkness, I can't stop my mind from drifting back to Connor and how much I want things to be good again between us—but how terrified I am of talking to him about it.

How terrified I am that I'll have to stop pretending.

CHAPTER THIRTY-THREE

July 16, five months before

By Friday, my stomach is in knots. I should be excited—it's a blessedly cool day, which means Nikki and I can meet for a run in Falls Park after work. Plus, it's the weekend, and Connor will be home in two days.

"You're sure quiet," Nikki glances over, slowing to match my stride. "Am I going too fast? It's not your knee, is it?"

For once, that's not the case. A twinge shoots through my knee then, a reminder of its presence. Okay, for once it's not the *only* reason. "Nah, it's fine." I don't know if it's something about being out here on a run, cool breeze carrying me along, the rush of the falls muting out the nearby traffic—and being able to stare ahead and not look my best friend in the eye—but suddenly it's as if the truth will burst out of me. "But look, I need to tell you something."

"It's you and Connor, isn't it?" She shakes her head. "I knew something was weird. Did you have a fight?"

"Sort of. Kind of a one-sided fight, admittedly. And I'm sort of having doubts now. About . . . us."

Nikki's head whips over. "Okay," she says slowly, "let's unpack this. Does this have something to do with your visit with his family?"

I nod.

"Are you ready to tell me about that?"

I wince at the annoyance in her voice, then take a deep breath. "Well, Connor's mom basically told me I'm a burden to him, and then we had to watch a slideshow of him with his gorgeous and perfect ex-fiancée—and I didn't even know he'd been engaged, by the way. And all of this after I totally almost passed out in front of his entire family because heat and MS don't exactly mix well."

Nikki slows to a stop, hands on her hips. "Whoa, whoa, whoa. First of all, she said you're a 'burden'? Like, she actually *used that word*?"

"Well, no, not exactly that." I stop, too; then we walk together as I relay the story.

Afterward Nikki frowns. "Okay. Well, we'll come back to that, but you almost *passed out*? Was it an attack like last time?"

I shake my head. "No, not like before. But I'm more sensitive to the heat now and need to learn my limits."

She nods, still frowning. "And *why* are you just telling me all this now?"

I dart a glance at her, knowing my eyes look guilty. "Because I guess I kind of . . . wanted to ignore it."

She nods but doesn't chastise me, which I appreciate immensely. Then she sighs. "Look, I'm really glad you're okay. And I'm sorry his mom said that. But do you think maybe you're taking it too personally because you're—you know—sensitive to the issue?"

My eyes blaze. "What's that supposed to mean?"

"Well, to me it sounds more like she's trying to pat herself on the back for raising him to be a good guy. I mean, what did Connor say about it?"

I look away. "I didn't tell him about it."

"Ah, the one-sided fight." Nikki shakes her head. "Mone, why?"

"Well, I mean, I *did* tell him how I felt about the slideshow." My voice is so defensive now it's practically a whine. "He apologized and said it's ancient history. We just haven't talked about the other stuff."

"Why not?"

"Because I know what he'll say."

"And what will he say?"

"He'll apologize and assure me he doesn't feel that way."

"So what's the *problem*, then?"

I flush in anger at her scathing words. "The problem is I won't know if he means it." She stops, staring at me with frustrated bewilderment, but I press on, fear and anger and uncertainty spilling out. "Nikki, Connor is a really decent guy who has come to my rescue throughout our entire relationship. And apparently that's just his personality. So, what if he feels trapped now? What if he just feels sorry for me and is staying with me out of obligation? What if he doesn't even realize that's what he's doing, but someday he does realize it and leaves me?"

Nikki blinks at me, dumbstruck, then suddenly bursts out laughing. "Do you *hear* yourself right now? Don't you think this is more about you and your insecurities than it is about him?"

My eyes widen in shock, her laughter slicing tiny cuts into me, and I can't take it anymore—I explode. "You don't understand, okay? You don't know what it's like to have to wonder if someone is only with you because they feel sorry for you. To have to wonder if you'll feel fine tomorrow or if you'll wake up unable to walk. To wonder at what point you're going to steadily progress until you lose all mobility, or worse."

Nikki sighs, but her voice softens. "Simone, any one of us could get hit by a bus tomorrow."

"Yeah, well, my bus is following me around, waiting to slam into me. I just have no idea when."

Nikki throws up her hands. "*God dammit*, Simone. It's like everything is the fucking Martyr Olympics with you."

My mouth opens but shuts again, the biting reply dying in my throat and my heart shriveling. Then, the longest silence there's ever been between us.

Nikki lowers her head, and when she looks back up at me, her eyes are glistening. "Claudia's mom was diagnosed with breast cancer."

"What? When?"

"We found out over Christmas. It's why we've been gone a lot."

"Why didn't you guys tell me?" But I know the answer, and the knots in my belly twist harder, squeezing the life out of me.

"Because you don't have room for anyone else's suffering right now." Nikki's voice is soft; she's dealing the blow gently. "And I get it. But it leaves no room for anyone else to ever have any pain around you."

I stare at her, too dumbfounded to say anything else. She sighs. "Look, I need to get going—I promised Claudia we'd go out to dinner. Do you . . . do you want to join us?"

But her eyes are on the ground again, so I shake my head. We both need space right now. "Nah, I've got some stuff I need to do."

She nods and turns to go, and I watch her jog away from me.

I stroll around Falls Park, letting the breeze carry me where it wants to, and eventually the roaring water lures me closer. I climb down onto one of the rocks and sit, letting Nikki's honesty roll around in my mind.

I have been a terrible friend.

I've held my own pain out as being more important than anyone else's. All the ugly thoughts, the judgments I have cast upon others, swirl through my mind.

I take a deep breath, watch the breeze push relentlessly against the trees. The leaves sway, but they don't fall. Sunlight sparkles through them, down to the water, a dazzling display.

My pity party needs to come to an end. No more—what did Nikki call it?—Martyr Olympics. God, the truth hurts.

My gaze flits toward the direction where Nikki left. Best friends are honest with each other. Best friends fight. We'll be okay. We *have* to be.

I need to apologize to her.

I need to start seriously thinking about seeing a different neurologist.

I need to talk to Connor.

The wind blows harder then, as if satisfied I've finally come around.

I stare out at the water. I don't know what I'll say to him. I don't know if, as Nikki said, this truly is more about me than it is about him. But I know I love him, and that's worth fighting for.

I take the deepest breath I have in a long time as I smile out at the water. Suddenly Sunday can't come fast enough.

CHAPTER THIRTY-FOUR

July 18, five months before

Sunday morning, I wake up to a ringing phone. Connor. I roll over, clear the sleep from my throat, croak, "Hello?"

"Well, good morning, sunshine." The rush of air surrounds his voice—he's in the car—and I smile.

"Good morning, yourself. How was your weekend?"

"Ah, it was great. I mean, it was a lot to take in and I'm exhausted, but I really feel like I'm finally on the right path again, you know?"

"That's great." I swallow. "So you're on your way home?"

"Yes. Well, sort of. Arielle texted last night to say Ella has a dance recital this afternoon. I got my ass up super early so I could swing through Aberdeen in time to see it."

"Swing through Aberdeen?" I rub my eyes. I haven't had my coffee yet, so I can't keep the pout out of my voice. "Connor, that's way out of the way."

"I know. But I haven't missed one yet. Not since . . ."

He trails off, and I want to punch myself. "Of course, you should absolutely go," I say quickly. "Have a great time and say hi to them for me. So I'll see you tonight, then?"

He pauses. "Well, I won't be getting back until super late, and then I have to be at work crazy early tomorrow. It's gonna be long days all week on two different job sites to make up for all the people who covered while I was in the Cities. I'm sorry, babe."

God, I am just so ready to talk to him, get it out in the open. "It's okay," I say at last, trying to hold back my disappointment. "We'll see each other soon, right?"

"Absolutely."

"Promise?"

"I promise."

As the week goes on, though, that promise proves difficult to keep. Connor works into the evening every day, going directly from the on-campus residence hall site to a new housing development going up northeast of Sioux Falls.

By Thursday night I'm anxious. We haven't made any concrete plans to see each other yet—we haven't even talked all week, dammit, only quick texts back and forth. I'm aching to talk to him about our relationship—rip it off like a Band-Aid.

Finally, fueled by two glasses of wine and a late-night viewing of *Bridget Jones* on Netflix, I decide to call him the only time I know he'll be home: after midnight.

He picks up on the third ring, breathless and disoriented. "Simone? What's wrong?"

A pang of guilt hits, but I squash it away. "Everything's fine—I just haven't talked to you all week."

He lets out a breath. "Shit, you scared me. I fell asleep on the couch. Just a sec." I hear shuffling; then the laugh track of a late-night show in the background clicks off into silence. "I know, this week has really sucked."

"It just seems like we could've at least seen each other by now. Like, even a quick coffee or something."

He sighs. "I promise I'm doing my best. Between picking up extra shifts and my classes, I've just had no time."

His voice is patient, yet pointedly so, like he's a saint for appeasing me—it stings, but I move on. "Do you have to work this weekend?"

Connor sighs. "Another long day tomorrow, but then Saturday won't be as long. So how about dinner Saturday night?"

"That sounds great." I hesitate, suddenly feeling shy, vulnerable. "I miss you."

"God, I miss you, too, babe." His voice is husky. "A lot. I'll see you soon, okay?"

I smile. "Okay."

I'm still smiling when I end the call, confident that, despite the twinge in my gut, everything will soon be back to the way it should be.

PART TEN

Betrayal

Monday, December 6, 10:17 a.m.

They say you spend more time with the people you work with than your own family—they might annoy the hell out of you, but when it comes down to it, you're in the trenches together every day, and there's a certain solidarity to it. A certain loyalty.

Not anymore.

Because the second voice belongs to Stan.

Stan is the other shooter.

Outside the closet the argument continues, but in here my mind races, the sting of blind betrayal hot and sharp. I trace back through the past several months. *How did I miss this?* Stan seemed sad sometimes, and things were likely rougher with Louise than he was letting on, but there's been *nothing* that would point to him going on a shooting rampage at our office.

Across from me Hayley sucks in a breath, and it pulls me back—I focus on their conversation outside the closet.

"Where's the body?" Chet barks. "Somebody moved it."

I meet Hayley's wide eyes again, and terror floods me.

"I . . . thought you did," Stan says timidly.

"You fucking idiot—the door was blocked when I got here."

"I don't—" Stan begins, but Chet suddenly shushes him.

The room drops back into an eerie silence, and my entire body goes cold with a terrible realization: Nikki's blood is all over the floor.

It's surely left a path, pointing them right to the closet.

They know where we are.

CHAPTER THIRTY-FIVE

July 24, five months before

I wake Saturday morning feeling more energized than I have in a long time, like I'm moving in the right direction and it's pointing directly to Connor. The combination of deciding to take action, knowing exactly when I'm going to talk to him, and realizing how much I miss him and he misses me makes me think maybe we'll be okay after all. Maybe this is a conversation we should've had right away. Maybe my fears could've been alleviated sooner.

I'm not meeting Connor until this evening, but by late morning my adrenaline is primed. I need to get out of my apartment. Nikki and Claudia are out of town again visiting Claudia's mother, so I drive downtown and set out on a solo run. It's early enough not to be too hot, but I won't push myself today anyway—just a nice leisurely jog to let out some energy. Phillips Avenue runs me straight into downtown Sioux Falls, and I lope breezily past shops and restaurants, dipping out of the way of window-shoppers and dog-walkers.

On my left, a bridal store's glass front window winks sunlight at me, sparkly white-dressed mannequins staring from the display, their plastic frozen smiles flashing the promise of possibility. My heart beats faster, adrenaline and optimism forming a dangerously confident concoction.

Maybe a happily ever after with Connor is possible.

I was wrong to worry about what his mom said, or that stupid slideshow. Like he said, that was in the past.

However uncertain my future is, maybe I'm meant to spend it with him.

At the next corner the orange Don't Walk sign is lit up, so I take the opportunity to stop and stretch—I've slacked on that today since taskmaster Nikki isn't here to crack the whip. When I turn to the left, stretching my neck, I blink. *Is that Connor's truck?*

I can't be 100 percent certain—I don't have his license plate number memorized, for crying out loud—but something sets the hair on the back of my neck prickling. He's working, I remind myself, but I turn to the right anyway. I'm in front of O'Malley's, where we had our first date. The sun is just right—no glare on the big front window—so I have the perfect view of the customers seated inside.

The perfect view of the middle of the room, where my boyfriend sits—not working at all, but leaning forward across the table toward a woman.

Even from out here, her long red hair shines, and it's like a hot flame of fire scorching my insides. I lean a hand against the window to steady myself, and the motion startles the patrons nearest the window. I step back, but it's too late. Connor looks over.

It's the widening of his eyes, really. Until then, I could've explained it away. But when I see the guilt on his face in full display before me, I can't pretend I didn't just catch my boyfriend on a date, with another woman.

I can't pretend anymore.

CHAPTER THIRTY-SIX

The door whooshes open, a bell jangles—a laughing couple walks out onto the sidewalk. The sound sets me in motion.

I run.

Back in the direction I came from, as fast as my legs will carry me, chased by the vision of them together—him leaning toward her, smiling that wide smile. The lies I told myself about the possibility of spending forever with him circle in my mind, taunting me for actually believing it could work out. All his excuses also swirl through my brain—*meeting with a distributor, Ella's dance recital, working late.*

Was any of it true, or was he with her the whole time?

I run until my lungs heave, until I'm slowed by my own sobs.

"Simone!" Connor's voice cries out behind me. "Stop!"

I don't—not until he catches me, running beside me, pleading. "Please, Simone. Stop. I need to talk to you."

I finally stop when he places his hand on my arm—and when the stitch in my side is unbearable. I turn and meet his eyes at last, my entire being radiating the pain of his betrayal, and he ducks his gaze. "It's not what it looks like."

"Oh God." I double over, hand to my mouth. Those words. *Those words.* That clichéd statement from every goddamned romantic comedy in the history of film.

"Please, Simone," he pleads. "She texted this morning—I had no idea she was going to be in town."

"I thought you had to work today." I don't look up, don't know how I get the words out.

"I did, but not as long as I thought, so I was going to just sleep this afternoon." He swallows. "But then Diana texted, and I mean, it's been years."

I look up at last. "Why didn't you tell me?"

He shrugs, runs a hand through his hair. "Because . . . shit, I don't know. Okay? I guess I remembered how you felt after the slideshow." I wince as he continues. "It's just . . . I haven't seen her since before Cam died, and she said she wanted to buy me a drink and catch up."

I bristle, my eyes flashing as they bore into his. "So you're drinking again."

"Christ, yes. I am, okay?" He rubs his face. "I've been so stressed— it's like I just can't handle one more thing right now, you know?"

Like he can't handle one more burden. I squeeze my eyes shut, and when I open them again, he's staring at me imploringly. "Is the drinking that big of a deal?"

I set my jaw. "I don't care about that. I care that you *lied* to me."

He flinches. "I'm sorry. I know I screwed up." Then he takes a step toward me, eyes eager. "But hey, maybe you can come meet her? She's not a bad person. You'd like her. She just got back from a year in AmeriCorps, and now she's starting a medical residency at a neurology department in Boston."

I suck in a breath. "Neurology?"

His nod is cautious, like a puppy that senses danger but is willing to please at all costs. "Yeah. Maybe . . . maybe you two could talk. Maybe she has some advice, you know?"

The searing pain of humiliation bubbles over into a pulsing stew of red-hot anger. "I don't need you to fix me." The words spit like fire from my lips, and I flick my head back toward the bar. "And I certainly don't need her to."

He holds up his hands in defense, eyes wide. "Whoa, what? That's not what I meant at all." He takes a step toward me, but I lean away, as if a barrier has shot up between us, formed by the blinding truth.

I was right about everything.

At best, I'm a diversion who makes him feel good about taking care of someone—it's what he does, as his mom said. At worst, I'm his way of proving himself to a fiancée he never got over.

My shoulders sag now as anger gives way to pain. "Look, Connor, I really wanted to talk to you about something."

He takes a step back at the change in my voice. "About what?"

"About the fact that maybe we rushed into all this." His eyes widen again, but I don't stop. "Maybe it's time to take a break."

His voice is barely a whisper. "Simone . . . I don't want that."

"I think our timing was just off. I never really had a chance to find my normal again after my diagnosis." I swallow the lump in my throat, praying my voice doesn't crack. "And maybe you never really had a chance to get back to normal after losing Cam."

"But *you* are my normal." His pained eyes bore into mine until I look away.

"Look, maybe you never had a chance to get over losing her, either." I gesture back toward the bar, where she sits, waiting for him. I can't say her name. She probably is a good person—a great one, even—but right now saying her name would break my heart more than it's already broken. "Maybe you need someone like her."

His frown deepens. "What does that mean?"

"It means you need someone who's not a burden."

He reels back like I've slapped him. "What? Simone, no—where is this coming from?"

I squeeze my eyes shut. "It's coming from the fact that I don't know what my future holds, so it'll be easier if this happens now. For both of us."

Connor stares at me in pain and confusion, tears in his eyes, too. "But I love you."

His words are desperate, defeated, and I can't bear it. "I have to go," I mumble before sprinting off toward my car. It's still five blocks away, but I push myself forward as fast as my knee will let me—it's throbbing now, as if it wants in on all this pain consuming the rest of me. I will my sobs to wait until I'm safely behind the wheel and driving away from downtown, away from him.

I don't look back.

PART ELEVEN

DARKNESS

Monday, December 6, 10:20 a.m.

There's no going back now. They know we're here, and they're coming for us.

There is nothing I can do to stop this.

Darkness washes over me like a blanket, warm and smothering, and suddenly I'm so indescribably tired. My body folds over Nikki like it's sinking. Like I'm sinking.

Outside the closet, Chet's and Stan's footsteps rush toward us, but my body refuses to fight. So I close my eyes, and I wait. "I'm sorry." I'm not even sure if I say the words out loud.

A hand squeezes my arm gently, and I open my eyes in surprise. Hayley says nothing, just gives a determined nod—I wish I could capture the moment our eyes meet, wish I could bottle it up, save it. But before I can even process what's happening, she has a hand on the doorknob, the other still clutching the scissors.

Oh God, no.

But she's out the door, pushing it shut behind her, screaming with a fury I've never heard before. For one heartbreaking moment, she is every woman who has ever stood up to an abusive man—and God dammit I wish I had given her a chance, looked past the exterior to see the woman inside, brave and true.

But it's too late now.

I hear her catch them off guard, hear the yelling and cursing when she stabs one of the bastards. But within moments a gun blasts, a deafening boom that sucks all the air, all the life, out of this room.

And I know that Hayley is gone.

CHAPTER THIRTY-SEVEN

August 20, four months before

The rest of the summer passes, cruel and unbearable, and then it is almost gone, leaving only the ghost of its presence, fleeting moments of sunshine that seep into shadow.

But I continue to run.

My training becomes my solace, my healing. There's something about the rush of air through my lungs, the strain of my muscles, my body testing its limits. It's the rhythm of it, the pattern. The swing of my arms, the scrape of my feet hitting the pavement. *Left-right-left-right.*

My mind clears and I hit the zone, that stride, about a half mile or so in—the runner's high I always assumed was a myth—and suddenly I'm not straining so hard; suddenly I could go for miles. I could fly if I wanted to.

It's what I do every evening when it's finally cool, guided by the waning sunshine as summer finally breaks into autumn. I shut off my phone, stop counting the calls and texts from Connor I've been ignoring.

And I run.

Because if I don't, the pain of missing him—the way his strong hand enveloped mine, the way his eyes focused so intently on me when I spoke, the way he'd scratch his stubbly chin when he was excited to tell a joke, the way his laugh, so deep and booming, filled up a room, filled up the empty places in my soul—might catch me.

But the combination of late nights and early mornings, the fatigue of it all, does catch up with me. I'm staring at my computer at work one late-summer day when Nikki is down the hall cleaning out the photo studio, a gentle breeze rustling the leaves outside, soft ballads crooning from my speakers, and my vision starts to blur.

Two sharp raps on my open doorway—I jolt up, blink, disoriented.

"Were you seriously just sleeping at your desk?" Raj's nose is crinkled, as if he can't decide whether to be amused or concerned.

I shake my head, smooth my hair. "God, I can't believe I did that. Sorry."

He chuckles and slides into the chair in front of my desk, flopping his shiny black hair away from his forehead. "Nikki said you've been in beast mode training for this race. Badass."

I snort. "Yeah. It's pretty badass to be caught napping in your office."

He shrugs. "Well, at least you weren't snoring or drooling or anything."

"True," I concede. "So, what can I do for you?"

He flashes a crooked smile, cocks his head, and I blink, wait. Then he shakes his head and pulls out a file. "Uh, I'm just here because we, the grammatically challenged, could use a little help with the copy on this next postcard."

"Well." I make a show of cracking my knuckles. "You've come to the right place."

He sets it down and points to a paragraph on the back. We both lean over to get a better view. "See, I'm pretty sure Chet didn't mean for it to say, 'Students can get *they're* degree in four years.'"

We giggle together at Chet's expense. "Sure, I'd be happy to take a look."

"Great." Raj clears his throat. "So, uh, Simone, can I ask you something?"

"Hmm?" I grab my red Sharpie, already hunting for other typos, but I look up when movement in the doorway catches my eye. "Connor."

He's standing there holding a bouquet of flowers and looking from me to Raj, and I can't read his expression. "Guess I'm interrupting something," he says quietly.

Raj leans back with an awkward smile. "Uh, hey, man." He turns to me. "I can come back later?"

"No, it's fine," I say quickly. "Just wait for a minute, okay?"

Raj freezes in place and I push myself up, head spinning, torn. Connor's here—he showed up at my office door with *flowers*, for Christ's sake; that has to count for something—and yet I'm so flustered I don't know how to feel. I step toward him, my voice low as I usher him out into the hallway. "What are you doing here?"

"I had to see you." He glances back toward my office. "But is that . . . are you . . . seeing someone else now?"

I cross my arms. "Raj is my coworker. We're just friends."

He nods. "And it's the same with me and Diana."

I wince when he says her name, and it all comes flooding back—the image of them together.

"Why won't you believe me?" Connor takes a step toward me, and I look down. "Please, Simone, can we just go somewhere and talk about this?"

I look up at last, and his eyes are so pleading—I am so desperate to trust this is real, that his love won't fade no matter what the future holds—that I fear I can't hold it back any longer. *Because I'm afraid. I am absolutely terrified you're a fixer who is going to leave me one day when you realize I am a burden and you should be with someone like Diana, not someone like me.*

Down the hall, a door clicks open. Tense voices float out, and Stan and Chet follow them, red faced and gesturing. "We don't know for sure, yet, right? We shouldn't do anything until we know what these meetings—" Stan stops when he sees us, then looks from Connor's frown to my sorrowful eyes. "Uh, Simone, is there a problem?"

Farther down the hall, Nikki pokes her head out of the photo studio, and her eyes widen, flicking between Connor and me. The floor squeaks behind us, and I whip around—Raj has moved to my office doorway and is peeking out, looking like he wants to melt into the floor.

I can't take it.

"There's no problem." I manage to hold my head high, though inside I'm dying. "Connor was just leaving."

The crushing look on his face steals my breath, and I can't watch him walk away. Instead I turn and flee down the hall in the opposite direction, past Stan and Chet, past Nikki and into the bathroom, where at last, behind the safety of the locked door, I let my tears fall.

CHAPTER THIRTY-EIGHT

September 19, three months before

As the heat eases and the chill of fall slips into the city, Connor's calls and texts stop as if carried away on the prairie wind, and I pretend it doesn't hurt anymore. Besides, I have to focus now: we're getting closer to race day, and the weight of its importance presses heavily on my shoulders.

So does my best friend's disapproval.

Nikki's frustration is a tangible thing today, barely contained. "Connor called Claudia again last night."

I grimace. Guess he hasn't given up entirely.

"And unlike you, we actually answer once in a while." She looks over at me without breaking stride. "I mean, I still don't understand how you could just cut him off like that."

We round a corner. The falls are in sight, and I push myself faster as if I'm trying to outrun Nikki, as if I'm trying to outrun my pain. My own callousness shocks me, too, makes the pain of missing him cut even deeper. But it's like a window was opened that day when I saw him with her, like I'd surfaced from a beautiful dream into harsh reality. And I couldn't let it go on any further. I could no longer pretend it could work out between us—that things could work out for me.

"It's easier this way."

"For you." There's an edge to her voice.

"For both of us." My voice has an edge now, too. "We rushed into a relationship during tough times in both of our lives without stopping to think about where we were going. About the future."

She pauses, and I know the question is there, the one she's been wanting to ask for weeks. "Even if that's true, don't you think you should've talked to him about it?"

"I planned to before I caught him with his *ex-fiancée*," I snap.

Nikki glances over, and her voice is gentler. "Simone, do you really think he was *cheating* on you? I mean, honestly?"

My chest burns and I can't answer. But even if it wasn't cheating, it could've been precheating—like I caught him with his hand on the lid of the cookie jar, knowing he would eventually take the plunge. "It doesn't matter. He lied to me."

"But you could still talk to him," she insists.

"Look, we were heading down separate paths anyway. He needs to focus on going back to school, and I need to focus on being as healthy as I can."

There's a pause but it's heavy, like she's gearing up for something. "Simone, I love you, and I know you're hurting more than you let on, but I have to say: that is complete bullshit."

I whip my head over, slowing at last. "Excuse me?" She matches my pace but doesn't look at me, so I press on. "For your information, *you* are the one who said I was burying my head in the sand about my illness, and now I'm trying to fix that."

"But that doesn't mean you can't also try to fix this with Connor."

My eyes flash. "Oh yeah? Well, how about you? Have you talked to Claudia about moving?"

Her eyes narrow. "Don't turn this shit back on me."

"Well, have you?"

"We've been busy with her mom."

I nod—I've found my opening and I'm taking it. "And now she's unsure if she wants to move farther away, right? Have you told her how *you* feel about it? How you're withering away in this conservative little city that pretends to be so progressive but you really feel like you can never be yourself?"

She slows to a walk now, and her face shrinks like I've slapped her. Shit, I've crossed the line. "Nik, I'm sorry." I stop, too, reach forward and hug her. I don't want her to move away, but I see how she and Claudia change depending on the situation, depending on the part of town, depending on the crowd, and I hate that it's the reality of living here. But it's their choice, not mine. "I'm an asshole."

"You *are* an asshole." She hugs me back and laughs a little. "But I don't want to leave you."

I squeeze her tighter. *And I don't want you to go.* I manage to hold the words in, though, because I've been selfish enough already. We pull apart and Nikki gestures toward the falls, and we walk over and sit down on the grass. The water is mesmerizing, the rush almost drowning out the racing thoughts in my head.

Finally, Nikki sighs. "I just want you to be happy, Simone."

"I want the same for you," I say. "But no matter what, I'm here for you."

She takes my hand, eyes still out on the water. "Me too."

I stand up and pull her to her feet. We run on together, silent but strong, lifting each other up through the darkness.

PART TWELVE

Chaos

Monday, December 6, 10:24 a.m.

I'm holding Nikki down in the darkness of this closet, but the truth is, she is anchoring me, her heartbeat the only tiny sliver of hope keeping me going through this nightmare.

The closet door is now open just a sliver since Hayley's departure, light peeking through, and Stan is having a breakdown on full blast. "You can't . . . you can't just do that. We never agreed to *kill* people!"

"Calm down," Chet spits. "Shit, she cut me good. You got a first aid kit in that closet?"

My body stiffens. Please God, no. I force myself up onto my knees, gathering any last shred of strength.

The door opens a crack farther, and I look fearfully up into Stan's face. His eyes widen in shock and shame, then a wild sort of resolve. He whips around. "Nope, we don't have anything like that."

The door shuts, but I hear a scuffle, and as it opens again, I do the only thing I can think of—lay motionless over Nikki.

"Jesus Christ." Chet's voice is a growl, like a predator ready for another kill, and I squeeze my eyes shut harder, chest hammering.

"No!" Stan cries.

There's a beat in slow motion; then both guns go off in thundering succession. My eyes fly open in shock; then I squeeze them shut again, bile rising in my throat. Because in that brief moment I saw Stan slumped on the floor—the left side of his face gone, a vision doomed to haunt me for the rest of my life, dark and gaping, a human inside out.

I hear footsteps now as Chet turns back toward us—and this is it, I think.

This is when it ends.

CHAPTER THIRTY-NINE

November 26, ten days before

Race day dawns bright, the blazing sun illuminating the last of the fading orange leaves on the trees, clinging to the branches as if fighting for their lives—as if they don't know they'll inevitably fall.

I'm up earlier than I need to be, dressing methodically in my black running pants and red shirt, lacing up my running shoes. I stare at the woman in the mirror. The quiver of anxiety in my belly is expected—almost a welcome companion after nearly three decades of introversion and social anxiety, present in all my life's milestones, from piano recitals to college graduation.

Today, the anxiety is a reminder of the importance of this accomplishment, of how far I've come. That no matter how uncertain my future is, no matter how much it hurt to lose Connor, if I can just cross that damn finish line, then maybe I'll be okay.

Nikki's reflection appears behind me in the mirror. We're matching this morning—black and red. Our smiles match, too, determined. "No matter what happens, I'm proud of you."

I nod. "Thanks."

Then we're silent as we make our way through the hazy, lightening morning toward the start of the race.

The parking lot at Veterans Memorial Park is filled to the brim, and as we walk across the crunchy brown grass to join the throngs of fit, agile bodies, nerves consume me. "What if there was a blizzard or something? It's late November, for Christ's sake—there could be tons of snow by now."

Nikki smiles. "But there's not. The path's all clear."

"Or there could've been ice," I add pointedly.

"But there's *not*." She smirks, her eyes darting to me. "It is going to be a beautiful, unseasonably warm day in Sioux Falls, South Dakota, Simone. We will be *fine*."

I roll my eyes. "Guess someone watched the weather this morning."

"Damn right I did." Nikki chuckles and links her arm through mine as we reach the crowd.

Amid the chatter around us, a voice calls out. "Mone!"

I turn, and my mom waves frantically from behind the taped-off viewing area. Behind her, Dad stands stoically—even a tired-looking Emmett rubs his eyes with one hand, the other gripping a cup of coffee. A surge of love for them—for all the chaos, for their semi-dysfunctional but fiercely supportive nature—propels me over, and I attempt to wrap all three in a hug.

"Good luck, honey." Mom rubs my arm, smiling. "We're so proud of you."

"I can't believe you guys made it."

Emmett shrugs. "They made me come." I smack his arm but laugh, and he grins.

"Now, if you pass out from exhaustion, I am CPR certified," my dad says. I blink at him, terrified for a split second he's seriously concerned

I can't do it, and doubt seeps in. But then his lip quivers, and he busts out laughing. "I'm kidding, Mone. Give 'em hell."

"I will, Dad," I say, turning to head back.

"Just don't go too fast!" Emmett calls. I turn, and he grins. "I've got money on you coming in last place."

"Jerk!" I yell over my shoulder, but I'm laughing when I get back to Nikki, who's frowning at her phone. I peer down and catch a glimpse of her text.

Guess we'll see what happens at the finish line.

She looks up at me and stuffs her phone in her pocket. I raise my eyebrows. "Claudia stationed at the finish line?" She nods, but her face is red, and she won't meet my eyes. "Don't tell me *you* are actually nervous about this."

She looks up then and winks. "Yeah, nervous I've trained you so well I won't be able to keep up with you."

"Yeah right," I scoff. "We both know that is *not* gonna happen."

Nikki drops her smile and fixes me with a determined gaze. "We got this, Mone." Then she smirks. "Just think about those beers Claudia has waiting for us at the finish line."

I laugh, but she cocks an eyebrow. "I'm serious. They have Oktoberfest on tap, and I intend to chug one of those bad boys immediately after the race."

"Well, then. We'd better run fast."

"Damn right."

We're relaxed then as we stretch among the throngs of runners, the scent of sweat in the air. Still, my stomach flutters when the runners are called to the ready. I'm sure I've made a terrible mistake, but in one surreal moment, the race begins and we are moving forward, lost in the sea of black spandex and bright cotton, leggings and tank tops, headbands and armbands and Fitbits and earbuds.

One foot in front of the other, my legs hit the pavement, and maybe I can really do this. But soon, too soon—have we even gone the first tenth of a mile?—my muscles start to tire. My lungs gulp for air. Dammit, what about all my training? Have I improved at all?

I can't do this—I can't.

A nudge at my right elbow. I glance over at Nikki, who nods. "Give it another quarter of a mile."

I nod back. Yes. Relax. Give it time. My pulse slows, and I look around at the way the morning sunshine filters through the trees, their branches waving in the breeze as if encouraging us. *You can do this,* they seem to say.

And soon my legs have found their rhythm. My muscles quiet; my lungs ease. My thoughts clear.

I can do this.

We slow enough at the first checkpoint to let tiny cups of water quench our dry throats and to let the encouraging words of the volunteers propel us forward.

At two miles, my knee twinges, but I'm feeling good. Nikki recounts stories about the old days in college—holding each other's hair back when we partied too much, drinking coffee until dawn when we did actually study—and I laugh through my puffs of breath.

At two and a half miles, it hits me that I am going to finish. We're nowhere near the front, but we're also not last. The pain in my knee is stronger but bearable.

I am going to finish this race.

The thought leaves me giddy enough that when Nikki leans over, raises her eyebrows, and asks, "Should we kick it in when we see the three-mile marker? Finish strong?" my nod is enthusiastic.

Euphoria takes over. I push myself forward, faster, harder. I am going to finish this. I am strong. I can handle this disease.

I am in control.

But as if that thought has summoned the cruel gods of neurological diseases, my knee lets out a vicious throb. My leg buckles and I stumble—I catch myself, but the pain slows me to a limp-jog.

"What's wrong?" Nikki slows, too. "Shit, I shouldn't have pushed you. I'm sorry."

"No, it's just—my stupid knee." I wince. "Oh God, I can't run anymore."

"Is it like before?" She's alarmed now. "Are you able to walk?"

I shake my head. "No—it's not numb and seizing up. It hurts, but I can walk. But I can't run."

Relief washes over Nikki's face. "Thank God."

I glare at her. "I can't *run*, Nik."

"We can walk the rest of the way—we're almost there."

"But I want to run this race." Her calm voice makes me even more shrill, panicked, as runners fly past us. I stubbornly try to speed up, wincing with each step. "I promised myself."

Nikki matches my pace. "Simone, you promised yourself you'd *finish* this race, and you will—whether it's walking or crawling or even if I have to carry you across that goddamned finish line. It's still finishing."

My shoulders slump. "But . . . I was going to beat this."

Nikki pulls me to a stop. More runners pass us, but she doesn't seem to notice. "Simone, this is one day. *One day.* All you can do is the best you can. All you can do is keep fighting every day. And I'll be right there with you. Okay?"

A shiver ripples through me, releasing my fear, my expectation. Making room for resolve. Determination. "Okay."

"Let's finish this race, eh?"

I nod, and hand in hand, we walk forward together. The finish line is in sight now. No more runners pass us—only those walking haven't finished yet. But even if we were the last ones in the race, it wouldn't matter.

I'm going to drag myself across that white line and finish. I'm going to conquer this challenge, and then tomorrow I'm going to get up and face the next one. And the next, and the next—I will keep going every day, no matter what.

I will not give up.

We're close to the end now, and I hear a clap. Then another. Then the whole crowd is clapping.

A voice shouts: "Come on, sis, you got this!"

I smile—I can't see Emmett, but he's there in the crowd, cheering me on, and I pick up the pace slightly. A high-pitched whistle—that has to be Claudia; no one can whistle like her. Everyone is cheering now, and their encouragement is enough that I can limp-jog across the finish line, hand in hand with my best friend.

Nikki wraps me in a fierce hug. "You did it."

"I couldn't have done it without you."

We pull apart when Mom, Dad, Emmett, and Claudia descend on us. Claudia hug-tackles Nikki while Emmett places his hands on both of my arms, looking down at me solemnly. "Sis, I just have to say . . . I totally called the last-place thing."

I slug him, and he wraps me in a hug. "Proud of you."

Mom steps forward to hug me, but there's worry in her eyes. "You did great, honey."

"Thanks. My knee was giving me a little trouble, but no worries—it wasn't even bothering me at the end, thanks to our wonderful cheering section."

"Yeah, we have a few cheerleaders here today." There's something about Nikki's voice, the way her brow furrows and her eyes dart over Claudia's shoulder. Then Claudia gives an almost imperceptible shake of her head.

I gasp, pop up on my tiptoes, scan the crowd, but there are no familiar faces—only happy strangers, exhausted and exhilarated. Then, on the edge of the parking lot, I see him. I want to call to him, but he's already so far away, so I hesitate, turning to Claudia and Nikki, unsure, desperate. "Was that text about Connor?"

Nikki sighs. "I'm sorry, Mone. We didn't know he was going to be here."

"But why is he leaving?"

Claudia clears her throat. "He said he didn't want to take away from your big day."

My shoulders sag, and Nikki reaches for my hand with a sad smile. "Come on, let's go get those beers."

Pain settles in, but I follow them, my knee and my broken heart now an excruciating match. With each step away from Connor, I remind myself I was the one who let him go—I was the one who *told* him to go, who ignored his calls and texts, who shut him out, over and over again.

I remind myself it is too late.

CHAPTER FORTY

Beer is great for quickly replenishing the lactic acid in your muscles after a race—Nikki says something to that effect, at least, but all I care about right now is that it's cooling my throat and dulling the pain. So after my family heads back to Aberdeen to pick up Grandma from the neighbors' house, I buy another round for Nikki, Claudia, and me.

I'm swigging a refreshingly hoppy IPA when someone steps in front of me. "I thought that was you." The woman beams, winded from the run. "Simone, right?"

I nod, wipe the foam from my mouth as I squint at her familiar face. Tall, with long dark hair—ah, she was at the support group meeting. "Danielle?"

She nods. "Didn't know you were a runner, too."

Her smile is careful as she feels me out. The buzz from the run and the beer is coursing through my veins, so my laugh is easy. "It's a newly acquired skill. Trying to stay as healthy as possible."

"I understand. I was the same way." Then she bites her lip. "Listen, I wanted to say I'm sorry about the way that support group meeting went."

My smile falters, my buzz killed. "No problem." But my voice cracks, and I swig my beer in a feeble attempt to cover it up.

She swallows. "Well, I hope it hasn't stopped you from coming back. I mean, some people don't need a support group—I understand. I hesitated at first, but it's been nice when I have questions. When I'm trying to decide what choice to make about something."

"Do they jump on you if your choice isn't what they agree with?" My biting words come too fast for me to stop them. I wince, and my hand tightens around the cup.

But when I look up, Danielle is smiling. "Sometimes. But almost five years in, I've learned to take anyone else's opinion with a grain of salt. I'm the one living this life, you know?"

I blink, the tension easing from my shoulders. "Yeah."

She sighs, her jaw set as if she's decided something. "Look, Simone, I remember what it was like, newly diagnosed. Nothing makes sense. There's all this advice and yet nobody is experiencing this illness in the same way you are." My eyes are wide, my nod enthusiastic, and it seems to help her gain momentum. "You just have to learn to make the best, most informed decision you can. Trust your doctor, but trust yourself, too."

Our eyes are locked, and relief courses through me, but questions do, too—so many questions swirling through my mind. I take a deep breath. "Can I ask you something?" She nods, so I press on. "Do you . . . have a good relationship with your neurologist? Do they answer your questions?"

"Absolutely. I've been seeing her for several years now, and she and her nurses are very helpful. Why do you ask?"

I let my anxieties and frustrations pour out. "Because when I called my neuro's office, the nurse made me feel like a bother for calling. So I'm wondering if I should look into switching . . . do people do that?"

"Sure. It's your life. You have every right to see a neuro you're comfortable with."

Relief floods through me. "Thank you."

"Of course. Do you need any help finding a new one?"

I picture my fridge at home, where a Mount Rushmore magnet holds up the note Walter gave me all those months ago. Dr. Bukhari is in Minneapolis, but so is Dr. Montgomery and his unhelpful nurse—and at this point I would drive to the ends of the earth if it meant I could see someone I could relate to. I shake my head. "No, thanks. I have a recommendation from a friend."

It's my life. My future. And I can at least control this one part of it.

"Mama!" The small voice cuts through our moment, and Danielle reaches down to scoop up the little boy who has thrust himself against her leg.

"Frankie, this is my friend Simone." A man walks over, tall, bronze skinned with dark hair, and leans in to kiss Danielle. She turns to me. "Simone, this is my husband, Shane. I might be biased, but I think I had the best cheering section today."

He smiles wryly. "The older kids are a little cheered out, so they headed to the van with their iPads." He smiles at me. "Nice to meet you."

I nod, the vision of Connor retreating far away in the parking lot seared into my mind.

"Is it time to go home?" Frankie asks.

There's an unmistakable whine to his voice, and Danielle kisses his forehead, then turns to me. "We probably should get going. But it was great seeing you."

I nod again, another question swelling within me that I can't seem to get out. I watch as Shane, already carrying one backpack, deftly scoops Frankie out of Danielle's arms and takes the backpack off her shoulder. "You doing okay?" he asks quietly, and she nods.

My breath stops as they turn away—the words finally burst forth. "Danielle, wait." She turns back in surprise. "Could I . . . could I ask you something else?"

Her eyes flit to Shane, and he says, "I'll see you at the van."

When she turns back to me, my insides flip-flop, suddenly nervous. "So, um, how long have you two been married?"

She smiles. "Going on ten years."

I can't seem to find the words. The beer and the run combined have made me uninhibited, and suddenly I'm afraid I'll cry if I even say his name.

"Are you seeing anyone?" she asks quietly.

"I . . . I was."

Her eyes soften. "I'm sorry."

"I was the one who ended it. Because I didn't know how he truly felt." I meet her eyes, try to keep the intensity and desperation out of mine. "How can you be sure that . . . they won't think of you as a burden?" My voice trails off at the end; my eyes glance in the direction her husband walked. "I'm sorry, I don't mean—"

"It's okay, Simone," she says, cutting me off. "We all have those feelings sometimes."

"How do you get past them?"

Danielle doesn't hesitate. "If you love someone, they're never a burden. You take care of them no matter what. That's what loving someone means." She glances over her shoulder toward her family. "We take care of each other. It might be in different ways, but it's all important."

I nod slowly and she smiles. "I should get going." She cocks her head, then reaches into her pocket for her phone. My own phone buzzes. "There. I just friended you on Facebook. If you want to accept my friend request, you can contact me anytime with questions, okay?"

I nod, grateful, and as she walks away I stare after her, relieved, but questions still burn—and underneath it all, pushing its way up, a deep exhaustion settles in from the physical challenge I've conquered and the emotional hurdles still before me.

When Nikki walks up and puts her arm around me, I sag into her. I'm so tired; fatigue is sapping my strength now, but so are the visions swirling in my head of Connor walking away from me. And the doubts—so many doubts—but also accusations. *It's my fault. It's too late. It's better this way.*

Is it?

Nikki squeezes my shoulder a little tighter. "You did great today."

I take a breath and it catches. "Should I . . . I mean, do you think . . ."

She reads the storm in my weary eyes. "Right now you need to rest and celebrate," she says softly. "One challenge at a time, okay?"

My eyes are fixed on the horizon, the way Danielle left. The way Connor left. But finally, I swallow back the fears, the doubts. "Okay."

My MRI is next Monday—when I called Dr. Reynolds, my primary doctor, to schedule it, she set it up for right around the one-year mark of my diagnosis. I know now that I want to switch neurologists, so I'll definitely ask for the MRI results to be sent to Dr. Bukhari.

One challenge at a time. Right now I'll just focus on getting through MRI day. A lot can change in one day, in one moment.

Everything can change.

PART THIRTEEN

COURAGE

Monday, December 6, 10:27 a.m.

All I can focus on right now is remaining still—our only chance of surviving is if Chet thinks we're already dead. Behind me I hear him fiddle with the weapon, cuss in frustration. Then, the sound of the rifle opening—he's reloading.

Terror pulses in my gut. I have seconds.

I can't give up, not when Nikki still needs me. I have to try, but everyone who has rushed Chet has failed; why would it be any different for me?

A wave of dizziness hits—then a bolt of lightning, a random scrap of memory. *Weakness doesn't give you a pass.*

We're lying here—injured, *weak* women—and it just might be enough for me to catch him off guard.

It just might be enough to save us.

My heartbeat rams against my chest, legs tingle—but now it's like a message. *We did not make it through all of this to go down without a fight.*

And that's what I'm going to do. I'm going to *fight*.

I hear him now, peering over us, and a brief flash of fear and doubt floods through me. But then I feel Chet's foot jab into my side, like he's a hunter checking his kill. The pain makes me wince—and sets me in motion.

I lurch up and shove Chet back, raising my knee up swiftly into his groin. He cries out and doubles over, and I latch my hands on to his wrist, thrusting the gun away from us as it goes off. I scream and scream and keep screaming, muscles aching with the effort of holding him back.

Suddenly my office door bursts open—and as I turn I realize this is it; I can't fight off anyone else. It's either the end or a new beginning, and I can't control it either way.

I cannot control a single thing.

But I see Officer Jackson in the doorway, gun raised and pointed at Chet. He yells and whips his arm away from me, but it doesn't matter now. She fires three times, and he goes down; then it's silent, so deafeningly silent, and I fall.

My guardian angel hovers over me when I open my eyes in the ambulance, struggling to push through the thick, velvety veil of fatigue. I whimper, but Officer Jackson shushes me, pushes back my hair. "Shh, you did good, Archer. Time to rest now."

"Nikki," I say.

She smiles. "She's in the other ambulance. She's still fighting, don't you worry. Try to relax—you've been through a lot, and you fell pretty hard when you passed out in there."

I close my eyes, a tear escaping, and immense relief blends with grief over the loss, the betrayal, the sheer exhaustion. I'm in and out, restless, visions of blood and guns and races and *the randomness of it all.*

The scream of the ambulance jolts me awake, and even though fatigue clings to me, threatening to pull me back into the darkness, my focus is suddenly razor sharp.

I almost died today. I almost *died* from something I never could have foreseen.

One moment can change everything. A shooter. A devastating diagnosis. A handsome stranger. The terrifying truth about life is that you never know which one you're going to get.

What a terrifying, beautiful truth.

We are all living on the edge of a cliff without even knowing it, and one fragile movement can push us over the edge or pull us to safety.

I won't ever be free of this disease, of what it might do to my body, my mind. I won't be free of fear, or worry about the future. I can't control what cards fate deals me, but I can choose how I play them.

Today, I chose to keep living.

Somehow from deep within, the words Danielle said to me after the race that day come back to me: *If you love someone, they're never a burden. You take care of them no matter what.*

Maybe Connor and I can take care of each other.

Maybe it's not too late for us.

At the hospital, I'm rushed into a room, and fatigue rears forward as a flurry of nurses descend on me with blood-pressure cuffs, monitors, and questions, so many questions.

"The woman brought in with me," I finally manage to say, grimacing as a nurse with gray hair and kind eyes inserts the IV needle into my arm. "How is she?"

Her smile is sympathetic. "We can't release information on other patients, dear."

I huff, then try my next pressing concern. "Well, can I at least have my phone?"

"We've already contacted your family. They're on their way."

My family. For a moment everything is overshadowed as I picture my terrified parents flying down the interstate at a hundred miles per hour. "Oh God."

"Shh, dear, just rest, okay? We're going to take good care of you."

And I finally listen, at last succumbing to the fatigue.

When I wake, my parents and Emmett are standing around my hospital bed. "Mom." My voice is thick with sleep and emotion, and she leans forward, red faced and puffy eyed, showering me with kisses. She doesn't let me go, and I half expect her to crawl in with me.

Dad places a hand on my arm, clenching his jaw in that way he does when he's trying to hold in any show of emotion, but his eyes well up. Even Emmett takes my hand. He looks gaunt. "Love ya, sis," he whispers.

"I love you guys." My eyes blur. I'm overwhelmed, and for a moment I just let them hold me, surround me in the protective, loving cocoon of family. Then I pull myself up so I'm sitting. "Nikki?"

"She's okay, sweetie," Mom murmurs. "Claudia texted to say she's out of surgery and stable. She's recovering in the ICU."

Oh thank God. My shoulders sag in relief, but still my eyes plead, and finally Emmett nods. "I'll take you up there."

I get up, grateful, and take his arm. "We'll let your nurses know," Mom says. "I want to talk to your doctor anyway."

I nod, relieved, as we walk out into the hallway, then dart another glance at my brother. "Did you . . . did you hear anything about the shooting?"

He winces, doesn't look over. "Yeah."

I take a deep breath. "How many . . . ?"

Emmett pauses, glances over as if deliberating, then stares ahead again. "Five confirmed," he mumbles. "So far."

I squeeze my eyes shut, my stomach heaving. Chet. Stan. Charlene. The poor man upstairs. And Hayley. *Oh, Hayley.*

"You okay?" Emmett asks, tightening his hold on my arm, and I nod, force a sad smile as we continue our slow procession through the hospital.

When we reach Nikki's room, I take a deep breath, brace myself, but my knees still buckle when I see her lying there, all tubes and beeping monitor, so frail. Claudia turns when we walk in, and her face crumples. She rushes over and we're hugging tight, crying. We stand like that for a long time before she pulls back, wiping her eyes.

"How is she?" I ask quietly.

"She's going to be okay. Surgery went well. The doctor says she needs to rest now."

From behind us, a small voice calls out: "I need a fucking drink is what I need."

We chuckle, and I walk over to her bedside, take her hand. "Hey, Nik."

Her eyes are slits, but she smiles. "Hey."

Emmett clears his throat from the doorway. "Uh, I'm gonna go down and get something out of the vending machine in the waiting room."

Claudia takes a shuddering breath. "And I think I'll go grab a coffee. You two okay?"

I nod, and after the door whooshes shut behind them, I turn to my best friend. We stare at each other, eyes brimming, until she speaks. "Hayley?"

I shake my head. "She saved us."

Nikki's face crumples. I grab a tissue from the box sitting by her bed, then dab at her eyes carefully. We sit in silence for a long time, mourning this life cut unbelievably short, this incredible gift we've been given. Finally Nikki slides her hand into mine and squeezes. "Thanks for coming back for me."

"You would've done the same. You've stayed with me through this entire past year." I take a deep breath. "And I actually think it's about time you left. You and Claudia."

Her brow furrows. "What?"

I will myself to have the strength to say this. "You need to go to Minneapolis." My voice breaks. "Life is short. No day but today."

Her lip quivers. Then she opens her eyes wider, as if she's trying hard to peer into mine, make sure she sees me clearly. "Will you be okay?"

I sit up straighter. For the first time in a long time, I am sure of the answer. "Yes."

The door opens behind us, and when I turn, it's not Emmett who returns with Claudia, but Mom. They're talking in hushed, tense voices, but when they look up, they both smile. "Rest time," Claudia says.

I lean in and hug Nikki gently and awkwardly around her IV and tubes. "See you tomorrow."

As Mom and I walk back, I am still full of grief about the horror of the day, but I am also hopeful, grateful.

We survived. We're still here.

Life is short. I don't want to let another moment pass without taking my shot at the life I deserve. When I get back to my room, I'm calling Connor.

But when we walk through the door of my room, the tension is thick; something is off. Dad's standing in the corner, head down; Emmett's sitting, staring at the floor intensely, his hands balled into fists.

"What's going on?" I glance at Mom, who's giving my dad a look. She catches me looking and smiles sadly, almost guiltily. "Mom?"

Her eyes dart from me to Emmett, who finally throws his hands in the air. "Shit, just tell her, okay? She deserves to know."

"Emmett." Mom frowns at him. "Language."

An alarm in my head, soft but rising. "Know what?"

When I look at Mom, she breaks. "Oh, Simone. Connor was here."

I gasp. "He was?" I turn back to look through the door and out into the hallway, but there are only doctors, nurses, the normal hustle and bustle of an emergency room. "Why didn't you come get me?"

"Well, because, he, uh . . . he left."

"What? Why?"

"Because I told him to get the hell out of here," Emmett blurts out.

I whip my face toward my brother, the sting of betrayal equal to my confusion. "Emmett, why would you do that?"

Silence again as they all look at each other, and a cold ache seeps through my body, as if it's bracing for the blow.

Mom looks down as she whispers, "Honey, he wasn't alone."

I blink, unable to process these words, put my hand to my face. Dad is quick, rushing to me and steering me toward the bed. Sitting now, I stare at my hands as if they hold the secrets of how to deal with this news. "Who was with him?"

"Emmett saw her," Mom says softly. "A redhead, right, Em?"

I sit, frozen, as my heart shatters.

I look up, and Mom's watching my face, my pain reflected back at me in her eyes. And somehow, even though I know it might never go away, not fully, a word pushes forward.

Enough.

There has been enough pain today, enough sadness. I can't endure any more, and neither can my family.

I draw a shaky breath. "Thank you for telling me."

Three sets of wide, suspicious eyes stare at me. "Are you okay, honey?" Mom asks.

She sits down next to me, and I lean on her shoulder. "No." I sigh. "But I will be."

I'm still here. I survived. I have a lot of life left to live—a lot more goals to accomplish, and I'm no longer afraid my illness will stop me.

I may never get over him, but I plan to keep going, no matter what.

PART FOURTEEN

SERENDIPITY

CHAPTER
FORTY-ONE

Christmas Eve, 2:32 p.m. After

My car jerks to a stop in front of my parents' house, and I curse at the radio, turning it off with a feline flick of my wrist. I swear to God if I hear "Blue Christmas" one more goddamned time I'm going to scream.

I meet my own weary eyes in the mirror, take a deep breath. "I'm fine," I say, but the woman staring back at me calls my bluff.

Of course I'm not fine. When I got out of the hospital, the next few days were a whirlwind of police station visits, questioning, reliving. With both shooters dead, it's not like I'll need to testify at a trial of any sort. But the ordeal is far from over.

For now, thankfully, I'm allowed to be free of it. That meant heading north to my parents' house for the holidays. It might become permanent—maybe not actually living with my parents, but living in Aberdeen.

I can't go back to that office. Nikki and I were granted an immediate leave of absence, but I intend to make it permanent as soon as Aunt Kit verifies that her job offer at the library still stands. It'll be hard enough to go back to campus after the holidays for the memorial service. The fear, the pain, the memories—I place my forearms on the steering wheel and double over against it. But I have to go back. I owe it to Hayley. To Raj, who will be speaking at the service. I owe it to myself.

But after that, with Nikki and Claudia planning to depart to Minneapolis, I'll put my apartment on the market and move back here. There's nothing left for me in Sioux Falls.

I lost him.

Another wave of pain, the biggest of all, and I slump even farther against the cold steering wheel.

I squeeze my eyes shut, wait for the pain to pass, focus on the good news of this month: Dr. Reynolds—God bless her—came through with my MRI results.

No new lesions since my diagnosis. No disease progression.

I smile now as I sit up and glare fiercely at the woman in the rearview mirror. Maybe I'm not *fine*. But I'm *here*. I *survived*. And every day gets a little easier than the last. I don't know what my future holds—someday, my MRI results might not be so positive. Someday, treatment might be an inevitability. Someday, I might need to once again adjust to a new normal as I navigate the ups and downs of this disease.

But even if it slows me down, it'll never stop me.

A gentle *rap rap rap* against my window, and I jolt upright. My parents' faces smile in at me, waiting to welcome me inside.

Two hours later, my parents' living room couch is enveloping me in its comforting embrace. I inhale the scents of ham, mashed potatoes, and pie wafting from the kitchen. Then I scowl—happy holiday tunes also begin blaring toward me as Mom turns the music up, their lie of joyful promise grating against my ears.

I crank up the TV to drown it out as I sip from the dwindling wineglass in my hand. I wrap my afghan more securely around myself and try to focus on the only Christmas movie I can bear to watch right now—*Die Hard.*

My phone beeps. Nikki:

Merry Christmas! See you in three days.

I smile. Mom and I are planning to meet them at the truck stop in Summit and then travel on together to Minneapolis—Nik and Claudia are going apartment hunting; Mom will go with me to my neuro appointment, my first time seeing Dr. Bukhari. For a moment I'm overcome with love for them, with gratitude that they are all in this fight with me.

I sniff, wipe my eyes, then type my reply.

Merry Christmas to you, too! Can't wait to see you two.

I settle back against the couch, and Bruce Willis has just reached Nakatomi Plaza when Mom walks in and sits next to me. "Don't worry, it's network TV—they'll bleep out the f-word," I say with a teasing grin as I turn, but I blink—it's not Mom. It's Grandma.

She smiles, her eyes crinkling at the edges. "I'm so glad you made it, dear."

A twinge—again, it's almost as if I can pretend she still knows me. "Yeah, the snow's supposed to hit pretty soon, but the roads were good for me today."

"Is your sweetie going to be here?"

I don't know who she thinks I am—a long-lost friend or relative, perhaps—but the reminder of Connor cuts like a knife. "Not this Christmas, Grandma," I say softly.

I turn back to the TV, trying to focus on Alan Rickman's skillful portrayal of the villain, but a few seconds later I glance over and find that Grandma is still smiling at me. She leans in, takes my hand, and gives it a gentle squeeze. "Don't you worry, he'll make it. It's Christmas."

The wine, the fragility from trauma, and the fact that it *is* Christmas, dammit, have all combined to raise some small sliver of hope within me. I squeeze her hand back. "Thanks, Grandma," I whisper.

A coat flies onto my lap, and I whip my head toward the door that leads into the hallway. Emmett stands there, keys in hand. "Mom needs more eggnog. Let's go."

I wrinkle my nose. "I just got here."

"Come on—you're not doing anything."

"But I'm comfortable," I whine.

Emmett smirks at my twisted-up hair and the baggy sweatshirt visible under the blanket. "I think you could stand to get out of the house."

I grumble, throw off the blanket dramatically, then switch the channel so Grandma can enjoy some old *Bonanza* episodes in my absence.

I shrug into my coat, leaving it unzipped, but as we step out, I quickly correct that mistake. The wind has picked up, and snow has begun to fall. "Sheesh, that escalated quickly." I yank on my hat and gloves.

"Yeah, they say it's going to be even worse than last Christmas." Emmett winces and shoots me an apologetic look. I shrug, and we walk to my parents' sedan.

We ride in silence at first; then Emmett glances over. "So, uh . . . I'm seeing Kaley again."

I whip my head over. "Emmett, that's great!" I beam at him, so happy he's sharing something with me, and he smiles before turning back to the road. "So is she coming over? Or are you going over there?"

"Nah, we're both spending time with our families. We want to take things slow, make sure this is the right thing to do."

I stare at him—at my little brother, who is not so little anymore—and am so proud of him in this moment. "Well, that sounds like a very mature, levelheaded thing to do."

Emmett rolls his eyes. "Yeah, don't go telling too many people."

I laugh, and we continue on through the increasing snowfall.

As expected, frantic shoppers roam throughout the store, plugging up every aisle, holiday music blares through tinny speakers, and the echoes of the Salvation Army bell follow us deep into the building like an eerie warning alarm.

"Good God, let's get this shit and get the hell out of here," Emmett mutters.

We stick close together and head straight for the back coolers, but we're halfway there when my phone buzzes. "Oh no." I look up at my brother in horror.

His eyes widen. "What?"

"She needs aluminum foil, too."

"Shit." He runs his hands through his hair. "That's all the way on the other side of the store."

"I've got it. You get the eggnog, and we'll meet at the checkout."

"Okay." Emmett places his hands on my arms solemnly. "Godspeed, sis."

I roll my eyes and turn to make my way through the throngs of shoppers until I find the aisle I need. The bright-blue boxes beckon me from the bottom shelf, but a woman in a gray parka has her cart blocking my goal.

I clear my throat awkwardly. "Um, excuse me, ma'am?"

She doesn't turn, doesn't move at all—maybe she can't hear me because her hood is up? I clear my throat, speak louder. "Could I please get past you?"

"Oh!" She jumps, and I feel bad for startling her. "Shit—yes, of course you can, sorry about that."

The voice is familiar, but when she turns around, it takes me a moment because her hood is pulled tight so only her face shows. I blink, take her in—young woman, Latina, very pretty. When she smiles a dimpled smile, I gasp in surprise. "Arielle!"

"Hey, Simone. Kinda wild in here, right? Way too many people." She shrugs, and I finally notice her face is haggard, eyes puffy.

"How are you?" I ask softly.

She scoffs, but then her face crumples. Without thinking, I reach forward and hug her. After a few seconds, though, she pulls back, wiping at her eyes with an embarrassed laugh. "Goddamn holidays."

"Where's Ella?" I ask.

"With my in-laws. Con—" She stops herself, looks down. "She'll be home later."

We're silent now; then she reaches out her hand. "Hey, what am I thinking—I wanted to say I'm so glad you're okay. What a nightmare."

"Thank you."

"I thought about texting or something, but I didn't know, you know, after what happened . . ."

I cock my head to the side, questioning. Ah, between me and Connor. Well, screw that—I take a deep, impulsive breath. "So, I'm going to be in town for a while . . . possibly indefinitely." I swallow. "Would you want to get coffee sometime?"

She blinks in surprise. Then she breaks into her dimpled smile again. "Oh God, I would love to. Drinks would be even better."

I laugh. "Sounds great to me."

She opens her mouth to respond, but then her eyes shift to my left. There's a presence next to me.

"What are you doing here?"

I look up in surprise at my brother's harsh tone, and he's glaring at Arielle. "Emmett, what the hell?" I scold. Arielle looks almost frightened, and I'm mortified—and confused.

He twists his face up in disbelief. "Simone, you actually *know* Connor's new girlfriend?"

My eyes widen. "His *what*?" I say the same time Arielle says, "Uh, *excuse* me?"

Emmett's glare falters for a second, his eyes darting between us in confusion. I turn to Arielle and slowly reach for her hood. Her puzzled eyes are on me now, but she lets me loosen it and push it back.

She lets her long curls spill out—the long curls that are now a bright, fiery red.

A breath puffs out of me. "You dyed your hair."

She brushes it back, fidgets in embarrassment and annoyance. "Yeah, finally made a change. Had to bleach it first and everything. I hate it," she scoffs.

I turn wide eyes to Emmett. He's staring at me with equally wide eyes. "Oh shit."

"Emmett, this is Connor's sister-in-law, Arielle."

He squeezes his eyes shut. "I am so sorry."

I turn back to Arielle, and to my surprise she bursts out laughing. "Okay, well, everything makes a little more sense now. Dude, when we saw you at the hospital, I just thought you were, like, super intense."

"He didn't tell me who you were!" Emmett's voice is shrill, his defenses up.

"Uh, well, you sort of shoved him against the wall before he could say anything."

Emmett grimaces. "Sorry about that."

Arielle shrugs, smiling sadly. "He wasn't even mad. He knew you were trying to protect your sister." Her eyes flick to me. "He said all that mattered is that you were okay. But I know he really wanted to see you."

Oh God. I clutch my arms around myself, leaning against the shelf full of aluminum foil for support. "Does . . . does he still want to see me?"

Arielle smiles. "Of course."

"You're sure?" I wince, squeeze my eyes shut. "I'm not like Diana."

Arielle laughs. "So?"

"So, you said she's perfect."

"But not perfect for *him*," she says. "Simone, when Connor's with you, he's . . . well, he's *Connor*. Diana always made him feel like he wasn't good enough—that *he* wasn't enough. I've never seen him more himself than when he was with you."

Hope swells within me, but then I freeze. "So . . . there's no one else, even now?" I draw in a shaky breath, my entire being hinging on Arielle's response.

Her smile is wistful. "Oh, honey, there's no one else for him. That was clear to me from the day I met you. He's like his brother that way."

I'm overcome, oblivious now to the frenzy of shoppers pushing their carts past us, the loud holiday music blaring throughout the store. Arielle arches an eyebrow. "Well, I happen to know where Connor will be tonight. We have a few hours yet—he always has Ella call me on the way. I can text you when he's close?"

I nod my head vigorously, and it's swimming as we say goodbye. I follow Emmett to the front of the store, through the self-checkout, and outside to the car in a haze of disbelief and joy.

Connor still loves me.

Emmett eases the car out of its parking space, and as we set off in the thickening snowfall toward home, he clears his throat. "Mone, I am so sorry about this. I was just . . ."

I reach over and touch his arm. "You were just being my brother. And it's okay." I beam at him. "Everything is going to be okay."

At home I'm a ball of energy, whisking about in a frenzy, preparing to be reunited with Connor. I have an hour and a half now, and I can't let his first vision of me in months be in baggy sweatpants and greasy hair.

I leap into the shower, slather on lipstick, even curl my hair. I slip into the sparkly red dress my mom got me for Christmas last year that fits just right—much too fancy, but I don't care.

I pause suddenly as I'm applying mascara, take a deep breath as I stare at the woman in the mirror—the woman who is about to get the happily ever after she deserves.

I smile at her, confident and strong, and she smiles back.

With a half hour to spare, I bound toward the front door, shrugging into my coat once more. Behind me, Dad snorts. "Where do you think you're going in this weather?"

I turn around, still smiling. "I'm going to see Connor. Emmett can explain."

"Oh, dear," says Mom, coming up behind him.

My grin falters. "Oh, dear, *what*?"

"Honey, look out the window—there's no way you can get anywhere with the snow coming down like that."

I turn pleading eyes to my dad, but he shrugs, helpless. "My truck's still up on blocks until Dale gets that new part in. Sorry, kiddo."

No. No no no no *no*. I stare out the window, willing the snow to stop, for the banks to part like the Red Sea, to get me to Connor.

Please, I need a Christmas miracle. Just this once.

Next to me, a presence, breathing oddly heavily. I look over and nearly jump back—it's Emmett, wearing a snowmobile helmet. His head turns toward me, but I see only my own face reflected back at me, my mouth hanging open. "Did you get that old piece of shit running?"

"Hey, that's an old piece of solid gold shit out there." His voice is muffled, I still can't see his face, but I know he's grinning. "And *yes*, I did. So what do you think, sis? Are you in?"

I grin back, a spark in my eye. "Oh hell yeah. Let's do this."

We're going so fast, flying through the dark, nearly empty streets, but for one moment I get the nerve to open my eyes, to peek my helmeted head around Emmett's back, and I gasp.

Snowflakes rush by, a force of white against the black sky. Like stars.

Like we're flying at light speed.

And I am. I am shooting forth at the speed of light, straight toward my love.

I shut my eyes again as we fly on, until Emmett slows to a stop and sits with the engine idling. I think he's at an intersection until he nudges me. When I open my eyes, we're sitting in a driveway of a house I don't recognize. It's small, blue with white shutters, pretty twinkling Christmas lights strung along the roof.

And Connor's truck is parked out front.

I ease myself off the side and almost roll into the snow, then waddle my way forward in the oversize snowsuit I borrowed from my dad—so much for the sexy red dress. At first I don't see anyone, but then the front door opens and Arielle sticks her head out. I yank off my helmet, brush back my disheveled hair so she can see it's me, and she grins, then rushes back into the house.

I stand in the driveway, and as the cold air whips against my face, cruel doubt starts to creep in. *What if I waited too long? What if's he's still hurt? Or angry? What if he's decided he doesn't want to see me—that he doesn't want me after all?*

The door opens fully, light pours out, and there he is, standing in the doorway—black jacket with his collar turned up against the chill, eyes sweeping the yard curiously. When they fall on me, he blinks, as if he can't believe it's me standing there. Shaking, I take a tentative step forward. He does the same.

I draw a deep breath. "Connor." My voice breaks, and he takes another cautious step. Another breath, and I speak again. "I shouldn't have run away. I shouldn't have sent *you* away. There's so much I did wrong, that I wish I could take back. I wish I'd talked to you about how

I was feeling. I was just so scared I wasn't enough for you. Or that part of me was *too* much . . . my illness, and everything that might come with it, was too much for you. That you would be frustrated when you realized you couldn't fix me, and you'd leave me."

He shakes his head, his eyes intense. "You don't need to be fixed. You're perfect, just as you are. Every part of you."

His words wash over me, and a tear escapes. "I am *so* sorry."

"Me too," he says. "There was never anybody else—*never*. But I should've been honest with you."

I nod and let my tears flow freely. I open my mouth, struggling to control my voice. "Do you think . . . I mean, could you ever . . ." But my voice catches; I can't get the words out. I look at him helplessly, hopefully.

Connor walks toward me until we are inches apart, until I can feel the warmth of his breath, his body. He searches my face as if reacquainting himself, and I search his—the stubble on his cheek, the tiny scar on his brow. I've missed every last part of him, every corner of his heart and soul, and in that moment there is no doubt how he feels—it's there in the depth of his eyes, the gentleness of his fingertips as he wipes away my tears, brushes back my hair. "Yes," he whispers.

My heart warms; it has always known it would be safe with his. The rest of me just needed to catch up.

"I love you," I whisper.

He smiles. "I know."

A gust of wind blows us closer, together at last, and he kisses me as the snow sweeps up into the sky. My fears, my doubts, swarm upward with the snowflakes, joining in their frenzied pattern of beautiful chaos, not knowing where they will land but grateful for every thrilling moment of existence.

AUTHOR'S NOTE

Multiple sclerosis is a chronic autoimmune disease of the brain and spinal cord in which the immune system attacks myelin. The cause of this unpredictable illness is unknown, and there is no cure.

MS affects almost one million people in the United States alone—including me. In many ways, Simone's journey with MS mirrors my own. Writing this story helped me share part of that journey—the long road to diagnosis, dealing with unpredictable symptoms—while also letting me show that all of us deserve a happily ever after.

No two people experience this illness exactly the same, so this book in no way speaks for everyone with MS. My hope, though, is that it can open the door to more chances for people with MS to tell their own stories.

If you are living with MS, I hope this book has helped you see that your story matters. *You* matter. And you are never alone. To learn more or connect with others in the MS community, visit the National MS Society: www.nationalmssociety.org.

ACKNOWLEDGMENTS

My gratitude is endless. So many people have believed in me, encouraged me, and been there for me when I needed them over the years—most of all, my family and friends. Without their support, I would never have gotten to this point, and this book would not be a reality—this dream would not have come true. To my husband and children, Ted, Isabelle, Jack, and Ernie Dickey, thank you for being the loves of my life and my reason for everything. To Bill and Elaine Grossell, thank you for teaching me that parents are always there for their children. To my sisters, Erika Grossell-Evans, Eva Moore, and Elana Evans, thank you for always having my back since day one, and for showing me what sisterhood means. To my besties, Alisa Kocian, Kari Nurminen, and Meghan Kutz, thank you for accepting me in all my writerly introversion, and for being my first readers.

To my amazing agent, Sharon Pelletier, thank you for believing in my writing and in all my stories, and for being so supportive throughout this journey, but especially supportive of a story with a main character who has multiple sclerosis. To my wonderful editors, Danielle Marshall and Erin Calligan Mooney, thank you for truly getting this story and seeing its importance, for believing in it and pushing me to make it even better so that the world can relate to and love this story about a main character with MS. And to Gabriella Dumpit, Nicole Burns-Ascue, Bill Siever, Jill Kramer, and everyone on the entire team at Lake Union who had a hand in making this book and my entire debut-author experience so wonderful; as well as Tim Green with Faceout Studio for designing the gorgeous book cover—thank you so much.

To my brilliant Pitch Wars mentors, Meredith Ireland and Kara Leigh Miller, thank you for choosing my story and believing in my writing, and for teaching and guiding me so much along the way. To my critique partners / writing buddies—Emily Kelly-Padden, Samantha Leach, Angela Parker, and especially Gretchen Mayer, my writing partner in crime—thank you so much. I couldn't have done it without you. To friends and family who have read my words: Suzi Dickey, Angie Cleberg, Carrie Cole, Kelda Pharris, and Kate Brauning, who offered wisdom and guidance on my path to publication, thank you for your unending support.

To the Pitch Wars class of 2016, the 2021 debut author group, and the entire writing community—thank you for your encouragement and support, and for lifting me up when I needed it. To everyone involved in Pitch Wars and PitMad—thank you for making people's dreams come true, including mine.

There are truly so many friends, family members, and coworkers who have believed in me, taken an interest in my writing, and offered advice or simply a listening ear. Each and every one of you has played a part in my not giving up, and I thank you all from the bottom of my heart.

To my fellow MS warriors—Duby, Carol, Susan, Marcia, and so many others—you are all strong and amazing.

ABOUT THE AUTHOR

Photo © 2019 Jordyn Photography \ by Jordyn Volk

Elissa Grossell Dickey is a former journalist who now works in higher education communications. Stories have always been a big part of Elissa's life—from getting lost in a book as a child to now reading bedtime stories to her kids. As a columnist for the National MS Society, Elissa shares her personal journey of living with multiple sclerosis. Though she grew up among the lakes and trees of northern Minnesota, Elissa now lives on the South Dakota prairie with her husband and children. *The Speed of Light* is her first novel. For information, visit www.elissaadickey.wordpress.com.